BENNETT FALLS

Peter Stipe

Lavender Press
an imprint of Blue Fortune Enterprises, LLC

BENNETT FALLS
Copyright © 2022 by Peter Stipe.

For information contact :
Blue Fortune Enterprises, LLC
Lavender Press
P.O. Box 554
Yorktown, VA 23690
http://blue-fortune.com

Book and Cover design by Wesley Miller

ISBN: 978-1-948979-76-4
First Edition: July 2022

DEDICATION

To all my friends in Newmarket and other small towns.
Your stories inspired mine.

Fiction by Peter Stipe:

Bennett Falls
The Fairy Garden
The Art of Love
Remember Me
Finding Our Way

Metcalfe House
Metcalfe Mills
Upper River Road
Lake Street
Concord Road
Main Street
River Road
Maple Street
Washington Street
Meadow Glen Road
Woodland Road
Manchester Road
School Street
N
WELCOME TO BENNETT FALLS

No man ever steps in the same river twice.
Neither the man nor the river are ever the same.

Heraclitus, circa 500 B.C.

The river had flowed from the mountains since time began, cutting a channel through the granite, tumbling glacial boulders in its path, grinding down through the forests, always moving toward the sea. In narrow channels it roared; it flowed more gently through the wide meadows. The river defined the hard northern landscape and became a part of Bennett Falls.

Outside of Bennett Falls, there were calamities—economic recessions and major wars. Life in Bennett Falls felt these events. Farm prices fluctuated and the fortunes of the mill varied. Boys from Bennett Falls marched off to war and some never returned. Still, through it all, life went on as always in Bennett Falls. The river flowed steadily through the heart of the little town.

PART

One

CHAPTER
One
September

Debbie Forbes absently pushed the "start" button on the coffee machine, noting Warren Briggs' approach as he crossed the town common, following the shaded gravel paths that bisected the historic lawn. She pulled a thick, white mug off a shelf, turned to the coffee station, and called to the kitchen, "Warren's on his way. You can start his usual."

Billy dropped two eggs on the grill. "Got it going," he called to his wife through the window connecting the kitchen to the counter.

Warren walked into the coffee shop, the bell above the door announcing his arrival. Without a word, he picked up the mug of coffee Debbie drew for him and walked to his customary table and usual seat. He set his mug on the stained maple tabletop and eased into the chair across from his old friend. "Morning, Andrew," he said, taking his time with the greeting. "What's happening around town?"

Andrew leaned forward, both forearms resting on the tabletop, flannel bracketing his cup. "Good morning, Warren. Bit of a snap in the air today. No frost yet. Still early for that. But it'll be coming soon enough."

Warren nodded and tipped his Red Sox cap back on his head. Ragged threads of white hair slipped out on the sides. He took a sip of the hot black coffee and exhaled, satisfied as warmth filled his belly. "Yup. Labor Day's gone and so are the tourists. Kids are all back in school. Things are back to normal again, just the way I like it. Least it'll stay quiet till the leaf-peepers arrive."

Andrew nodded in silence.

Warren sat back in his chair, ready to bring up the question of the day, the one on his mind as well as on the minds of everyone in Bennett Falls. "You hear about what's happening up at the old Metcalfe place?" he asked, voice raised for the benefit of the diners. "Bit of gossip and rumors out there. Lots of whispering, lots of speculation, but I got no patience with idle talk. I figure if anyone would know for sure about that place it would be you, living right down the hill from it and all."

The coffee shop regulars became quiet and attentive. Who better than Warren and Andrew to know and share the news about the Metcalfe House, or about anything happening in town, for that matter? For a moment, the only sound in the crowded restaurant was the scraping of chair legs on the old wood floor as patrons shifted closer. Behind the counter, Debbie paused, stopping the clatter of filling the dishwasher. Billy leaned away from the eggs he was cooking on the grill.

Andrew took his time, basking in the awareness that the town was listening. He didn't waste words when they weren't needed, not in The Sunrise Café, or in town meetings, or in any large gathering. When there was something to say, or when he was inspired to tell one of his long, rambling jokes, he couldn't be stopped. But this was big news. Finally he spoke, raising his voice like Warren so all the early morning patrons and staff could hear him. "Yup. I might know a bit about that. My cousin Joe told me that his neighbor was up there a few days ago. You know. Young Jimmy Sanborn? Amos Sanborn's grandson. Big Jim Sanborn's boy? Well, Joe told me that Jimmy got a call to go up there and take a look at things. That guy who bought the place? Sullivan's his name, I believe? From

Boston or New York, some city down that way?"

Diners stirred, moving closer, waiting for more. Warren interrupted, warming to the story, adding what he knew. "I believe that fellow's from Boston. He was a banker or a lawyer or maybe in real estate. You know how they work down there. Made millions and retired young. I saw him driving through town the other day. He doesn't look a day over his mid-forties. Now he's dropped everything and moved up here with his wife. So what's he want?"

The café was silent, everyone hanging on Warren and Andrew's words. Encouraged, Andrew went on, enjoying the attention. "Well, Joe said that Jimmy came over after supper a few days back to watch the Sox game with him on the television. And he said that this Sullivan fellow wants a lot of work done on the place. Joe told me Jimmy's all excited. Says it could take him several months to do the work, and it'll be worth a lot of money for him. They want to take the top two floors and remodel them to have seven bedrooms, each with its own attached private bathroom. The plumbing work alone will pay Jimmy thousands. And this man Sullivan wants to keep the parlor and the living room and dining room the way they are but expand the kitchen downstairs and then build out a complete apartment in the back of the first floor where he'll live with his wife. Jimmy told him Sullivan wants to turn that old house into a bed and breakfast."

Andrew sat back, satisfied. He slurped a sip of coffee and surveyed the cafe, noting with satisfaction the excitement his news had engendered. The breakfast regulars murmured about Andrew's report. Debbie busied herself behind the counter, and Billy went back to work in the kitchen.

"Well, that's a fool idea if ever I heard one!" Warren laughed. "A bed and breakfast? Who would want to come to Bennett Falls and stay in the old Metcalfe House? Sure, it's a big old place, and maybe a bit elegant, what with that long front porch and the gardens and all. If Jimmy and his boys work on it, fix it up a bit, well, that might be nice. But why would anyone want to visit Bennett Falls? Nothing to do here."

Andrew disagreed. "People always come to look at the foliage in the fall. The leaf peepers, you know. And we get skiers in the winter. And people might like to take their vacations here in the summer. There's the lake and the mountains, and it's quiet. It might work."

"Come on, Andrew. The nearest ski resort is a half hour away. Even more when there's snow on the roads. And sure, we've got Clear Lake, not that it's much of a place to go except for us locals. Nothing to do there but swim maybe or fish or go out in a canoe. And Lake Winnipesaukee is a half hour away too. Only that one little boat ramp on Clear Lake and another one on the river behind the hockey rink. Nobody would want to come here."

"They already do come up here. They stay in the hotels and motels up in the mountains. They could just as easily stay here. It might bring some of that Boston money into town."

Warren shook his head and laughed again. "Bah! It's a foolish idea. We're just an old mill town. And Metcalfe Mills has been closed for years. Old man Metcalfe died a few years back. His kids moved away, and that house has been sitting empty ever since. So, what have we got? We're just a bunch of Yankee dirt farmers, you and me and the rest of us. Aside from us, there's a lot of old mill workers doing other things for work if they've stayed around. A lot of the mill people left. There's nothing to do here. Nobody will come."

Andrew took another sip of his coffee, his arthritic hands wrapped around the thick white mug. "I don't know. Those Metcalfe children owned the house after their father died but they've been gone for years. Moved someplace out west, I heard. I'll bet the Metcalfe kids were happy to finally find someone to buy it and take it off their hands. Maybe if this Sullivan fellow was smart enough to make the money it took to buy the place, maybe he's smart enough to make it work as a bed and breakfast."

Warren nodded. "Yup. Sure. I still say he's a fool. Let's wait and see. A bed and breakfast, huh? Who'll be cooking the breakfast up there?" Then he had a thought. "Hey Debbie," he called to the kitchen. "You and Billy better keep your eyes on this new business. If they start serving breakfast up the hill there at the Metcalfe House, you won't be the only place in town to get a bite to eat in the morning."

Debbie leaned out of the kitchen door, a hand on her hip, grinning. "If they turn that old house into a fancy bed and breakfast, will you stop coming here every morning? You'd probably have to stay the night there to get the breakfast anyway. And you and Andrew have been coming here every morning for as long as I can remember. Are you planning to stop coming if the Metcalfe place starts serving eggs in the morning?"

"Of course not!" Warren laughed. "That Sullivan fellow's got a long road ahead of him. How about it, Andrew? You going to abandon Debbie and this place to go try out the new Metcalfe breakfast place? If Sullivan ever gets it off the ground?"

"No, of course not." Andrew laughed. "Debbie, looks like you're stuck with us. We're never leaving." Andrew smiled and patted Warren on the arm.

"Not that I would wish for that!" Debbie stated. She brought out two plates, each with two eggs over easy, home fries, and wheat toast. There were two sausage links on one plate, two strips of bacon on the other. She set a plate in front of each of her two regular customers: bacon for Andrew, sausage for Warren. She handed over a bottle of ketchup from the next table for the home fries.

"I can't see you sitting up there in a fancy dining room with lace curtains, fine china and all, looking over the menu and trying to make up your mind between the Eggs Benedict or the spinach quiche," she said. "It would take you all morning to decide."

"What's Eggs Benedict?" Warren asked.

CHAPTER
Two
September

Jack and Keira Sullivan sat on new, white wooden rocking chairs with pastel floral seat cushions. Sarah, Keira's best friend from Boston, sat across from them on a wicker love seat with a matching cushion. The wide porch of the Metcalfe House was cool, shaded from the rising sun. Flowerpots hung from the eaves of the porch, the flowers beginning to fade, shedding petals, scattering them like bright pink confetti on the white porch railing and the weathered, splintering gray planks of the porch.

Two plates, one of sliced pears and grapes, the second of store-bought pastries, rested on the glass top of the round wicker coffee table tucked between their chairs. A square of blue-checked gingham cloth spanned the middle of the table. Three smaller crumb-covered plates sat on the gingham. Keira reached for a small, delicate cup, in shades of teal and blue, and sipped her tea. She set the cup down and brushed her light brown hair back as it blew in the breeze.

Looking out at the lawn and the landscaping, Keira spoke, breaking the hush of the bucolic dawn. "What a lovely morning, isn't it? It's peaceful here. Quiet"

Sarah leaned back on the love seat and sipped her coffee from a flower-painted mug. "It's quite a change from your little house in Quincy. This place is huge." She looked across the lawn, at the oaks and maples, their leaves beginning to turn, bright reds and yellows emerging. Among the hardwoods, heavy, dark pines guarded the yard, their boughs hanging low.

"It's beautiful," Sarah continued. "But what are you going to do with a house this big?"

Jack held a rough-textured, earth-tone pottery mug of coffee. "This is what we've always wanted." He sipped and smiled. "If things go the way we hope, this porch will be covered with guests by next summer. We want to turn the house into a bed and breakfast."

Sarah smiled. "Really! That'll be amazing. A big, beautiful old Victorian like this? It would be wonderful."

Keira nodded. "We've always dreamed of owning a B&B, but we still have a long way to go. Not just the house, but the furnishings. I'm okay with what we've bought already, but we'll need more."

Jack agreed. "We can hit some of the antique stores and consignment shops to get the place furnished. We'll serve breakfast in the morning. Or our guests can come onto the porch with coffee after breakfast if they've eaten inside. And we can serve wine and cheese late each afternoon."

"That'll be perfect," said Sarah. "I'd stay at a place like this if I was on vacation in New Hampshire."

"There's a lot we need to do to fix the place up," Jack said. "My background managing those high-rise buildings down in Boston will come in handy. I'll be overseeing a lot of work here. Once the construction work is done inside, we'll need to set up all the bedrooms and the dining room too. That's a lot of furniture. It'll cost a lot."

Keira smiled, set down her mug and took his hand. "Mom left us plenty when she died. Enough to buy this big old house. Enough to fix it up. And enough to furnish it. It'll be great when it's finished."

"We'll miss ski season this year," Jack said. "But we should be open when the snow melts sometime in the spring."

"That's the plan," Keira agreed and smiled. They were in this together, building their retirement dream.

"How late does the snow last up here in New Hampshire?" Sarah asked. "It's gone by late March, early April in Boston."

"Later I expect. Into April maybe? Late winter might be our slow season," Keira mused.

"Do you miss going to work?" Sarah asked, shifting the focus.

"No, not really," Keira answered. "I miss the people. I had some good friends there, you and a few others. If we were still in Boston, I would have been at work an hour already by this time of the morning. It's nice to ease into the day like this."

"You get a later start, but you're still working now, up here online, right?"

"Yes, of course," Keira said. "The difference is I do my marketing projects remotely and I can work my own hours now. I teleconference whenever there's a meeting. I'll still have to go to Boston for meetings once, maybe twice every month, but all the rest of my work will be done here."

"No more commuting. No more dressing up for work, right?"

"Right! Setting my own hours will give me time to start building our website and marketing this place. How about you, Jack? Do you miss it?" Keira almost laughed and took another leisurely sip of her tea.

Jack paused for a moment, analyzing their present status. He rubbed his chin, feeling four-days growth of dark whiskers. While he was still working full time in Boston, he'd shaved every day, even on the weekends. It was nice to be able to let it all go. He hadn't worn a tie in two weeks.

"Do I miss it? Not at all," he said. "I'm still going down there a couple of days a week. I'm meeting with my building and office tenants and with the guy who'll be taking over my accounts. I'll still get paid for another six months as a consultant to help with the transitioning of my accounts. But it's not the same. I loved my job in Boston. I still enjoy working there. But I'm ready to be a full-time manager of a bed and breakfast. The timing should work out perfectly. I'll end my Boston job contract in a few months, just about when we're ready to open this place."

He took a sip of coffee and watched four deer cautiously stepping from the forest onto the far end of the lawn. The deer looked to the house, assessing the humans on the porch. Then they began grazing on fallen fruit in the tiny orchard that bordered the lawn and gardens.

Jack put his mug back on the table. "I certainly don't miss the early mornings and the commute. And I'm done with the day-to-day hassles for the most part. No more neckties except when I'm in Boston. The office politics. The pressure of keeping all the tenants in my portfolio of buildings happy, even on the weekends. It's nice to sleep peacefully at night and not lie awake worrying all the time."

He paused for a moment, then he continued. "The only way this could have been more perfect would have been to be raising a family here. A couple of kids running around the lawn and all that. Maybe having this bed and breakfast will help Keira and me move past the loss of the babies."

Keira tucked her chin and stared at the family of deer. She said nothing.

Sarah reached over and took Keira's hand. "But Jack, this is such a great adventure. A wonderful business opportunity. And in such a perfect setting. No more big city Boston hassles."

"We'll be free and clear by springtime." Keira laughed, brightening. "Ready to run our little inn here in the mountains."

"That's true. I'll be free. And working with all the contractors and the unions down in Boston? Trying to get things done and not let anything fall through the cracks. It prepared me to know what I'm talking about with the locals here. Like this kid Jimmy I've found to work on the house. I've asked him to come over and take a second look at the place later this morning. It appears he'll give me a good price for all the work we need. The way he's talking about what I want done, he's not going to charge anywhere near what the same work would cost in Boston. And he should be a good guy to work with. None of the headaches I ran into back in

Boston. Jimmy seems straightforward and honest."

Keira smiled and gave Jack's hand a squeeze. "This is so good," she said. She turned to Sarah. "I'll miss you. And all my Boston friends. We don't know anyone in this little town. Not yet."

Sarah reached over and took Keira's hand again, linking herself with her best friend and husband. "Visit us in Boston any time you get lonely. We'll be quite a few miles apart when you're settled here, but we'll still be in touch. Can I come stay here again? I'd like to bring Tom and the girls."

"Of course," Keira said. "You can be our first guest in our little B&B. We really appreciate you taking a couple of days off to help us move in."

Keira gave Sarah's hand a quick squeeze. A breeze flipped Keira's hair as she looked out at their gardens. Mist rose in the sunlight from the field, damp with dawn dew. The gardens were beautiful, even overgrown, with late season flowers raising their heads above the tangle of weeds. They would need some tending to, weeding and pruning. Keira could take care of that with a few hours of work each week. She looked forward to the joy of being in the gardens, working with her hands, taking a break from the confining world of indoor desk work. Sunlight lit the landscape, revealing a clarity they had rarely seen in the smog of the city.

They sat quietly, Jack and Sarah sipping their coffee, Keira with her tea, watching the deer, the lawn, and the garden below the porch. A warm breeze blew up again, moving the yellow and crimson early autumn leaves on the trees. Above the tree tops, a chevron of geese honked past, seeking their traditional path south. Birds hopped on the lawn. Sparrows chased through the branches of a maple tree. High above it all, a hawk circled. Beyond the lawn stretched the narrow river valley, a white steeple and the rooftops of Bennett Falls a half mile away. Down the hill through the trees, a church bell tolled nine o'clock. Other than the bell and the birds and the breeze, it was silent.

CHAPTER

Three

Autumn

The covered bridge that spanned the river had become the iconic image of Bennett Falls. Originally built in the late eighteenth century, it burned in the autumn of 1835 when a farmer's wagon cracked a wheel on a rotten flooring plank. When the wheel broke, jolting the wagon, the hanging lantern fell and spilled oil and flames, first onto the cargo of hay then onto the bridge itself. The farmer escaped with his unhitched horse and his life. The wagon and bridge were lost to the fire in minutes.

It took most of the winter to rebuild the covered bridge that connected the town to a wide, packed dirt road into the hills. That highway was the main route into Bennett Falls from the mountains and the Connecticut River valley. For months, everyone detoured two miles upstream to the next bridge, a narrow one north of the waterfall and rapids, beyond the bright new brick textile mill, powered by the river falls. The rebuilt covered bridge into Bennett Falls opened late in the spring of 1836 and was dedicated on the Fourth of July with speeches, bands, and a parade.

The new bridge lasted, with some repairs, until a rowdy Friday night in 1968 when some of the local youth, inspired by too much beer, lit it on fire for fun. The kids were arrested but the bridge was gone. Federal highway funds helped restore it quickly.

The new bridge—a classic, wide, sturdy thing built of steel beams and concrete—was solid and serviceable, but ugly. It took a year more for the town to recognize the need to restore the look of the old, covered bridge. They clad the concrete with oak, built the shed-like roof over it to keep the snow off, and even laid in thick, wooden planks for the road surface, fastening them in place, but leaving them loose so they rattled romantically with nostalgia when cars crossed the bridge. Quaintly lettered signs were mounted above the entrances to the bridge on both ends reading, "Bennett Falls 1797".

A few members of the town council believed the bridge could become a lure for tourists. Small, gravel parking lots were added on either side of the bridge. Paved viewing points, ideal for taking photographs, were constructed. Benches and picnic tables were installed. A large bronze sign on a post detailed the full history of the covered bridge. It worked. New Hampshire Tourist magazines and websites included pictures of the bridge, and to the amazement of skeptical old-time locals, visitors started to drive through town, detouring off the interstate to see it.

Debbie's grandmother, and then her mother, saw a spike in business at their Sunrise Café. They added items to the lunch menu that appealed to the New York crowd: deli food, Reuben sandwiches, and soups, not just the regular cheeseburgers and BLTs. Debbie's mother even got a liquor license and began to offer bottled beer and a short list of red and white wines. Debbie inherited the café and now carried on a thriving family business with her husband, Billy.

The general store, two doors down from the Sunrise, also saw increased business. Along with moose-themed refrigerator magnets, maple sugar candies, and tiny bottles of syrup, postcards showing the covered bridge were popular. T-shirts with a picture of the bridge and the words "Bennett Falls 1797" usually sold out before the first snow fell each year.

This autumn morning, Lana Briggs and her old friend Michelle Lacroix sat on a bench beside the bridge across from the Town Common. For years, they had met at the bridge each morning for their walk across the town Common and along the brick-paved path next to the river. Best friends more than a half a century, ever since high school, growing up together in Bennett Falls, they had much in common.

Their families didn't. Michelle's family had worked in the Metcalfe Mill for generations. French-Canadian immigrants in the middle of the nineteenth century, they settled in one of the small houses on the narrow rows of streets across from the mill. Michelle still lived in the house where she had grown up, now sharing it with her husband Peter. The mill work was gone; textiles these days came from Asia. Michelle adapted quickly when the work left. She opened a craft shop on the first floor of the old Metcalfe Mill building, selling pottery, carved wood items, and quilts made by local artisans. Tourists crammed the store most of the year. Three nights a week, Michelle also worked in The Old Mill restaurant that filled most of the main floor of the looming brick Metcalfe Mill. Often, she served as the hostess, greeting diners at the front. When it got busy, she reverted to her original job serving dinners to the wealthy visitors. Locals ate there only on Valentine's Day, birthdays, and anniversaries.

For years, Michelle's husband, Peter Lacroix, was the only plumber in town. A new plumber had moved to Bennett Falls from somewhere south eight years earlier. Peter claimed to be retired, but he still did occasional plumbing, carpentry work, and other odd jobs around town. Most nights he drank beer. He watched hockey on television when the Bruins were in season. He had played defense for the Bennett Falls Regional High School team years ago when he and Michelle were high school sweethearts.

Michelle and Peter had raised three children in their small house near the mill. Two of them had gone to college and moved from Bennett Falls for careers, one in high-tech in Seattle, the other selling insurance near Boston. The third child, a boy who was always in trouble, had enlisted in the army during the Gulf War. He survived the war but never came home to Bennett Falls.

Lana was from an old New Hampshire family. Her father had been a truck driver, working for a lumber mill in the next town. She married Warren Briggs right after high school graduation and settled with him on his family farm; a narrow stretch of flat, fertile soil along the river, across from town, downstream from the mill and the covered bridge. Their house, a clean, two-story white clapboard, sat close to the road with a tidy farm stand next to it. Most of the farm stood idle these days, but they still raised a few vegetables which they sold at the farm stand late each season. They had one child, a girl who had gone to two years of college, married, and settled with her young family outside Manchester. There was a grandson. They gathered together on every holiday; Thanksgiving in Bennett Falls, Christmas and Easter at their daughter's house. Manchester was only an hour away, even when it snowed.

Lana and Michelle rested after their morning walk, sitting on a bench by the covered bridge, enjoying the sound of the water tumbling over the rocks behind them, basking in the peace of the New England autumn sunshine. When they walked, the brisk pace left them too out of breath for much talking. No longer out of breath, it was time for catching up.

"Lord, love him." Lana chuckled for a moment, giving a wry smile. "Warren's all worked up about this business up at the old Metcalfe House. Every night he's just fussing about it. 'What are they thinking?' he keeps saying. 'A Bed and Breakfast? Waste of money.'"

"He doesn't think it'll work?" Michelle turned from watching the river to face her friend. "I like tourists. If the Metcalfe House lures a few more into town, I say bring them on. It's money in my pocket."

Lana took a sip from her water bottle and smoothed her thick, black-and-white, curled hair. "No. He thinks it's a waste of money because nobody will come stay there when the folks who bought it are done fixing it up."

"So what? Peter will make a quick few dollars out of that work. Jimmy

Sanborn called him a couple of days ago asking if he'd be interested in doing some plumbing work up there. Jimmy doesn't trust that new plumber who came to town a few years back, and he wants Peter to work for him, just the way he always has."

"That's what I keep telling Warren. If the guy who bought the house wants to pay a bunch of us to fix up the old place, I'm all for it. I don't care if he can make a go of it. At least he'll put some money into the town's economy with all the construction work."

"If it works, my store will sell crafts like crazy. All those visitors. The Old Mill should be full whenever the tourists are in season. If I work evenings there, I expect I'll make good tips all summer. Not to mention the money Peter'll get for the plumbing work this winter."

"That's right," agreed Lana. "Bring on the work."

"I guess I'm lucky to have Peter," Michelle said. "So what's with Warren? Why's he so dead set against it?"

"Oh, you know him. Nothing's ever right for him. It gives him something to complain about. If it wasn't this, it would be the potholes in the roads every spring, and why doesn't the town patch them quickly enough."

"How do you put up with him?"

"I've been married to him almost fifty years. I'll give him a couple of more years to grow out of it. If he doesn't change, so help me, I'll throw him out."

"Sure you will," Michelle mocked.

Lana laughed. "You know I will! See you tomorrow morning?"

They stood. Michelle straightened her sweater, clipped her water bottle on her belt and checked her shoelaces. "Eight o'clock sharp, right here. I've got to go open my shop. It's almost nine."

The two women gave a cursory hug and headed off, Michelle to her shop in the mill and Lana to her farm. Warren would still be at The Sunrise. She would have some peace and quiet to get things done around the house.

CHAPTER

Four

Autumn

Jimmy Sanborn pulled his pickup off the Concord Road into the curving packed-gravel driveway leading to the Metcalfe House. He stopped on the turnaround circle at the front door. Jimmy was five minutes early. His appointment with Jack Sullivan wasn't until ten, but he liked to show new customers he was prompt. He picked up his clipboard box, got out of the F-150, closed the door quietly, and surveyed the wide porch, the three stories and the gabled roof of his new project.

The Metcalfe children had done a good job maintaining the exterior. The old clapboards were coated with a thick, fresh layer of gray paint with a sharp, contrasting white trim. Black shutters framed every window. The front door was a matching black with an etched glass panel and a shining brass doorknob. The new roof with black shingles matched the door and the shutters. The place was aged, but the paint and other touches gave it an air of freshness.

It was a big house, at least 4,600 square feet, Jimmy estimated, maybe even more. He'd measured the rooms he would be working on during his first visit at the house with Jack Sullivan. When he was done, there would be seven guest rooms, each with a private bathroom. And that didn't account for the new private apartment he had designed to build off the kitchen for the Sullivans to live in. That would add 700 feet of private living space.

The front door opened, and Jack came onto the porch, raising a hand in greeting.

"Good morning," Jimmy called. "I'm a few minutes early. I hope you don't mind. I don't like being late." He wanted to stress his promptness again to his new client.

"Quite all right," Jack said, walking down the steps to the driveway, long legs spanning the distance in a few strides. "I appreciate it. Let's talk about what needs to be done." No small talk for Jack when none was needed. It would be the same for him in rural New Hampshire.

They shook hands, a firm clasp. In his early forties, Jack was older, slightly taller, and heavier-set, used to office work and business lunches. Jimmy was lean, a body hardened by daily physical work. Jack was now clean-shaven, having prepared his business look for the meeting. Jimmy's red-blonde beard was thick but neatly trimmed.

Jimmy took a sheet of paper out of the box on the clipboard, clipped it in place, and clicked a pen open. "Let's get on with it. Where do we start?" He waited for Jack to lead with questions. Jimmy would steer the conversation when needed, but he left it up to the customer to explain what he wanted done.

For an uncomfortable moment, Jack said nothing. Jimmy stood patiently.

"Okay," Jack began, shifting to face Jimmy squarely, assuming command. "Let's talk about the house, point-by-point, and project-by-project. Let's start outside. What, if anything, do we need to do about the exterior?"

"With that you're good. The house is solid. It's better built than most newer homes in town. They don't build them this way anymore. Thick walls, solid studs, real plaster for the interior, not sheetrock, good insulation. The foundation is field stone, but you've got a concrete floor down there.

The cellar might be damp but it's not leaking. I wouldn't store anything important down there, and I doubt that you could finish it off, make it watertight without a lot of work, but it's not a problem. It won't flood. I don't think you'll need a sump pump."

"What about the roof?"

"A local roofer re-did it for the Metcalfe kids just three years ago. You should be fine with that. He's a friend of mine and I trust him. He's going to shingle the addition I'm building off the back for you." Jimmy hoped his trust in a fellow contractor might instill trust between Jack and him.

"Plumbing?" Jack asked, leading the way inside the house.

"There's a problem. It's original, possibly as old as the house. I doubt that it's still lead pipes but it's going to need a lot of work. You're connected to a good well, and the septic system's fine. But we're going to put in seven bathrooms with showers, tubs, toilets, the whole works, one with every guest room. You might as well replace all the old pipes. That could be expensive. I've got an old friend in town, Peter Lacroix. The best plumber around. He's fair and honest. He'll call you to set up an appointment. Here's his card. Let me know if he doesn't get back to you by Friday. Be ready to tell him if you want old fashioned copper pipes, which are expensive, or the PVC kind."

"I'll have him quote me for both, but I'll probably have to go with the PVC." Jack's statement implied the need for a cost-conscious approach. He hoped Jimmy caught the hint.

"Have him add in his quote the cost for the new bathroom in the apartment I'll be building off the back for you and your wife."

"Of course. How about the electrical work?"

Jimmy began tapping on the walls. "The walls are solid. I'll check to be sure I'm not taking out any load-bearing walls. You never know what you'll find when you start tearing out walls. But about the electrical work? I'm licensed for that. I'll take care of it while I'm framing in the new bedrooms. I'll include it in my overall quote, and I'll give it a separate line so you can see that cost."

"Good. And heat?"

"You'll need some work there. The heating system you've got isn't that old, but I can't imagine how it's able to heat a house this size. The house is well insulated, and you've got new storm windows, but an upgrade to your furnace could save you money in the long run. I've got a guy from all the way over in Concord, but he's good. I'd suggest you have him put in three zones, one for each floor. That way, you can close off the top floors when you don't fill them with guests. The first-floor zone would include your apartment. We'll want all the new duct work done before I frame in the rooms upstairs. And you'll want the new system finished and working before winter."

"How do we heat a place this big? What are we burning?"

"Oil. Be careful to use a good oil company and maybe get a contract for the year, locking in the price. I'll give you the name of the best guy for that."

"Should we do wood stoves here? Maybe put one in each guest room?"

"No. I wouldn't recommend it. You don't want your guests having to light fires in their rooms each night. And they'd be waking up in the middle of the night with the fire out and the room cold. That, plus you'd have to build a bunch of new flues and chimneys."

"Yes, you're right. I thought maybe it would be a nice, romantic touch for vacationers."

"That it would. Maybe you could put a wood stove in the downstairs parlor, set it right in the fireplace. You can buy one down in Manchester, and I'll give you the number for my firewood guy."

"I'd appreciate it. What else do we need to go over?"

"Licenses. I'll take care of all the licenses for the construction, the plumbing, and the electrical work. You just missed the fall town meeting, so you'll have to go to the town meeting in the winter to get your license to run a bed and breakfast. It shouldn't be a problem."

Jack made a quick mental note to attend the winter meeting and apply for the business license. He asked, "Is there anything else I've missed?"

"I think we've about covered everything. I know what you want for your apartment off the kitchen. I'll go over my notes and have a contract covering everything ready for you by Friday morning. What time could I meet you?"

"I'll be down in Boston till Thursday night. I could meet you anywhere, anytime next week. Here? Or at your office?"

"How about nine o'clock on Monday? There's a place downtown where we could meet or I could come here."

"Excellent. Let me know about the downtown place."

"It's a little coffee place right off the Common. The Sunrise Café. You can't miss it."

"Perfect. See you Monday morning at nine."

Jack led him back out on the front porch. They shook hands. Jack turned, surveying his new bed and breakfast. Jimmy drove around the circle in front of the old house and turned down the Concord Road, heading to the old, covered bridge back to town. He would pull a contract together over a cup of coffee at The Sunrise.

CHAPTER
Five
October

Well before eight on a chilly Saturday morning, Jimmy's grandfather, Amos Sanborn, set up a folding chair and a card table inside the gate to the Bennett Falls landfill. Elections for the town council were approaching, with Amos campaigning to retain the seat he had held for more than two decades. He placed a stack of papers under a stone on the table.

It was a New Hampshire ritual. Saturday morning, everyone went to the dump. Recycling was in a concrete pit to the left as drivers turned off Meadow Glen Road onto the muddy track that led into the dump. General trash went in the swampy marshland straight ahead. Anything else to be discarded was left in a dry meadow off the right side of the entrance road. The meadow became an impromptu yard sale with no prices. People congregated there with their coffee to inspect newly abandoned broken appliances and other items, sometimes taking them home in the back of their pickups. Broken bicycles were a popular take away. It was also a good place to come, meet people, and chat on a sunny autumn morning.

Amos had set up his campaign in the meadow with the discarded things, handing out the one-page campaign flier from the table. It featured his picture, a list of his accomplishments, and an outline of his proposed ideas for the future of Bennett Falls. It was unnecessary, except to inform the new settlers in town. The regular residents knew all about Amos Sanborn. He was a real estate agent who had collaborated a bit more than ten years ago with a developer from Manchester to build all those new homes up School Street, a mile south of town. The winding streets of this new community were filled with small capes and raised ranches. Although it was officially labeled "Mountain View Meadows", the neighborhood was now commonly referred to by the old-time residents as "Sanbornville".

Amos' son, Jim Sanborn, had built many of the houses, assisted by his son, Jimmy. Big Jim, as the father was called to distinguish him from little Jimmy, had died of a heart attack shortly after finishing the last of the houses in Sanbornville. Jimmy had taken over his father's business and thrived. He now lived in one of the Sanbornville raised ranches with his wife Lynn and their two children. His twelve-year-old boy Amos was a star in Little League and a promising youth hockey player. Fourteen-year-old daughter Christine had already brought home figure skating trophies.

Amos had also spearheaded the campaign to acquire state and federal funding to build the new school complex out from town off Washington Street. Additional classroom space was desperately needed to accommodate all the children of the many young families who had settled in Sanbornville. A new Regional High School sat at the corner of Washington Street and School Street. The elementary and middle schools were built on adjacent land, a half mile farther up School Street, across from Sanbornville. The original school building, a three-story brick edifice, stood in town, positioned across the street from the Town Common. In the old days, children were educated there through all twelve grades. The old school building now housed the Bennett Falls School Department and the other town administrative offices.

The mood at the dump was congenial. People dropped off their trash, and then swung over to where Amos campaigned to park and talk, enjoying the autumn sun and the bright foliage. Paper cups of coffee, banter, and laughter turned the dump into a party.

Warren Briggs arrived, pulling over at the general trash area. He got out of his drab truck and flung two black trash bags onto the mound of refuse in front of the town bulldozer. Warren then circled back to the cab of his truck and drove to the meadow where Amos and the crowd had gathered.

Warren turned off the truck, got out, and ambled with his careful, arthritic gait through the thick grass to the flock around Amos, taking his time.

"Good day!" Amos began congenially. "How are you this fine morning?"

"Could be better. What brings you out here to the dump so early, Amos? And why the crowd?" Warren knew the answers to his questions. It was just his opening volley.

"Campaigning for Town Council. General election in a few weeks, you know."

"That so? You're running again? I'm all for term limits. You've had your turn."

"We have term limits, Warren. It's called an election. Vote me out if you don't like what I've done or what I plan to do. Why don't you throw your hat in the ring and run against me?"

"I've got no time to be on the Town Council. You're running unopposed again, I suppose?"

"No, there's a new fellow running against me. He's a lawyer, I think, moved up here several years ago from Massachusetts. A Democrat, of course."

"Of course. So I'm left with a decision between some lawyer flatlander Masshole or you? Let me give it some thought." Warren kept a poker face, but a light in his eye showed that he heard the bystander's chuckles.

Amos extended his hand to shake. "Well, I certainly would appreciate your support, Warren. You've lived here your whole life and people respect your opinions."

Warren shook Amos' hand and held on. "Let me ask you a question, Amos. You built all those houses off School Street. And you got us those new school buildings. The town has doubled in size over the past few years. I suppose the added tax revenue is good. We need it to pay for the new teachers and police we've had to hire. But this isn't the Bennett Falls where I was born."

"True. There's a new look and feel to the place, a new energy. But I believe we've retained a lot of the small-town character that makes it a great place to live and raise a family. So, what's your question?"

Warren released the handshake. The crowd swiveled their heads, following the conversation back and forth between Warren and Amos.

"My question is this. What do you think about the plans for the old Metcalfe House? I know your grandson, Jimmy, is working up there, so I expect you support the idea because Jimmy's making money. But how do you think that place will change the town when they open?"

"I'm not opposed to it. Like you say, Jimmy'll be making money there and so will a few of the other folks in town who're getting some work with Jimmy. And when it opens, it will bring a lot more people into town, visitors who'll spend their money here."

"Why would we want all those people coming here? Clogging up our streets. Causing traffic jams. Disrupting everything. We'll need to hire more police to keep the crowds under control and that'll raise our taxes. Your expansion has gone far enough. We're all fine with that old house just sitting there. If a rich guy from Boston wants to live there, I say, 'good.' But we don't want a hotel up there."

"It's his decision, Warren. He bought the old house. He wants to fix it up. What he does with it once he's finished is up to him. There are no zoning laws in New Hampshire. Like they've always said, 'Live Free or Die.'"

"So you say, Amos. No, I'm not going to run for town council. But I'm going to do whatever I can to stop that place from becoming a bed and breakfast."

"You do that Warren. And come on down to the elementary school on election day and vote. I'm counting on your support."

"Don't count on anything, Amos."

CHAPTER
Six

Andrew Holmes came in the door of The Sunrise Café and stopped for a moment, furling his black umbrella, banging the end on the floor to shake off the water. It was a short walk from his house, over the covered bridge, across the Common to Washington Street and The Sunrise, but the gray rain that fell had soaked his shoes and the cuffs of his khakis. He propped the umbrella by the door and took his seat across from Warren Briggs.

"Least it's not snow," Andrew stated.

"Won't be long," Warren replied. "The Old Farmer's Almanac says we're in for a cold winter. The caterpillars are wooly this year. Never a good sign."

"Who knows for sure what winter will be like? They make it up when they write that almanac down the road in Dublin. It's all just guesswork. When it snows, we'll deal with it."

Warren nodded. "We always have. We always do. We always will." He sipped his coffee while Debbie brought a cup for Andrew.

Andrew took his first sip, slurping a little. "So," he said. "I heard you got into it with Amos out at the landfill on Saturday morning."

"Where'd you hear that?"

"Down at the VFW. Some of the boys at the bar there were talking about the Metcalfe place. Rodney says he might make a few dollars helping to fix the place up. Jimmy Sanborn's hiring him for some of the carpentry and sheetrock. They all said you went after Amos about it. You're still going on about the Metcalfe House?"

"Damn right. And if Amos doesn't see it, he needs to know."

Andrew paused before slurping more coffee, aware the morning regulars were listening. "You know about my cousin who lives over on the coast, north of Portland in Maine?"

Warren growled, "Yes, we've all heard about your cousin. And we all know where Portland is." He wanted to stop Andrew before he started. But Andrew was as unstoppable as the coming of the winter snow.

"He told me about something that happened down there in Maine a few years ago. It's sort of like what we see here with that lawyer fellow who's moved up to Bennett Falls and decided to run against Amos, or the guy from Boston who bought the Metcalfe place. You see, that little town where my cousin lives down Maine had 273 registered voters, all of them Republican, of course."

"Of course." Warren looked down at the tabletop, praying that Andrew would end this latest nonsensical story and knowing he wouldn't.

Andrew continued. "One day a new fellow moved into that little town in Maine. Just like the new folks we've got here. He was a retired lawyer from New York. Of course, he went down to the town hall and registered to vote. Everyone in town kept going on about how he was probably a Democrat and there goes the town. How it would never be the same."

Debbie came from the kitchen bringing the two men their plates of breakfast. Smiling, she goaded Andrew. She and everyone else in her café had heard this story before, but it was free entertainment. "Go on, Andrew. What happened on election day?"

"Aw, Debbie!" Warren grumbled. "Don't encourage him!"

Andrew ignored Warren. "On election day, they had 274 people go out and vote, including the New York fellow. And wouldn't you know it? When they counted up all the ballots, sure enough it was 273 Republican and one Democrat. And Ethel, the head of the League of Women voters, called out, 'just as we thought. That new fellow is a Democrat.' So everyone in town began talking about what they should do about this. They'd liked the New Yorker well enough when he first moved there, but now… Well, they still sold him his groceries when he went down to the IGA. And the postmaster still gave him his mail when he came in the post office. And people tolerated him when he went to church on Sunday. But nobody really spoke to him anymore. Not his neighbors. Nobody. So this went on for years. And every election it was the same thing. 273 Republican votes and one Democrat."

Warren sighed and gazed out the window at the rain. He knew that Andrew was approaching the end of his story. He'd heard it before. It would be over soon.

"So, after a few years, that New York fellow passed away."

"God rest his soul," someone on the other side of The Sunrise called out.

"That's right." Andrew gave a nod to the man across the café. "His family took him back to New York for the burial. And everyone in my cousin's little town thought everything would go back to normal. But you know what happened, Warren?"

"I haven't got a clue." Warren stared at his plate, took a bite of his eggs, and leaned back, his face placid as he chewed, waiting for the punch line.

"Election day rolled around and sure enough they had 273 people vote again. And when Ethel counted up all the votes… suddenly she stopped and announced to the town, '272 Republican and one Democrat.' And everyone took a moment to realize that the New Yorker was gone, but there was still that one Democrat voter in town."

Andrew waited, letting the moment sink in for everyone in the Sunrise. Warren turned to look out the window again, ignoring his old friend. Andrew continued. "And someone in my cousin's little town finally spoke up. 'My God,' he said. 'All these years we were shunning the wrong fellow!'"

The breakfast crowd roared. There was scattered applause. Andrew leaned forward and tucked into his breakfast.

"Dammit, Andrew," Warren mumbled. "You and your fool Down Maine stories. Will it never end?"

"Nope." Andrew dabbed a bit of egg from the corner of his mouth with his napkin and slurped some more coffee. He went on, emphasizing his words with waves of his fork. "But that story could be about right here in Bennett Falls, you see. No need to worry about that new lawyer running against Amos. He hasn't got a chance. But some people are all in a lather about this Sullivan fellow who's come up here with his wife. All upset about how he's fixing up the old Metcalfe house. Let it go, Warren. I've bumped into Sullivan once or twice, down at the supermarket and around town. He seems like a regular sort. His wife is nice, too. Why not leave them alone?"

"Oh, I don't have anything personal against the guy. And I don't really care one way or the other about his wife. I just don't want him to wreck our town by opening a bed and breakfast and turning Bennett Falls into some sort of a tourist Mecca."

"Come on. Jimmy Sanborn says he's putting in seven rooms, that's all. How bad can it be?"

"Seven rooms probably means at least fourteen people coming to town. They'll likely be couples. Some might even bring their kids with them. We'll be over-run. You don't see it, I know. But it's a situation waiting to happen."

Debbie passed by, dropping off two checks, one for each man. "It's a situation I won't mind. They won't come here for breakfast, but that's fourteen more mouths to feed at lunchtime."

"Nobody sees it but me," Warren fussed. "We're heading into trouble."

CHAPTER

Seven

October

Peter Lacroix stood in the parlor of the Metcalfe House. He was a short, thick-set man, his hair and beard black, but streaked with white. Writing with a pencil, he made a note in a spiral-bound notebook. Jack and Keira stood by, watching in silence, waiting for him to explain his plans. Peter mumbled something unclear about joints and pipes and pulled a tape measure off his belt. He laid the tape on the floor with an end abutting a wall and began extending it, striding sideways, holding it in place with his feet. He stretched it to the opposite wall and nodded.

"Twenty-eight feet. Thought so."

Jack pulled out his cell phone. "You can measure everything more easily and with more accuracy with this." He opened an app on his phone and aligned it with one wall, then scanned it across the room to the opposite wall. He hit a button and showed it to Peter. "There we are," he said. "Twenty-seven feet, four and a quarter inches."

Peter looked down and wrote in his notebook. "Twenty-eight feet," he said, looking up, straight into Jack's eyes. "You have to account for the extra space the line will take as it goes under the wall. And I need to allow a little wiggle room for when I connect everything."

"Okay. But this app on my phone could really help you."

"Tape measure works fine." Peter pushed a button on the side of the yellow plastic case and the tape zipped across the room, snapping back into the case. He climbed the stairs two at a time and began stomping along the hallway above Jack and Keira's heads.

Keira rested a soothing hand on Jack's arm. "Let it go. He seems to know what he's doing, and Jimmy says he's the best in town."

"I know. But come on. How accurate are his measurements? What if he doesn't order enough pipe? What if he overcharges us by quoting for too much pipe?"

"Wait for his estimate. Stay calm. See how he does."

Peter came clumping back down the stairs. "I think I've got all the information and measurements I need. Can I take a minute at the kitchen table to total everything up for you?"

"Of course," Jack said.

Without a word, Peter walked into the kitchen and sat at the table. He flipped through his spiral notebook. Looking over his shoulder, Jack and Keira saw that he had three pages covered with numbers and writing, one page for each floor of the house. He had a fourth page with numbers for shower stalls, tubs, sinks and toilets. They had already reviewed different fixtures with Peter and approved them.

Ignoring Jack and Keira, Peter worked through the numbers, patiently adding by hand and totaling with his pencil, and double-checking his math. He spoke quietly under his breath, talking to himself. He sighed heavily twice when things didn't add up.

After several minutes, he pulled a triplicate form from the notebook and set to work with a ballpoint pen, transposing items and prices onto a contract. Jack saw that the form already had their name and address filled in. There were also several lines completed, listing the fixtures.

At last, Peter sat back in his chair and looked up from the table. "Here's my estimate." He handed the triplicate form to Jack.

Jack looked it over in silence. Peter waited. Keira waited.

Jack took his pen out of his pocket, uncapped it, leaned down to the tabletop, and signed the estimate. "When can you start?" he said.

Peter took it back, signed it as well, tore off the front page, folded it in half and stuffed it in his notebook. Then he pulled off the yellow middle page and handed it to Jack. "First thing tomorrow morning," he said. He walked out the kitchen door, crossed the back porch, and left.

Keira smiled. "How was his price?" she asked.

"A thousand, maybe two thousand less than I expected. And Jimmy says he does good work. What can I say? I signed."

"He doesn't have a lot to say."

"No, he doesn't. Let's see how his work is."

Keira paused, puzzled for a moment. "How early do you think 'first thing in the morning' is?"

"We'll find out. But I have a feeling we'd better not sleep in. He could be doing demolition in our bathroom before seven."

"You never know. I'll set an alarm."

CHAPTER
Eight
Late October

The bell above the door to The Sunrise rang and everyone turned to see the person entering the café. Jack Sullivan. Heads turned as he walked to Jimmy Sanborn's table. Warren and Andrew sat two tables away, attentive, not talking, eavesdropping.

"Good morning!" Jack said, extending his hand.

Debbie hustled over with a cup of black coffee for Jack and a plate with two Danish. Jimmy already had his coffee. "On the house," Debbie said as she turned back to the counter.

Jimmy half-stood and reached across the table to shake hands. "Good to see you. Thank you for meeting me here. I use this place like my office. I like to meet all my customers here. It's been a few weeks since I last saw you. My crews have been working a lot up at the house. How are you and Keira doing, living in the midst of all my work?"

Jack sat. "We're getting along. We're sleeping in the front bedroom on the second floor, the one you've finished. Just for the time being. The rest of our things are packed in the first-floor parlor. I'm down in Boston most of the week, so Keira deals with all the workers and the noise. They started on the upstairs bedrooms. How is everything coming along?"

"All the work's on schedule. I expect you've seen that I've got things going on in the addition off the kitchen."

"Yes. Keira says your men arrive every day at dawn. You've framed everything on the new foundation. Any idea when that part of the work will be done?" Jack poured cream into his coffee and took a Danish.

"I'll get the windows in this week and have it weather-tight by the middle of next week. It's a little tricky sealing it where it adjoins the existing house. But I want to finish that by the end of October before the weather runs out. If the outside is done, I can do interior work regardless of the weather."

"Excellent. So we could move downstairs into the new apartment by early November?"

"I expect. I might still have a bit of interior painting to do the first week of November, but that seems realistic."

"I thought Peter'd come in and have all the bathrooms done by now. But sometimes we'll go days and not see him. Then he'll show up. Comes in without a word and carries fixtures up the stairs. I don't know where he is the rest of the time."

"Be patient. It's hunting season. He's probably off in the woods someplace looking for deer. He'll get the bathrooms installed in plenty of time."

"Okay. I'm used to the schedules of contractors down in Boston. I've never had to account for deer season before."

"Welcome to New Hampshire!"

Jack laughed.

Jimmy concluded their meeting. "Am I missing anything? Do you have any concerns about how things are progressing?"

"Not really. When Peter finishes the plumbing, you close up our apartment, and the new furnace is installed, we'll be almost there."

"That's right. I'll probably still be around 'til the end of the year, maybe early January taking care of painting touch-ups, baseboards, those details."

"Any word on the woodstove?"

"Oh, yes. My firewood guy talked to me last week. You'll have three cords of wood delivered within the next week or two. Deer season impacts that business, too. But the stove itself is back ordered. People buy those during the summer to prepare for the next winter, and he was sold out of the size that would fit in your fireplace. He's promising sometime around Christmas maybe. You'll have to use oil heat until then."

"That's fine. I wasn't counting on it for heat. Mostly just atmosphere for the guests when we open."

Jack got up to leave and shook Jimmy's hand, satisfied with the progress on the house. Once he left, conversation resumed throughout The Sunrise. Jimmy settled in to his breakfast and business notes.

Warren leaned across the table to Andrew. "It's a runaway train. Nothing I can do to stop it. And nobody even seems to care about it but me."

"Oh, come on Warren," Andrew said. "Why do you get so worked up about this? This Jack Sullivan fellow wants to open a bed and breakfast place. That's all. There's no reason to be so upset."

"You want to know why I'm upset? I'll tell you. I would think you'd be upset too. You remember how things were a few years ago? You ran the bank across the street from here, right? The place where they have that little bookstore now."

Andrew nodded. "The Granite State Savings and Loan. And your point?"

Warren knocked back the last of his coffee and banged down the empty mug, looking around the café, exasperated. Debbie hustled over with the coffee pot, but Warren put his hand over the top of his mug.

"Yes, please," Andrew said, holding his mug up. "Warm me up." Debbie topped him off. She turned back to the kitchen, but she remained attentive.

Warren went on. "My point is this. You worked at that little bank and financed everything happening in town. Your wife taught elementary school at the old school building down at the end of the Common. Your son Matthew graduated high school here. Life was good, right?"

"Yes, it was. Marilyn and I walked to work together every morning. Sometimes we met here for lunch. It was nice."

Warren nodded. "Yes, that's the way things were. And then a big Boston bank swooped in and took over your little bank and moved all the bank business down the road, next to the shopping mall. Put it in a brand-new building. And then that bookstore went in your old bank building."

"That they did. And the Boston folks bought me out. I retired a couple of years earlier than I planned, with a tidy sum of money from the Boston bank. Now that new bank down by the mall has a drive-through thing and a new, Boston-bred manager."

"That new manager doesn't even live here," Warren stated, his voice rising, face red and eyes large. "He has no idea what goes on in Bennett Falls or what we need. And you can't walk to work with your wife anymore. Hell, they closed the school where she taught and put the town offices in the old school building."

"Yes. So, she had to drive a mile to teach her last two years in the new school down off School Street. Your point?"

"Remember how good it was when you both walked to work and knew everyone in town? Remember when the old school was still a school and not the town offices and when the bookstore was your bank? No more. Those days are gone. It has to stop! Enough is enough. This bed and breakfast scheme is the latest thing. It's just another change, destroying what we had here in Bennett Falls."

Andrew shook his head. "I don't see all of it as a bad thing. I do miss my Marilyn. People pass. But as for the town, I like the new schools. I think the new bank building and even that new manager are good. I'm fine with the way things are now. I pay my bills, and I get out around town every day. I see my friends all over town. I meet you here for breakfast just about every morning. What more could I want?"

Warren dismissed it all with a wave of his hand, like he was swatting mosquitoes in the summer. "Bah! You don't see it. Nobody does. We've lost the Bennett Falls we knew. It's gone. And everything that's happening, like this new bed and breakfast, takes us further away."

Andrew tried to appease his friend. "Come on, Warren. It'll be okay. Give it time."

Warren stood, pushing his chair back, scraping on the wood floor. "I'm out," he said. "See you tomorrow morning."

He banged out the door, the bell tinkling cheerfully above him. Andrew took another sip of coffee and watched through the window as Warren stomped across the Common, kicking through the fallen leaves.

Debbie came over and sat with Andrew. "You okay?" she asked.

"Yes. I just wish Warren could accept that things are going to be okay. Things change. They always have. They always will. All any of us can do is make the best of it."

"True," Debbie said, leaning in toward Andrew. "You know as well as any of us that Warren's got a lot to deal with. Be patient with him. He and Lana ran their farm across the river for years. Now he's too old to farm. He can't do it anymore. And his daughter's settled over in Manchester. She and her husband aren't about to come back and run the farm. He sees it as the end of the line. He knows his family's farm is dying. I know Warren gets a call now and again asking if he wants to sell the land to someone who'll build new houses there on the river. He'll never do it. That land has been in his family for a century at least. He's scraping by, I expect, but he's sitting on a fortune in land, and money's tight, but he'll never sell."

Andrew nodded. Then he shook his head, resigned. "I understand all that. He's an old friend and I care about him and Lana, but I can't change his mind. He's in a tough situation and he blames it all on the way things have changed. There's nobody to blame. It is what it is."

CHAPTER
Nine
November

Keira and Jack had located several antique stores in nearby villages and one across the Common from The Sunrise. They purchased bedroom furniture: a four-poster bed, old dressers, bedside tables, and chairs. They squirreled all of it away in a storage unit they leased several miles down the road toward Manchester. Now, Keira decided to shop for accessories that would enhance the décor of their new guest rooms.

Jack left to work in Boston, leaving Monday morning at dawn as he had done every week since the construction was under control. Keira chose to use her time to explore the old mill building up the river in Bennett Falls. She parked her Lexus, noting faded paint covering most of the peak on the end wall of the tall brick structure. Huge red letters on a white background spelled out "Metcalfe Mills." Four stories tall and running the length of a city block, the Mill filled the space from the edge of Main Street to the shore of the river. The white-water river roared over rocks behind the mill.

Keira walked along Main Street and saw doors, some made of heavy oak, others of thick glass. Brass plates by the glass doors listed names of the tenants, law offices, and small businesses. A few people seemed to reside there. Behind the glass doors, elevators and stairs with polished brass rails ran up to what appeared to be condos on the top floors. Those, Keira imagined, might be luxurious lofts that would overlook the river.

She found several storefront shops, small retail spaces on the first floor of the vast building, their wood doors set between plate-glass windows. The shop doors opened directly onto the sidewalk, the brick wall looming above. A gourmet food shop carried a wide assortment of cheeses and spices in the window. An organic and vegetarian food store was next door. A used bookstore filled a narrow space. Tall glass doors showed the carpeted lobby of a restaurant. She saw a boutique with cute baby clothes and wooden toys. A thrift shop displayed faded and worn second-hand clothes. She passed these by after window shopping. The next store had a sign: "New Hampshire Artisan Crafts." Keira went in.

A diminutive woman with long waves of white hair greeted her. "Welcome to New Hampshire Crafts. I'm Michelle. Please let me know what I can do to help you."

"Hi. I'm Keira. My husband and I bought the big house across the river. We're fixing it up and I thought I'd look around to see if there might be anything to go with our furniture and colors."

"Oh! Mrs. Sullivan. Keira. My husband has been doing some work up there. Peter Lacroix. The plumber. He's told me all about you."

Keira noted the smocked peasant top, the long strings of wood and pottery beads around the woman's neck, the wide, loose cotton trousers, woolen socks with leather sandals. The tiny woman looked like an aged, smiling flower child. Keira tried to match this woman with the gruff, burly plumber who had been working at the Metcalfe House for several weeks.

"Oh, yes! Peter the Plumber. Yes, he's been spending a lot of time up at our place."

"Well, it's sure nice to meet you, Mrs. Sullivan. Welcome to Bennett Falls. How's Peter been treating you?"

"He treats us well!" Keira said, stressing optimism with a lift to her voice.

"It looks like he's doing good work. I stay out of his way to give him the room he needs to work. He's been putting a lot of piping inside the walls and ceilings, so I give him his space."

"That's a good idea. People say he does good work, but I know he comes across as off-putting at times. He doesn't have a lot to say to people he doesn't know that well. He's a good man, though. So, what can I help you find today, Mrs. Sullivan?"

"Call me Keira. We have seven rooms we need to set up, each with its own bathroom. We've picked out antique furniture, but we'll need accents. Soap dishes for the bathrooms, lamps for bedside tables, things like that."

"We have a few items that might do. Take a look at some of our pottery. Some of these might suit you. What do you think?"

Keira looked at the display of pottery and picked up one or two that could serve as soap dishes, or maybe just as accents on tables. "These are nice. Let me look around and see what else you have," she said.

"Those are all made by people who live nearby. We only stock crafts by local New Hampshire artists. That little dish you picked up was made by a woman over in Conway. She's very good."

Keira nodded and strolled to a table in the back of the store covered with quilts, macramé, and woven table runners. Behind the table, a tall window looked onto the rushing water of the river. Michelle followed Keira, ready to give advice.

"How do you like our little town so far, Mrs. Sullivan? Keira?"

"I like it. It's charming. We haven't had time to meet many people yet. Mostly just Jimmy Sanborn and some of the men he has working for him on our house. Your husband and a few others. They seem very friendly."

"Yes. That's good. It takes a while for some of the people here to warm up to newcomers but give it time. It's a wonderful place."

"I think so. Honestly, I haven't been able to get out much. I should, but I've been busy, staying home working. Have you lived here your whole life?"

"I could answer with one of those old northern New England jokes and say, 'not yet', but that would be foolish. Maybe even rude."

"Not yet?" Keira contemplated Michelle's statement for a moment. "Oh, as in you're still living here day-to-day. Your life's not over so you haven't lived here your whole life yet. Ha! Okay." Keira laughed briefly.

"Yes, I know. It's a dumb joke. People here say things like that, and I expect it can be hard for newcomers to understand. Have you met Andrew Holmes yet? He's famous for telling old New England stories and cracking stupid jokes."

"I don't believe I have. Is he one of the men working on our house?"

"Oh, I doubt it. He's a spry little man, as old as the hills. He lives in that big house straight ahead as you go through the covered bridge from town, right down the hill from your house at the corner of Concord Road and River Road. He's alone there now. His wife passed away a few years back and his son moved away. But Andrew's all over town. I'm sure you'll bump into him sooner or later. He's got too many stories and jokes like that. You'll see. About me, yes, I've lived here my whole life. So far, that is," Michelle added with a quiet laugh.

"That must be nice. To know everything about a place, know everyone in town."

"Oh, I don't know everyone. You're not the only newcomer. Some of the people in the condos upstairs here in the mill are new. They stay to themselves, and I haven't really met them yet. Most of the folks up in Sanbornville are also new here."

"Sanbornville?"

"It's that big, sprawling neighborhood up School Street by the high school. Go down Washington Street about a half mile after the Common. Turn right before you get to the high school. Your Jimmy Sanborn's granddaddy and dad got it built and now everyone calls that neighborhood Sanbornville. Jimmy lives up there."

"Where do you live? Are you up there too? You say you've lived here your whole life. So far," Keira added with a smile.

"No. My parents were mill workers here in the mill, and so were my grandparents and great grandparents, too. A lot of the people who worked in the mill lived in the neighborhood right across the street from here. People call my section of town 'Frenchtown' because most of us are French Canadian. Peter and I live in the house where I grew up. Peter grew up two blocks away."

"You've known each other since you were kids. That's beautiful!"

"Yes, we were high school sweethearts, I guess you could say. And still together."

"Children?"

"Yes, three kids. Two of them went to UNH," she said proudly. "And they're all gone off on their own now. Do you have children, Keira?"

"No."

Keira looked away, dismissing the question. She picked up two quilted table runners, turned and stopped back at the pottery table for three more small items. She carried them to the counter by the door. Michelle followed.

While she waited for the credit card approval, Michelle said, "I'm so glad you stopped in. Welcome to Bennett Falls. Come visit any time. Even if you don't need to buy anything, stop in. We can chat."

"That's so nice of you. I will."

"You know what you should do? If you're around next Monday, come down to the Common for our Veteran's Day parade. Everyone will be there. The parade starts at the high school at nine, goes along Washington Street by the Common, and ends at the VFW right down the street from here. You'll enjoy it, and you'll probably see everyone you know in town."

"I don't really know that many people. You'll be there?"

"Of course."

"Then I'll see you at the parade next Monday at nine."

CHAPTER
Ten
Veteran's Day

Jack and Keira left Metcalfe House in the early morning sunshine and walked down the hill to the covered bridge and the Common. They believed they had plenty of time to get there for the nine o'clock parade and didn't expect a big crowd in such a small town. The brisk walk kept them warm. Both were bundled against the sudden arrival of cold weather: Jack in a thick fleece jacket over a sweater and Keira with a down parka and a wool hat pulled down to her eyebrows.

As they came through the covered bridge, they noticed cars and trucks parked in a line along the road and a dense crowd stretched along both sides of Washington Street for the length of the Common. It was their first time on the Common. They had a few minutes before the parade began and decided to use the time to explore. Though they had driven through the town many times in the months when they were looking for a place to open a bed and breakfast and had lived in their new home for two months, they hadn't been out much. Jack was still consumed by his career in Boston, and Keira was reluctant to go out in the strange place by herself.

At the near end of the Common, across from the bridge, stood a patina-blackened bronze statue of a marching soldier dressed in a World War I uniform: a flat helmet and leggings down to his boots. He carried a rifle and a rucksack. His forever gaze stared up Main Street toward the Metcalfe Mill.

Jack and Keira paused for a moment and looked at the pedestal of the statue. Plaques with lists of the dead from several wars were bolted to the base. There were long lists for the Civil War, World War I, World War II, and a shorter list for Korea. A newer, less tarnished plaque listed two short columns of local boys lost in Vietnam. There was only one soldier listed on a shiny plaque for the Gulf Wars, a man with a French name. The birth and death dates listed next to his name showed he was young when he died.

A wide crowd had gathered at the far end of the Common around a gazebo-like white bandstand. Jack and Keira followed the path down the middle of the Common, past the flagpole. As they approached, a woman called from the crowd.

"Keira? Is that you?"

Michelle broke from the crowd, smiling, and came to them. Her waves of white hair were wrapped at the neck with a purple wool scarf. "I hardly recognized you with the hat covering half your face. I'm glad you came down. And you must be Jack. I'm Michelle, Peter Lacroix's wife. I met Keira a few days ago at my shop."

Jack reached out to shake her hand. "It's nice to meet you, Michelle. Keira told me she met you at your store. Peter's doing good work for us up at the house."

Keira asked, "When does the parade get here? What's the plan?"

"It begins at the high school, just a short way up the road. They should be starting soon. There'll be speeches here at the bandstand, then they go down to the statue and lay a wreath. At least that's the way it always goes."

Jack looked over the sprawling crowd. "I didn't expect this many people. I didn't think the town was this big."

"We're not a very big town, but absolutely everyone who lives near here comes out for our parades. We do it again on Memorial Day and the Fourth of July. A lot of the town will be in the parade, and everybody knows someone who's in it. So, if you're not marching, you're watching."

The rat-a-tat of drums and bleeping sirens sounded, causing the crowd to start pushing toward the street. Michelle led them into the press of people. "I'm here with one of my friends and her husband. They'll have saved my spot on the curb," she said as she elbowed through the crowd. "Hey, Lana, I'd like you to meet some people. This is Keira Sullivan and her husband Jack."

Lana turned and smiled. "Welcome to Bennett Falls! I'm Lana Briggs. I've heard about you, of course. Not just from Michelle. You two are the talk of the town, what with the work you're doing up at the Metcalfe place."

Lana turned to Warren, preparing to introduce him, but he had turned and moved away as much as the crowd would allow. He intently watched for the approach of the parade, pointedly ignoring the two newcomers. She turned back to Michelle and her new friends.

"It's nice to meet you, Lana," Jack said. "It's great to get out and meet some of the people who live here. I'm still working down in Boston a few days each week, and I'm spending most of my time at my house when I'm home, overseeing the guys working there. It's nice to have a day like today and take time off to come into town and see what's going on."

Warren muttered, "Should have stayed in Boston."

Jack ignored the remark, puzzled but pretending not to have heard over the sounds of the approaching parade.

"Here they come!" Michelle shouted.

First to arrive was the Bennett Falls Regional High School band, surprisingly large for a small town. Working with a regional school, drawing students from the outlying farms and villages as well as from Bennett Falls, the band director had assembled more than a hundred musicians.

Rank after rank of students marched by in crisp red and black uniforms, trimmed with white braid and brass buttons. They were very good, playing a Sousa march and keeping their lines straight as they marched past.

A fire truck labeled Bennett Falls Volunteer Fire Department followed the band. Its siren blared, picking up the noise once the high school band stopped playing. Peter Lacroix sat in the front seat, and he leaned out the window, grinned and shouted, "Hey, Michelle! Light a fire for me to put out!"

"See you as soon as you get home, my brave firefighter!"

A second fireman, riding outside the truck, tossed wrapped candies into the crowd, watching for children, and waving at people he knew. The children scrambled in the street behind the fire truck, screeching and grabbing candies.

Several flat-bed farm trucks, dressed up with crepe paper streamers like floats, followed the fire truck. They represented the Grange, the Rotary, and the Lions. Two lines from the VFW came along, old men in tight uniforms, marching in step, eyes front, quietly calling a cadence as they marched smartly by, boots echoing on the pavement. Then the Cub Scouts and Boy Scouts wandered by, followed by the Brownies and Girl Scouts, all of them milling out of step. A small group of Little League baseball players came next, even though it wasn't baseball season. They were dressed in their baseball uniforms over sweatshirts but wearing mittens and stocking caps. A larger group of youth hockey players came along, also in uniform. Jimmy Sanborn walked beside the young hockey players, wearing a hockey jersey that matched his team. He saw Jack, pointed, smiled, and waved. "Good to see you out here, Jack," he called.

"Good to see you too, Jimmy," Jack shouted back, happy to be engaged in the parade. It felt great to know someone marching in his new little town.

Jimmy saw a woman and a young girl in the crowd. He waved again, "Hey there!"

Michelle explained. "That's Jimmy's wife, Lynn, and his daughter,

Christine. He and Lynn have been together forever. His son is one of the hockey players."

Led by Amos Sanborn, a flock of the local politicians strolled along next, wearing dark overcoats, neckties showing behind the lapels, waving and calling to supporters. Amos had been re-elected a few days before. Suddenly, the parade came to a stop with the end of the parade, the middle school band and the second volunteer fire truck next to the bandstand. "That's the fire chief driving the second truck," Michelle explained. "Wilbur Jackson. He's been with our Volunteer Fire Department as long as I can remember."

With the parade paused, a moment of silent anticipation grew. A large boy in the middle school band set the bass drum on the pavement and sat down in the street next to it.

Amos led the group of politicians and clergy off the street, through the crowd, onto the bandstand. The ceremony began with three short prayers, the first delivered in a resonant bass voice by Reverend Thompson, the white-haired Congregational Church pastor, the second by Father Girouard, the gaunt priest from the Catholic Church, and finally, a short prayer by Paul Brown, the young, eager minister from the Baptist Church. Then Amos stepped to the microphone and gave a heart-rending oration explaining the sacrifices made by too many of the young men of Bennett Falls over the decades. He told how their service had preserved freedom for Bennett Falls and was a debt that could never be repaid and should never be forgotten. Applause, muffled by mittens, followed his speech.

The politicians and clergymen left the bandstand and rejoined the parade. The middle school boy climbed to his feet and picked up his drum. The high school band, waiting at attention halfway along the Common, got ready. The band director called out a command, their drums started again, and, playing another march, they led the parade farther along Washington Street. The crowd followed alongside them, tramping across the frozen lawn of the Common.

"What happens now?" Keira asked Michelle.

"They lay a wreath at the statue. Then the parade finishes up the road at the VFW hall."

The high school band turned the corner onto Main Street at the end of the Common, marched a short way, and stopped again. The rest of the parade followed and stopped.

The politicians and clergymen left the parade route a second time and cut through the crowd to the statue. Amos Sanborn stepped away from the line of dignitaries and laid a ribbon-decked, laurel wreath at the base of the statue. He moved back a pace and paused in silence, hands folded, solemnly contemplating the wreath and the statue. Finally, he saluted, and returned to the parade route.

The drums started again and the parade was on its way. As the last rank of the middle school band passed the statue, the crowd began milling about in the road. Some of the spectators followed the parade up the Main Street hill to the VFW hall, possibly going to gather their children who were in the parade. Or maybe they planned to join the veterans for an early morning beverage at the VFW.

"Now what?" Keira asked again.

Michelle replied, "That's about it."

Lana added, "It might not be as big as parades you might be used to down in Boston. But we like it."

Jack grinned. "It was great! True, the parades are bigger in Boston. But your bands are really good. It was a lot of fun."

"Bah!" Warren said.

"Are you a veteran?" Jack asked Warren.

"Vietnam."

"And you're not in the parade?"

Warren mumbled, "I don't march in parades or hang out at the VFW."

He turned and walked away, heading for The Sunrise Café.

"That's my husband," Lana said. "Don't mind him. Things are never good enough for him. I'll go have a cup of coffee with him now, calm him down, and then take him home. It was nice meeting you two. I'm sure I'll see you around town."

She chased after Warren. Andrew Holmes appeared from the crowd and trotted across the Common, following Warren and Lana.

Michelle hugged Keira. "I'm glad you had a good time. It was so nice to meet you, Jack. Keira, come up and see me at the store sometime. We can talk some more."

"I will. You enjoy the rest of your day."

As Jack and Keira walked back over the covered bridge and started up the hill to their house, Jack asked, "What was that one guy all about? He didn't seem to enjoy the parade at all."

"I don't know. He seemed upset from the moment we got there. Maybe he and his wife lost someone in Vietnam or another war?"

"Maybe. Maybe he has trouble thinking about his time in Vietnam. Who knows? Aside from him, it was a good time. I'm not going to let his attitude wreck the whole day. Let's get inside where it's warm."

"Would you like me to fix a cup of something to warm us up?"

"That would be perfect."

They walked the rest of the way, holding gloved hands, happy.

CHAPTER

Eleven

November

Peter Lacroix banged through the door to The Sunrise, looked around, and found Jimmy. He walked over and dropped into the seat across the table. "What's up, Jimmy? You wanted to see me?"

"Yes. Let's have breakfast and talk about the Metcalfe House."

Debbie appeared at their table. "What'll it be?"

Jimmy answered first. "My usual. And Peter, get whatever you want. I'm paying."

Peter stuffed the menu behind the salt and pepper shakers and said, "I'll have the Supreme Breakfast. Ham, onion, and three eggs scrambled with cheese. Wheat toast. And coffee."

"Got it." Debbie hustled back to the kitchen.

"So…?" Peter asked.

"So, give me an update. Where are we on all the work up there?"

"I've got four of the seven guest rooms done, the fixtures in place. And the apartment for the Sullivans, too. All the pipes are in, of course. I got all the plumbing work done a while back so you could finish off the walls. The remaining three rooms are rough plumbed, ready for the fixtures."

Jimmy smiled. This was a time to manage his plumber with subtlety, taking his time, keeping his man happy. "How do the finished guest rooms look? I saw what you did with the apartment. That turned out really well. The Sullivans are settled in now that the water's running in their apartment."

"The guest rooms look good. They've all got those rain showers where the water falls straight out of a big head on the ceiling in oversized shower stalls. They're fine."

"That's good. Which three rooms still need to be finished?"

"The two on the third floor and the one on the back of the second. If the Sullivans wanted to open for business, they probably could right now, just with the four rooms that are done."

"I don't think they'll be opening till spring. They need some furniture and their business license. They'll have to wait for the town meeting to get approved for that. But I'll let them know you're done with all but those last three rooms."

"Yeah. Jack can probably see that. He seems to understand what I'm doing. I don't know if his wife understands what I'm up to."

"Oh, Keira's pretty aware. I expect she sees it too. Any idea when you can finish off those last three rooms?"

"I've got the fixtures in my warehouse. I bought everything at one time, so I got a volume discount. I take things up there one room at a time. My truck's only so big and then I have to haul everything up the stairs."

Jimmy nodded. "I understand. Do you need help carrying it up the stairs?"

"No, I can manage. I can probably finish in a few weeks."

"A few weeks? But it shouldn't take more than a day for each room."

"Yeah. Just about a day for each one. Carrying everything in. Hooking it all up. Turning the water on and testing it for leaks. I've got a lot going on. I can do the work in three or four days, but there's other things happening."

"Of course. I understand. What else have you got going?" Jimmy knew the answer to his question, but it was a gentle way to deal with the delay.

"Well. There's a lot happening right now. It's deer season, for one thing. I've been up north."

"Did you get anything?"

Peter smiled and leaned back in his chair, tipping his Bruins cap back. "Yeah, as a matter of fact. I got a little buck last Tuesday. I've got it in with Archie now, preparing the meat. I should be ready to pick up more than a few pounds of frozen venison on Friday."

"Very good. Congratulations!"

Debbie came over with two plates. She handed Peter a big platter covered with scrambled eggs, ham, and toast. Jimmy got a small plate with a toasted English muffin around a fried egg, a slice of cheese, and bacon. Debbie placed a check by Jimmy's plate.

As she turned to go back to the kitchen, Andrew left his usual seat across from Warren and walked up to the table. "Did I hear you say you went deer hunting, Peter?"

Debbie stopped and turned to watch and listen. Silence filled the Sunrise as all the regulars waited for Andrew's next story.

"Yeah," Peter replied. "Up in the mountains. Got myself a little buck."

"Well, good for you. Did I ever tell you about when Warren and I went bear hunting?"

Across the room, Warren fussed. "Aw, Andrew! We never went bear hunting!" Warren shook his head and had a sip of coffee. "He's a damn fool," he said to no one in particular.

Andrew ignored his friend. "Yes, Warren and I went up there in the mountains to go bear hunting. Packed our guns on the rack in the back of my truck and drove up in those mountains."

Andrew paused, looking around to be sure everyone was paying attention.

Jimmy led him on. "So, what happened, Andrew? Did you two get yourselves a bear?"

"Well. As long as you asked. We came to a fork in the road. And there was a sign. And the sign said 'Bear Left.' So we turned around and came home."

Silence. No one in the café laughed. No one said a word. Andrew turned and walked back to his seat across from Warren. Debbie sighed and went back to the kitchen.

Warren shook his head. "That's the dumbest joke I've ever heard. The dumbest thing you've ever said, Andrew. And that's saying a lot."

"Well, if it's a joke, why didn't anybody laugh?" Andrew asked. "I'm hurt."

"Nobody laughed because it's the worst joke you've ever told. And everyone's heard you tell it a thousand times already anyway."

"Maybe I'll save it for that new Sullivan fellow. He's never heard it. He'll laugh."

"Bah. It's such a dumb joke even he won't laugh."

Back at their table, Peter and Jimmy dug into their breakfasts. "Where were we?" Jimmy asked.

"Oh, the deer I got. And then Andrew stopped over."

"Oh, yes. Do you think you could finish those last three bathrooms now that deer season is over?"

"Sure. Give me a couple of weeks?"

"That's fine. You can be done by the first week in December? I want to give you the last payment, but I can't until you're finished."

"Sure. End of the first week of December. I could use the money for Christmas."

"That's right. First week of December then. Congratulations again for your deer. I'm sure you and Michelle will enjoy the venison this winter."

Chapter

Twelve

Keira and Jack woke at dawn on Thanksgiving, chilled in their new apartment off the kitchen. It was unusually hushed. Usually, they could hear the quiet sound of cars passing nearby on Concord Road, sometimes even the roar of the big trucks that cut through, shifting down to climb the hill, avoiding the interstate as they passed through Bennett Falls and other small towns. Today was silent, maybe because it was a holiday.

Jack rose and looked out the window. "Oh! Keira, come look!"

She joined him and watched soft snow falling, weighing down the pine boughs, fluff covering the lawn. She leaned her head on his shoulder and pulled her robe close. "It's beautiful," she said. "We've had flurries, nothing more than an inch deep, nothing that even slowed life down."

"What about my parents and my sister?" Jack asked. "They're supposed to be coming for dinner today and to see the house."

"You'd better call them. I don't know how bad it is in Boston, but maybe we should postpone?"

"The forecast was only for one to three inches."

Keira laughed. "Isn't that what they always say? We've got about three inches already and it doesn't look like it's letting up."

"I'll check the forecast again. My folks aren't supposed to arrive till two anyway. It's a two-hour drive from Boston. I'd hate for them to get stuck."

Keira headed for the shower and Jack checked the forecast again. It now predicted two to four inches with more in the mountains. He wondered if Bennett Falls qualified as "mountains." Certainly, the hills around the town and to the north were higher elevation than Boston, or even than Manchester, where the broadcast originated.

He waited until after breakfast and called his parents. "Hi. It's Jack. How's the weather down in Boston?"

His dad answered. "Light snow. They don't expect much and figure it will stop later this morning. What's it like up there?"

"We've already got about six inches. I can dig out the driveway, but I don't know if you can get here or if you'll be stuck, even if you make it. We've got space for you to stay if you have to. Four of our guest rooms are ready. But do you want to end up spending the weekend?"

"No. We want to see the place now that you've got it almost all fixed up, but maybe we should wait. Maybe in a week?"

Jack sat down, elbows on the kitchen table, resting his forehead on his palm. "That's probably for the best. I really wanted to see all of you. Maybe let's wait a week and do it then. I really miss you guys. I miss the whole Boston crowd. Let's wait."

After the call, Jack slumped. Looking at Keira, he said, "I feel very alone here right now. You know how close my family is. Being up here, I miss my parents. And you know me and my sister. Colleen's my best friend, other than you." He hugged Keira. "Thanksgiving was always a big thing. Watching the parade on television. Football games. Dinner."

"At least you still have a family. I've got no one now that my mom died. And I'm stuck here all week, supervising carpenters and workers. You go down to Boston every week. Not that I have that many friends left there. Most of my college friends have moved away from Boston."

"Sure," Jack fussed. "My family is like your family now. But now they can't come, and it looks like the whole day is ruined. No turkey, nothing."

Keira pushed aside her own troubles and soothed him, wrapping an arm around him, pulling him close. "We'll do all that. I know you miss your parents and your sister. We'll make it a good day here, just the two of us. If your family can get up here a week from now, I'll cook another turkey."

"Sure." Jack looked out the frosted window at the snow. "If we'd been able to have kids, we could go out and play in the snow with them. We could make a snowman. But now, with no kids, the snow is just an annoyance."

"Look on the bright side!" Keira tried to cheer him up, ignoring the mention of their childless life. "It's beautiful. Look how it is on the pine trees across the yard."

"It's just cold and wet. I hate it."

Keira put the turkey in the oven. Around noon, the snow changed to rain. There were eight inches of snow on the ground. By early afternoon, the sun was out, and the snow began to melt. Snow slid off the roof, thudding to the ground behind the house. The pine branches released their loads of snow, springing back.

Jack and Keira spent a relaxed day alone in the big house together, never going outside.

Friday morning, it was sunny again. When Jack stepped out the door onto the porch, the air was fresh and warm. Most of the snow had melted. Only traces remained beneath the pines, and in shady spots. The grassy lawn was wet and muddy. Jack set to work in shirtsleeves, shoveling the last traces of wet snow off the long driveway and the turnaround in front of the house.

While Jack tidied up the driveway, Keira mused. She called Sarah, her friend from college back in Boston. "We were snowed in yesterday. Jack's parents and his sister Colleen were supposed to come up for the day and for dinner, but they couldn't."

"What did you do?"

"We had a quiet day. Had a turkey dinner and watched football. It wasn't that bad, but Jack misses his family."

"How about you?"

Keira leaned her elbows on the kitchen table and sighed. "My mom's gone now. I've got no family. Jack's family and my friends, people like you are all I have left. And you're all in Boston." Keira paused, fighting back tears. "Sometimes I feel very alone in the middle of nowhere, stuck in this little town in the mountains. I don't know anybody, really. Jack goes to Boston every week. But I'm alone. It's hard."

"You get back to Boston from time to time, right? We should do lunch the next time you're down."

"I don't come down that often. Maybe once a month for a meeting I can't handle remotely. I'm still working, but it's all virtual. Anyway, either Jack or I have to be here for the workmen. Jack's still working down there, so it's my job to stay and be with the carpenters."

"But you've found new friends in New Hampshire, haven't you?"

"Yes." Keira thought about Michelle for a moment. "But it's not the same. I'm by myself. Could you come visit sometime?"

Sarah heard her distress. "Maybe I can come up after Christmas. But with Tom and our kids, and all the holiday craziness, I don't know if I can get there until January. Maybe New Year's? Would you like me to come up for a long weekend at the first of the year?"

"Yes."

"Let's plan on it. We'll all come up, maybe do New Year's Eve together. Are you ready to put us all up for a few days?"

"Yes, the house is almost finished. We have plenty of room."

"Then we'll do it. Hang in there, Keira. We'll talk to you soon."

The call ended and Keira sat back in her winged armchair in the parlor, looking out at the wet lawn and at Jack, in his shirt sleeves, pushing the slush off the steps to the front porch. He was smiling while he worked.

She felt terribly alone.

Colleen leaned against her brother on the sofa in the wide parlor of the Metcalfe House. "How are you and Keira doing?" she asked. "The house is beautiful. Are you settling in?"

Jack kissed the top of his sister's head. "We're doing well!" he said with enthusiasm. "The house is almost finished. There are three bathrooms to finish upstairs and some painting and trim work needs to be completed. That's all. We've started meeting neighbors, people from around town, not just the men who've been working on the house. It's a small town, so it won't take us long to know everyone. So, aside from the fact that we've cooked a whole turkey for the second time in two weeks, we're fine."

Jack's dad laughed and joined the conversation. "Nothing wrong with turkey. When we missed dinner here on Thanksgiving, we had a feast of whatever we had in the freezer. Let's think of this as Thanksgiving all over again."

Jack laughed. "And with less traffic getting here from Boston, I expect!"

"Yes. A bit of Christmas shopper traffic near a mall in Manchester, but nothing to worry about."

Late in the afternoon, after the turkey dinner, when the dishes were done, they all packed into Jack's SUV for the trip to St. Mark's for Mass. Jack parked on the street next to the Common. Since dusk had settled in, lights glittered on the trees scattered across the Common. Wreaths hung on every lamppost. Pine garlands and lights circled the entrance to the covered bridge. Matching garlands and lights framed Main Street up the hill toward the Metcalfe Mill.

St. Mark's was a brick church that looked like it had been built in the same era as the old Metcalfe Mill building, probably more than one hundred fifty years ago. The brickwork showed old mortar and the windows were framed with white-painted wood. The main door was tall, heavy oak. The church was half the size of their parish church back in Quincy. The Mass was the same as everywhere, but St. Mark's held a sense of intimacy hard to find in the vast space of their familiar church in Massachusetts.

When the Mass finished, as they all walked back to Jack's car, Colleen suddenly stopped. "My God! Look up!"

They did. In the clean, cold New Hampshire night, the Milky Way made a bright band across the sky. Even the small Christmas lights, set out in the trees on the Common, couldn't obscure the brilliance of the stars. They stood silently, looking up at the sky.

"I've never seen the stars so clearly back in Boston," Colleen whispered.

"Keira! Jack!" Their silent contemplation broke as Michelle came out of St. Mark's and hurried over.

"Michelle," Keira said. "It's good to see you. This is Jack's family from down in Boston. His parents and his sister Colleen."

"Welcome to Bennett Falls," Michelle said, shaking each of their hands. "I'm Michelle Lacroix. It's so nice to meet all of you. We love having Jack and Keira as a part of our little town."

Jack's father replied, speaking for the whole family. "Why thank you, Michelle. It's good to be here and see where Jack and Keira have settled."

There wasn't much more to say before the cold drove them to their cars.

Back in the warmth of the Metcalfe House, enjoying a light dinner of leftovers, Colleen asked, "The woman we met after Mass? She's one of your new friends here?"

Keira nodded. "I met her when I went shopping for things for the house. She has a little shop in the big mill here in town. All local crafts by New Hampshire artists."

"Her husband is the plumber who's done the work on the house," Jack added.

"You've met a lot of the locals?" Jack's father asked.

"Yes," Jack replied.

"A few," Keira corrected. "You know me. I've never been that outgoing. It's not easy for me to become acquainted with new people. But we've met a handful. There's Michelle and her husband, Peter the Plumber, and Jimmy Sanborn, the contractor, and the other carpenters and people who've been working here. And we've bumped into a few more around town. We met Michelle's friend Lana at the Veteran's Day parade. And there's an old gentleman, Andrew, who lives right down the hill by the covered bridge. I don't remember his last name, but he's friendly."

"Andrew Holmes," Jack clarified. "He seems to be the town's storyteller. I didn't know you'd met him, Keira. I met him at The Sunrise Café one time when I was there with Jimmy."

"He saw me at the grocery store last week and came over," Keira replied. "Very gentlemanly. He tipped his cap and introduced himself as my neighbor. He said you and he'd met at The Sunrise."

"What's The Sunrise?" Colleen asked, looking puzzled.

Jack explained. "It's a little breakfast place on the Common. It seems to be the center of everything happening in town. The contractor working on our house uses it as his office."

Jack's father smiled. "Isn't that the way with small towns? Your grandfather ran his construction business out of a bar in Southie when you were a little boy. Do you remember that, Jack?"

Keira shook her head. "Yes, it's a lot like that, but Boston's a big city. Not like here."

Jack disagreed. "Southie's like a small town on the edge of Boston. Everyone there knows everyone else. It's probably the same here."

Keira tried to agree with Jack but found it hard. "I guess," she said. "In South Boston, it takes time to get into the flow of the town if you're not from there. Even if you're from Boston, it takes time. I hope it doesn't take us that long here."

"It won't take long," Jack assured her.

Keira slumped in her chair. "It will," she said. "We really don't know many people, and we've been here since August. I don't expect it'll get any easier to meet people in the winter when everyone stays in their houses."

"So go out. Spend time downtown. Talk to people," Colleen said.

"It's not that easy," Keira repeated.

"We'll be fine," Jack asserted.

Keira mumbled to herself, "You're in Boston all the time. You don't know what it's like stuck here alone all week."

Again, Jack scolded. "So, go out and meet people. I'm never home but I probably know as many people here as you do. I already feel like I'm part of the town."

Trying to keep the visit with Jack's parents cordial, Keira said nothing more on the topic.

CHAPTER

Fourteen

Jack had left before sunrise Monday morning for the drive to Boston. Keira remained alone again in the quiet house, picking up from the family visit, getting ready to vacuum. The clump of footsteps on the porch preceded a knock on the front door. She opened it to find Peter standing on the porch looking back at his truck on the drive.

He turned back to the door, head down. "I've got the fixtures for your three bathrooms. Can I come set one of them up?"

"Of course. Come on in."

"I'll be right back." He walked to his truck and picked up a bulky box from the tailgate. He brought it back to the house, grunting with the exertion, pushed past Keira, across the hall and up the stairs.

Keira heard bumping on the second floor, and a mumbled curse. Then Peter came down, went out and took a hand truck off the back of his truck, setting it on the gravel. He climbed in the bed of the truck and pushed a bigger, heavier box onto the tailgate. Back on the ground, he slid the big box off the tailgate, onto the hand truck, strapped it on and rolled across the frozen gravel driveway to the porch steps.

"Can I help?" Keira called.

"No. I've got it. It's the toilet. Just make sure the front door is open and stay out of the way."

He pulled the hand truck, banging up the steps and across the porch. Then he bumped up the stairs to the second floor, one step at a time. He made several more trips back and forth to his truck. Finally, he settled in upstairs.

Keira spent the morning vacuuming the downstairs. When she finished, she set to work on the internet. Preparing marketing campaigns required a lot of solitary time on the computer. She had found that, without the interruptions that were part of her days in the office in Boston, she could be very productive. Working remotely, she completed most of her weeks' assignments in less than twenty hours; two, maybe three intense days of concentrated work.

With her newfound free time, she had begun to work on a website for The Metcalfe House Bed and Breakfast. Even though it wasn't finished, still lacking photographs and descriptive prose, it looked beautiful. She couldn't wait to link it to various lodging and tourism sites for visitors to the White Mountains.

Today though, with the constant noise of Peter working in the second-floor bathroom, she couldn't concentrate. It was as distracting as if she were in her office in Boston, but without her co-workers. She felt more alone than usual, even with Peter bumping and clanking and cursing as he worked upstairs. At noon, Peter came down the stairs and stopped in the kitchen where Keira was eating her lunch.

"Everything's just about set up there," he said. "I'm going to get lunch. I'll be back in an hour or so to finish up."

"Okay. Would you like me to fix you a sandwich here?"

"No. That's okay, thanks. I'll be back to finish up that bathroom sometime this afternoon. And I'll try to finish the third-floor bathrooms later this week."

"Oh. Good. I'll see you this afternoon. I might be out running errands, but I'll leave the door unlocked. Just come in and do what you need to do."

Peter nodded, gave a short wave, almost a salute, and went out the front door without a word. Odd man, thought Keira. I wonder what's bothering him. Maybe it's just his nature.

Keira finished lunch and went upstairs to inspect the bathroom. The shower fixtures and toilet were installed. The sink was in place, but it lacked faucets. Peter's toolbox sat in the middle of the floor next to a big mat he must have used when he crawled under things. The other two bathrooms on the third floor had boxes of fixtures, but nothing was installed. Keira looked over everything, though she had no idea what to look for.

The house was quiet again. Keira considered going back to work on her computer but found no inspiration. She needed fresh air. Out the door she went, leaving the front door unlocked for Peter. She expected unlocked doors were a common, safe practice in a town like Bennett Falls. Not so in Boston of course, or even in their small house near the city in Quincy.

Keira thought for a moment, considering where she might go. She knew so little about Bennett Falls. Maybe sightseeing, she thought. This is a chance to learn my way around the town. I've lived here almost four months, but I've never really taken the time to explore. She drove down the hill, through the covered bridge and along the edge of the Common, noting Peter's pickup parked near The Sunrise. Someday, maybe I should go back and check out the Sunrise with Jack? We could get breakfast. Not today. Maybe this weekend. She continued along Washington Street past the bandstand, out onto the Manchester Road. As she approached the high school, she turned right onto School Street.

Keira passed the middle school, elementary school, and a series of streets turning into a new residential area. This must be Sanbornville, she pondered, the neighborhood Michelle told me about that Jimmy Sanborn's grandfather built. Maybe I should stop in Michelle's store while I'm out. She's invited me to come back, and I'm always too busy. I spend all my time working and being at the house for the carpenters.

School Street climbed for a half mile past the last street in Sanbornville.

Keira came to a crossroad. The street sign at the intersection read Woodland Road. She turned right again, assuming that would bring her back to downtown Bennett Falls. She passed the Grange Hall, its dirt parking lot empty. The road rolled over low hills, weaving through farm fields with long grass bleached by the cold winter sun, leaning and bobbing in the chilled wind. Patches of woods, bare trees, rock walls, and scrub pine bordered the empty fields. It impressed Keira how much open space there was in Bennett Falls only a mile from the center.

She passed small clapboard houses, many of them appearing to be very old with weathered paint and battered trim. Others, larger and newer looking, were set on landscaped lots with perfect lawns, cleared of leaves and still green despite the winter. Shady spots on the vast lawns were dusted with remnants of snow. Woodland Road wound over a steep hill, through a heavily forested area, and began to descend from the hills into a grid of narrow streets crowded with small houses. Frenchtown. Straight ahead, Keira could see the tall brick front of the Metcalfe Mill building. She turned right again on Main Street, parked, and walked to New Hampshire Artisan Crafts.

"Keira!" Michelle called when she saw Keira come through the door. "How are you?"

"I'm good. Your husband's up working at the house. I thought I'd go for a drive, see the town, drop by for a visit."

"I'm glad you did. Have you eaten? I was about to grab a bite for lunch."

Keira shook her head. "No, I already ate a sandwich back at the house."

"That's okay. Come with me. Get something to drink while I eat. I'm going to close up for a few minutes and run next door."

Keira nodded and followed Michelle out. Michelle hung a small white sign on the door that read, "Closed for lunch. Back in an hour." She locked the store and led Keira two doors down the street to double glass doors labeled "The Old Mill."

They went in and up three stairs to a hushed, carpeted foyer. A young hostess greeted them. "Hi Michelle. I see you've got a guest. Two today?"

"Yes. Can we have a seat by the window?"

"Of course. I'll give you the table between the window and the fireplace. The fire will keep you nice and warm."

The hostess led them to their table. Out the window, Keira noted a massive waterwheel against the river-side wall, the crest of the wheel level with the dining room ceiling. More than half the wheel was hidden below floor level. Next to the wheel, insulated windows ran from near the floor all the way to a high, wood-beamed ceiling, giving a view of the rapids and small waterfalls that had powered the waterwheel and the mill in its day. Across from their table, a wide brick fireplace offered a wood fire, crackling and hissing, heating the restaurant.

"What do you think of The Old Mill?" asked Michelle.

Keira looked around at the white tablecloths, the widely spaced tables, the charm of the brick walls and wood beams. She smiled. "This is not at all what I expected. I thought The Sunrise was the only place in town to eat. I didn't know you had a restaurant like this in Bennett Falls."

"The Sunrise is a good spot, too," Michelle said. "Everyone goes there for breakfast. And a lot of locals go there for lunch, as well. But there's a different crowd at the Old Mill for lunch." Michelle tossed a glance at people at other tables in the restaurant, and Keira followed her look. She saw business people, men in neckties and women in dresses.

Michelle continued. "The local bankers, lawyers, and some of the real estate people eat here. I believe some drive all the way over from Concord. It's a little more expensive than The Sunrise, but I get a deal because I work here."

"Really? What do you do here?"

"I'm the hostess a couple of nights a week. Sometimes in a pinch I still wait tables. Most nights this time of year, Peter goes down to the VFW to watch the Bruins games at the bar. That leaves me alone, and I come here for a few hours in the evening. I've worked here since the place opened, not long after I got out of high school, so that's a lot of years. I enjoy it."

"You've got your job at the little shop next door and then this? You're busy."

"I guess. What else would I be doing? I own the store and it does all right in the summer with the tourists. We get a lot of business in the fall too. People come to New Hampshire to look at the leaves. Right now, we have a few Christmas parties scheduled here in the restaurant. Some businesses book us every year. Except on the weekends, it'll close soon after New Year's Eve until the first of April. My shop is slow that time of year too, and with the restaurant closed, I relax all winter."

"I wondered when you closed the store for lunch. I wouldn't want you to miss out on customers." As she said it, Keira recalled Michelle locking the door to the store. She worried, was I wrong to leave my house unlocked? I had to leave it unlocked so Peter could finish his plumbing. I hope everything is all right.

Michelle carried on the conversation. "I'm missing nothing. I opened at nine today as I always do. All morning I only had two customers, two little old ladies who came in together, walked around a few minutes whispering to each other, and then left without buying anything. I don't know why I even stay open after Thanksgiving. I keep expecting Christmas shoppers, I guess."

The waitress approached, eager for their order but tactfully waiting a distance from the table for them to pause. When she saw a break in the conversation, she came closer and smiled. "Are we ready?" she asked.

Michelle ordered a chicken salad sandwich, then caught the waitress by the arm and said, "Please bring my friend a cup of the cream of broccoli soup."

"Sure, Michelle," the waitress said as she headed to the kitchen.

"I told you I'd had lunch."

"Yes, but you've never tasted the soup. You're going to love it!"

They settled in to wait for their meals.

"How are your kids?" Keira asked.

"They're fine. My daughter and her husband and our granddaughter will be coming up from Boston for Christmas. Our son is out in Seattle. We'll talk with him on the phone of course."

"You have two children?"

"No. Three. We also have a son who's in Texas. We don't hear much from him."

Tactfully, aware from their earlier conversation that Keira and Jack had no children, Michelle asked, "You said you have no children?"

Keira remembered telling Michelle earlier. It couldn't be avoided. "No," she replied. "For a while we put our careers first. Then, a couple of years ago we tried. No luck."

Michelle nodded. "Oh. Okay." It was clearly a topic not to be pursued.

"So what do you do up at Metcalfe House?" Michelle asked, changing the subject. "How do you fill your days?"

"I work remotely with my old marketing company in Boston. It was hard when we had a lot of construction work up at the house. It was always noisy and people coming and going. I'm just about finished with my Boston job, now. I have a contract for a couple of more months. And Jack and I have hit a bunch of the antique stores to buy new, or should I say old furniture for the place. We're setting it up with antiques. So I've been really busy until the last week or so. It's getting quiet up there now."

"So now what?"

"I spend a few hours a week working at my old job. And I'm building a website for the house, a place where people can make reservations when we open. That's about it."

"Well, if you're ever restless, come on down to the store. I'll put you to work if you're not careful!"

Keira laughed. But the offer sounded enticing. She couldn't imagine how else she might fill the days ahead, alone in the house with Jack still working in Boston and her consultant contract winding down.

The waitress brought their lunches. Keira tasted a small spoonful of the soup. "Oh! You were right! This is wonderful!"

Michelle smiled. "This place gets reviews in foodie magazines and news columns all over New England. People say it's really good. All I know is it's the best food in Bennett Falls."

"Maybe Jack and I should come here for New Year's Eve."

"Make your reservations now," advised Michelle.

"What will you and Peter do for New Year's?"

"I know we won't come here. We might have a couple of people over to the house. My best friend and her husband. Remember Lana from the parade and her husband?"

"Oh. Yes." Keira remembered the sullen man who didn't seem to want to talk to her or Jack.

They took an hour at lunch, talking, lingering over the food and splitting a heated brownie with vanilla ice cream for dessert.

Keira thought about her afternoon. She had left the Metcalfe House on a whim, wanting to learn a little about her new town. More than the exploration of the back roads, Keira was thankful for the companionship she found with Michelle. It eased her loneliness.

It was nearing sunset when Keira got back to the Metcalfe House. She went in, locking the door behind her. The house was silent. Fearfully, she checked that nothing was missing, confirming that her jewelry was still in its box in her dresser and her computer undisturbed. Relieved, she went upstairs to see how Peter's work was coming along. His toolbox sat in the middle of the bathroom next to the mat, the same as when she left. The sink still needed faucets.

CHAPTER

Fifteen

Keira settled in for the winter. Every morning she greeted the few workmen who came by to put on finishing touches. She waited for Peter LaCroix to come back. He didn't. His toolbox waited in the middle of the second-floor bathroom. The box with the faucets still sat beside it. Keira spent most of each day finalizing her consultant work for her old Boston job. She did her Christmas shopping online and developed the Metcalfe House website to be ready for the day when they would finally open for business.

Every few days it snowed, small overnight storms, flakes falling silently through the darkness, glistening in the faint sunlight at dawn. Keira woke many mornings to find several inches on the steps and the driveway. She pushed the snow away, working around the workmen's trucks, annoyed by having to dig over the packed-down tire tracks. She expected there'd be a real blizzard sooner or later and dreaded that eventuality. How would she cope if Jack remained in Boston? Once, as she was finishing shoveling the long driveway to the Concord Road, pushing the snow to the lawn, she mumbled, "I hope Jack is home when we get a big storm. I can't handle deep snow by myself."

Keira noticed that when the snowfall totaled less than a few inches, Bennett Falls hardly slowed down. Schools opened on time. Traffic ran up and down Concord Road just as it did on any other morning. "It's a nuisance," one of the carpenters told her. "That's all. We can't let the weather boss us around, now, can we?"

Many of the trucks the men drove when they came to work at the house now had gargantuan tires with thick tread. They also carried plow blades mounted on the front.

Anyhow, she mused, the crisp snow, freshened several times a week, gave the town the pretty look of an old Currier and Ives print. It lent itself to the Christmas season ambience of the little town set on a river in the mountains.

For all the beauty of Bennett Falls in the snow, and in spite of being busy with her consulting work, Keira felt increasingly isolated. The loneliness was worst at night, going to bed alone in the cold, quiet house. She craved the weekends when Jack returned, full of his stories from his job, exciting tales that made her homesick for Boston.

*P*eter Lacroix came to the house three more times, always entering without a word, hauling heavy boxes up the stairs by himself, bumping around on the second and third floors. By the middle of the second week of December, he had finished. He took his toolbox to his truck, came back in the house, and found Keira working on her computer at the kitchen table.

"Your husband's down in Boston?" he asked.

"Yes. Is there anything I can help you with?"

"No, I don't think so. I'm done with the bathrooms. You've got my estimate. I'm a couple of dollars under. You pay Jimmy. Jimmy pays me. I'll let him know I'm done."

"Okay." She hung her head, her hair hiding her face. Peter's abrupt manner distressed her, but she couldn't let him see her struggle to answer. She turned away, trying to think of a strong response. Before Keira could continue the conversation, Peter was out the front door and in his truck.

She turned off her computer. She had finished her work for the week, and the website she was developing for the Metcalfe House was almost done. She had taken photos of the house exterior in October when the foliage surrounded the grounds with a glorious glow. She planned to add romantic ones with unplowed snow gleaming on a sunny morning, but the workmen's trucks always arrived early and got in the way of her vision. There were still photographs to be taken inside every guest room.

After the terse conversation with Peter, Keira needed to get out of the house and interact with friendlier people. She pulled on her parka and walked out to her car, breathing the hard, cold air, unlike the damp, stale winter air of Boston. Looking up, she saw a white, thinly overcast sky. Was that what it looked like before snow came? She had never checked the sky for a forecast in Boston. The weatherman on the evening news was good enough. Now, in this white, gray, and dun-colored landscape, the weather forecast mattered more.

Keira got in her car and turned down the hill toward Bennett Falls. The woods beside the road were bare, a gaunt study in shades of black, gray, and white. Traces of the dusting of snow that fell a week earlier lingered in the fields, deeper in the shady spots. The snow-filled woods were barren, lacking any traces of life. She felt desperate for Jack, for her few friends in Boston, for Sarah. Her own small family was lost with her mother's passing less than a year ago, and it had been two weeks since Jack's family visited for the belated Thanksgiving weekend.

Maybe it would have been better if she and Jack had been able to have children. She tried to imagine little ones running around the house, filling it with their noise and their happy clutter. That would never happen. I need to stop thinking like that, she chided herself.

Keira passed through the covered bridge, turned right at the soldier statue, drove up Main Street and parked across from the VFW. Peter's truck was there, and she guessed he must be inside celebrating the completion of his work at the Metcalfe House. She walked up to the New Hampshire Crafts shop and went in.

"Welcome back! It's a cold one today. How are you?" Michelle hugged her.

Keira held on for a moment. "I'm fine."

Michelle let go and stepped back, evaluating her friend. "Are you sure you're okay? You seem concerned. What's wrong?"

"No, no. I'm fine. Your husband finished up at the house this morning. He's parked at the VFW now, probably having lunch there."

"I expect. Hope he has a burger with his beer. So, aside from the plumbing, how's the house coming along?"

"I think we're done. Maybe Jack and I'll bring in the last of the new furniture this weekend. We have it in storage."

"He's down in Boston today?"

"Yes. He usually leaves early Monday morning and gets home Thursday night. His company has him staying in a hotel down there. He'll be done with his work in Boston by the first of March."

"Okay, then. Let's get lunch. I recommend the Shepherd's pie."

Michelle locked the door and led Keira to the Old Mill. They sat at the same table, next to the window by the massive waterwheel.

Keira stared out the window. "What was this place like when it was a factory? What did they make here? Tell me about that big wheel."

"Textiles. The place was booming for decades. That big waterwheel turned all the looms. I think the gears might still be in the basement, but they locked the wheel in place once the factory closed."

"It's too bad they stopped the wheel. It would have been neat to see it turning."

Michelle shook her head. "It was noisy. When the river ran hard at the end of the winter, it made this wall shake. It's probably for the best that it's been stopped. But I suppose it lends a bit of nostalgia to the restaurant. This is my favorite table with the view of the rapids and the wheel."

Keira watched the rushing water. "Was it hard when the mill closed?"

"Yes. A lot of people were put out of work. Some had to move to get work elsewhere. I was settled here, and Peter had his plumbing, so we got by. Then I opened my little shop."

"That's fortunate."

"Yes. I believe things are always changing. Nothing lasts forever. What matters is how flexible you are, how well you adapt. Peter would go off to work every morning and our kids were in school, so I was home alone every day. I had a lot of time to sort things out and decide what I'd do next."

Keira thought of her own situation, alone all day at The Metcalfe House.

Michelle went on. "I had a few friends from school. They were artists and they were all doing things, making pottery, weaving, painting. But they had no idea how to make money from their art, how to sell it. I'm not a very good artist, but I had all these artistic friends. So, I rented the little store and set it up to sell my friends' work. I landed on my feet. We've all prospered. If the mill hadn't gone out of business, none of that would have happened. It was a godsend when it closed. I do still think about the mill workers who weren't as fortunate."

The rest of their conversation was subdued, Michelle asking about Keira's days alone in the big house.

After lunch, Michelle asked, "What are your plans for the afternoon?"

"I don't have anything planned. Why?"

"Spend the afternoon at my store. You seem like you need some company and you don't need to be sitting in that big old house all by yourself."

Keira started to say no, but the door to the store opened, the bell jingling, and a half-dozen women came in, chatting noisily. They spread through the space, picking up pottery and checking the jewelry cases.

Michelle walked into the midst of them. "I saw you all down at The Old Mill having lunch a few minutes ago. Where are you ladies from?"

A tall woman, with carefully styled white hair, dressed in a fashionable blazer and khaki slacks, replied. "We're from down outside of Boston. We take a day every year and come up here to the mountains for Christmas shopping. Do you have any decorations?"

"Not true Christmas decorations. We're not a Christmas shop. But we have a lot of wonderful things, all made by local artists and craftspeople. A lot of what you'll find here is perfect for decorating a home in the winter. Take a look at these mugs. And these candle sticks."

Michelle led the woman to a table loaded with pottery in winter colors.

The woman nodded with appreciation and picked up two mugs. "Can you hold these at the counter while I look around?" she asked.

"Of course. Keira, could you save these up by the register?" And just like that, Keira became an employee of New Hampshire Artisan Crafts. Less than an hour later, the group of women left the shop, all carrying bags.

Keira sat down and watched Michelle sort through the receipts. Finally, Michelle looked up, clipped the receipts together, and smiled. "Almost a thousand dollars of business in less than an hour! Thanks for the help. A lot of artists are going to be very pleased with what just happened."

"Glad I was here to help out. Is it always this busy?"

"Not this time of the year. In the summer and fall, yes. I usually hire a high school girl over summer vacation. Sometimes one of the local craftspeople help when it's busy. The artists prefer to stay home making their things. They don't want to sit around this shop all day. When they come in, I have one of them set up and work here. Customers like to see them working and maybe the artist sells a bit more because people can meet them."

"I had fun. It was nice to be busy. I felt a real energy when we were working with all those women."

"And now you're on the payroll. I might stay open a day or two a week after the New Year if you'll help. Maybe I'll do some clean up, painting, polish the floors, things like that while business is slow. Would you be able to come in? Your bed and breakfast isn't open yet."

Keira thought about it. She had never worked retail. Not during college, and certainly not since she graduated. "I'd be happy to come in a couple of days a week. Maybe not on the weekends though, when Jack's home."

"Of course not. So, you'd help me fix the place up after the New Year?"

Keira smiled. For the first time since she and Jack had moved to Bennett Falls, she felt welcome. "I'd love that," she said. She stood and went to Michelle, reaching out to shake her hand.

Michelle took her hand and pulled her close for a warm hug. "It's good to have you here," she said.

CHAPTER
Seventeen

Jack and Keira spent four days at Christmas with Jack's family in Quincy. It was the first time Keira had been away from Bennett Falls overnight since they had settled in the Metcalfe House. *Why haven't I been to Boston more often in the last few months,* she thought. *I've had to be there to let the workmen in the house with Jack away all week. But the work's done. I miss Boston. I love Jack's parents, and his sister Colleen is one of my best friends, but I miss my own family and friends. Maybe because I'm an only child and my father's been gone for years, the hole left by mom's passing nine months ago seems unbearable. The noisy fun with Jack's family helps, but sometimes it accentuates the emptiness I feel.*

While she visited Boston, Keira met Sarah for lunch, describing her new life to her old college friend. But Keira had the odd sensation of missing both her home in New Hampshire and her roots in Boston. She felt out of place everywhere, lost between her two homes. "Do you have plans for New Year's Eve?" she asked Sarah. "We talked a while back about you coming up for New Year's."

"No. We'll probably stay home. The girls are too old to accept a babysitter and too young to be left alone."

"Come up to New Hampshire. See our new house. Bring the girls."

The plans were finalized moments later. If Keira was unable to get to Boston, maybe she could bring her friends to Bennett Falls.

That evening after dinner with Jack's family, Jack's father asked, "How's the house coming along? Are you done with the construction?"

Jack answered, "Yes. That's done. Jimmy Sanborn, the contractor, stopped in a few days ago. He inspected all the work and seemed satisfied."

Keira added, "He joined us for lunch in the kitchen. I made him a turkey sandwich with the leftovers from our second Thanksgiving."

Jack took a sip of his drink. "We're still waiting for a wood-burning stove to be installed in the fireplace in the living room. And we still need to pick up a few more odds and ends to furnish the place. I expect we'll be ready to open by spring. We'll wait to move the remaining furniture in, what with winter and snow everywhere."

"We need to get the furniture in soon, Jack," Keira said. "We need to be ready for business, even if it is still winter."

"When does spring start up there?" Colleen asked.

"I don't know," Keira said. "I think we should be ready to open in a few weeks, even if there's still a bit of snow. People might book rooms during spring break. I'll launch our website and start promoting the place."

"So you have a bit more work to do, but you're ready?" Jack's dad asked.

"Yes. I believe so. We still need a business license. Maybe I should have taken care of that before we started fixing the place up. We have to pay a ten-dollar fee, and I can't imagine getting approved will be a problem. I'll be working in Boston until early March anyway," Jack said.

"And I'm done with my job here in Boston," Keira added. "Friday was my last day, so I can concentrate on marketing the house."

"Will that be enough to keep you busy?" Colleen asked.

Keira said nothing. "I'm so alone now," she mused. "There's nothing I need to do in the big house while Jack finishes his last weeks here. I hope I'll be able to find a way to fill the empty time. Of course there will be work to do when we open the B&B."

Jack nodded. "We'll be plenty busy. I'm always slammed with my work, and that's good. I love the interaction with all my building tenants. Anyway, you saw that Keira and I gave each other new ice skates for Christmas? There's a pond not far from our house where everyone in town goes ice skating. I think we should go skating when we're back in Bennett Falls."

"I think we should," Keira agreed. "It's called Clear Lake, and I guess there's a little park on the shore and the town cleans the snow off the ice in the winter so people can skate. Jack will probably dazzle everyone in town with his old hockey moves from high school."

"Do you miss Boston?" Jack's mother asked. "We miss seeing you on Sundays for supper after Mass."

"We miss that too, Ma. And once I stop coming down for work, I expect I'll miss Boston too."

"I already do," Keira said. "This is really the first time I've been able to come back here and relax since we moved. The few times I've come for work meetings, I've driven down early in the morning, spent the day, and driven back in the evening."

For the first time, Jack saw Keira's discomfort. It puzzled him. He pulled her to him with an arm around her shoulder as they sat on the couch. "Sarah and her husband and kids will be up for New Year's. You'll be fine."

"Yes, and after the New Year, I might be working regularly down at the little craft store in town. You remember Michelle, the woman you met after Mass when you were up to visit? She has a little shop where I'll be helping out a bit."

Colleen smiled. "So you're practically a native already! Going skating on the local pond, working in a little store up there."

Keira smiled grimly. "Natives? Hardly."

⊰⊱

They were on the interstate heading north, both eager to get back to Bennett Falls, and both missing their old life in Boston. Jack asked, "When did you decide to work at Michelle's little store?"

"A few days ago. I stopped in and we had lunch and she asked if I'd be interested in helping out a bit there."

"That's great. I know you've been feeling a little out of place in Bennett Falls. This should help."

Keira tucked her chin in the collar of her parka and looked out the window. Snowy fields and bare trees rushed past. "You have no idea how I've been feeling," she said petulantly. "You have no idea what goes on up there most of the week. You're in Boston, always busy. You have the best of both worlds. You get the best of Bennett Falls on weekends and the best of Boston during the week. And you have your big family. What do I have?"

"My family's not big. Just me and Colleen and mom and dad."

"You've got all your uncles and everybody. But that's not the point. You come home every weekend and all you talk about is the great things going on in Boston. All the things you do at work and with your family. Meanwhile, I'm alone in Bennett Falls. I had the workmen coming and going, but they're done. I've finished my projects and I'm closing out my contract for my work with my old company. And with my mom passing away last year, I have no family. I'm alone all day in that big old house…"

She stopped. She didn't know how to say what she wanted to say without starting a fight. She never wanted to fight with Jack, but sometimes he seemed clueless about how she felt.

Jack pondered how to proceed. They had talked for years about opening a bed and breakfast somewhere in the mountains. Now they were almost ready. But Keira was so moody when he came home on the weekends. He couldn't make sense of it. She missed Boston. That was obvious. What could he say to make her feel better about things now that they were almost ready for business?

"You'll be working at Michelle's store. Everything's going to be fine. Sarah and her family are coming up in a couple of days for New Year's Eve."

"You don't get it, Jack. I'm lonely in Bennett Falls. I need you to be there with me. I've never made friends easily. I'm not like you. I don't become friends overnight with everyone I meet. And now, there I am, in the dead of winter, alone in the middle of nowhere."

"So, what do you want to do? Sell the house and move back to Boston? We talked a long time about how we'd like to run a bed and breakfast. Now we're ready to open and you get cold feet?"

Keira laughed sardonically. "Cold feet. Funny thing to say when I'm abandoned in the middle of Nowhere, New Hampshire in the winter. No, we can't quit. We sank all our money into the house. After all the work we've had done, after spending even more money fixing it up, I doubt we could sell it without losing our shirt. No, we're stuck there now. We'll have to muck through and make the best of it. I just wish you could be there with me. It would make it so much easier. I'll need you there once we open."

Jack tried again to be encouraging. "Remember when we were starting with this adventure? We talked about how wonderful it would be to own a bed and breakfast in a small town in the mountains. It's still our dream. Nothing's changed. So settle in. Meet some more of the locals. Make new friends. It'll all work out."

Keira sank further into her coat, slumping in her seat in the car. "Sure," she said. "This is what we wanted. This is our fantasy. Me alone all week in a big old cold house. You in Boston with your friends."

Jack sighed, hunching over the steering wheel. "Let's not fight. We worked through things when we tried to start a family and couldn't. We'll get through this."

"When we tried to start a family? I lost two babies. You can't imagine what that does to a woman."

"I lived with you through all of it. I understand."

Keira shook her head, and they drove the rest of the way without talking. The house was icy and dark when they returned to Bennett Falls.

arah, her husband Tom, and their two sullen adolescent daughters, Lisa and Kristen, arrived at Metcalfe House in the middle of the afternoon on New Year's Eve. Keira and Jack met them on the porch with hugs and laughter. While the adults chatted on the porch, the girls slouched into the house and pulled out their phones.

"I don't have any bars on my phone," said Kristen, the older daughter. "God, what are we going to do without internet?"

Lisa turned to Keira. "You've got WIFI, right? They must have something civilized out here in the middle of nowhere."

Sarah started to scold her girls but Keira interceded. "Of course we've got WIFI. I'll get you the password." She led everyone inside the warm house.

Once they were set with the password, the girls retreated to the parlor and huddled over their phones. They refused to take off their new parkas, Christmas gifts, wearing the jackets loosely cradling their thin shoulders, as though they were prepared to bolt from the house into the cold if the adult's conversations became too tedious.

With Michelle's intervention, Keira finagled a dinner reservation for six people at the Old Mill early that evening. They all dressed for the occasion, the men in jackets and ties, Sarah and Keira in dresses they might have worn to the theater in Boston. The two girls, reluctantly, wore dress slacks and sweaters rather than the hoodies and ripped jeans they wanted to wear.

Compared to Boston restaurant prices, The Old Mill seemed inexpensive. The adults' meals were exceptional: prime rib and leg of lamb for the men, duck for the women. The girls got burgers. The party was back to the Metcalfe House before nine. They waited for midnight and went to bed shortly after they watched the ball drop in Times Square. Sarah and her husband, and Lisa and Kristen filled three of the new bedrooms on the second floor. Jack and Keira went to their apartment.

The next morning, Keira prepared a special casserole combining eggs, hash brown potatoes, cheese, and bacon. The six of them ate a late breakfast at the long, newly polished table Jack and Keira had found at an antique store in the Berkshires. After breakfast, Lisa and Kristen went to the parlor to watch the parade on television. The adults remained in the dining room with second cups of coffee, Keira with her tea.

Tom helped himself to another piece of coffee cake and said, "That casserole was amazing! And this coffee cake…" He closed his eyes rapturously while he chewed a bite of the cake.

Keira smiled.

"I'll need the recipes," Sarah said. "Where did you learn to cook like this?"

"I've been researching recipes for breakfasts ever since we decided to run a bed and breakfast," Keira said. "I've been trying new ideas every weekend since Thanksgiving. You'll love the scones I've started making. I make several types from recipes I found and they're really good."

"You're a lucky man," Tom said, clapping Jack on the shoulder. "Living like this, eating like this all the time."

Keira laughed. "We don't usually eat like this. Once we have guests, this might become our way of life. Right now, even when Jack's not in Boston, we just have regular meals. It'll change when we're ready for business."

"Not quite yet," Jack admitted. "I've still got a couple of more months to go in Boston, staying in a hotel there, grabbing a bite whenever I can."

"I'll feed you like this if you ever come home to stay," Keira said. She looked pointedly at him. Jack and Tom missed the look, but Sarah didn't. She reached over and rested a comforting hand on Keira's arm.

Later in the afternoon, Lisa and Kristen went upstairs to their rooms, bored and fussy, begging the grown-ups to leave them alone so they could text their friends in Boston. Jack and Tom settled in the parlor, watching bowl games on television. Sarah and Keira went to the small sitting room off the bedroom suite in the addition Jimmy had built. Out of earshot of their men, they could talk.

Sarah asked, "When we had lunch that day after Christmas down in Boston, you talked about how hard things were here in New Hampshire. It's only been a few days, but have you adjusted to living up here better now than when we talked? It seems like a pretty place to live."

"I don't know. Maybe yes. I'm really trying to settle in. It's a very pretty Currier and Ives setting here. I keep expecting a horse-drawn sleigh to come down the road just like at the end of the White Christmas movie. Jack and I might go skating some weekend, whenever he's home. We're adjusting, I guess."

"Skating should be fun. Tell me all about New Hampshire. Details," said Sarah, brushing her cropped blonde hair back. "All the good things, all the bad. Spare me nothing. What do you and Jack do for fun?"

What do we do for fun? Nothing. But Keira relaxed, comforted by the presence of her best friend. She took the bottle of red wine she'd brought from the kitchen and poured them each a glass. Still, she said nothing, trying to decide where to start. Sarah waited.

After a sip, Sarah pressed again. "How are you? I know you were struggling. Things must be better?"

Keira sighed. "A bit better, I guess. There are still a lot of things that fall through the cracks, things that I took for granted back in Boston that aren't here. Or if they are here, I simply haven't found them yet." Keira sat quietly, saying nothing more.

"Like what? What do you need here that you haven't found?"

Keira slumped for a moment in her seat, then looked away from Sarah. Finally, she opened up. "We don't need anything. We've got everything, really. There's a supermarket a little over a mile away on the other side of town, so we've got food. The house has well water, and it's a solid, well-insulated and well-heated place. All the basics are taken care of, food and shelter. It's just stupid little things I miss. Pizza. There's a little local pizza shop down in the middle of Bennett Falls, right on the Common. It always seems to be busy, but I don't know if they're any good. And there's another pizza shop, one of the big national chains, out in the plaza where they've got the Walmart, right next to the supermarket. I don't know. I knew our pizza shop back in Quincy. I don't know these places yet. And there's no Chinese restaurant at all. I miss Chinese food. Don't even ask about a Mexican place. And there's this. Look at my hair. When I lived in Boston, I got my hair done every month, never went longer than six weeks. I haven't found a hair salon anywhere in town. The last time I had my hair cut was in October after I went to a business meeting down in Boston. I shouldn't have to go all the way to Boston to get my hair done. And there's no dry cleaner in town. Either people here don't wear clothes that need dry cleaning, or I just haven't found one yet."

She looked up, imploring Sarah's support. Sarah hugged her and held on. "You and Jack are okay? You and he aren't fighting about this, are you?"

"No, we're fine," Keira said, wondering if it was the truth. "It's just hard being alone all the time in this barren little town."

"It's going to be okay. You'll figure it out. Give it time."

When Sarah let go and leaned back, she saw that Keira's eyes were glassy and her flushed cheeks were wet. "Come on," she said, holding Keira's hands. "You'll find a decent pizza place. There's got to be a dry cleaner here. Ask some of your friends here in town. There's probably a place you can get your hair done. I don't know about Chinese restaurants, but there's got to be a dry cleaner."

Keira sniffled for a moment and pulled a tissue from her pocket, wiped her nose, and tossed the tissue in the trash. "I know," she said. "It's all so foolish. I'm being foolish. I know."

"No. It's not foolish. These little things make all the difference. You do have friends here, right? Ask them for advice."

Keira thought of Michelle. Maybe she could help, but she's so much older. Michelle's hair looks like it hasn't been trimmed for a year. She knows all about Bennett Falls, but does she know good pizza? Does she like Chinese food? Does she cut her own hair?

"I don't know," Keira said. "Yes, I've got one or two friends here. Not enough. Not as many as I had back in Boston. No one like you." She gave Sarah's hand a squeeze. "I could ask them for direction. It might help. But I feel so alone sometimes."

"It certainly couldn't hurt to ask your friends here where to go for things. You'll find your way around. You've only been here a few months. You'll figure it out. Give it time."

Through the kitchen they heard the men whoop in the parlor. A scream from Tom, "Unbelievable! I can't believe that. Interception and a score!"

Jack suddenly appeared in the door to their suite of rooms. "You girls need to come watch! The Rose Bowl is tied with five minutes to go!"

Their alone time was over. The two women smiled and stood, picking up their glasses to go join their husbands.

The next morning, while Tom packed their bags in the car, Sarah came to Keira. "You'll be fine, Keira. Talk to your friends in town. Ask them for directions to places. You'll find your way around. Call me. Next week. I'm always there for you."

After a long hug, Keira pulled back. "I will. I'll call you. Stay in touch."

Tom hugged Keira first and then Jack. "I admire what you two are trying to do," he said. "Any time you start a new business there are risks. But I see you two throwing yourselves into this bed and breakfast idea all the way. I hope it works out for you."

"It will," Jack said. "We're almost ready."

Sarah wrapped her arm around Keira's shoulders again. "It's a great adventure for you two. Moving up here, fixing up this old house. I know Tom and I could never have done this."

"I hope it'll all works out for us," said Keira. Her voice betrayed her fear.

"Can we go?" whined Kristen, climbing in the back seat and clicking her seat belt.

Lisa followed her sister. "Finally! Back to civilization. There's nothing to do here. This town is dead."

Sarah packed herself in the front with Tom. Then, waving, they circled in front of the house and turned down the hill toward the covered bridge and Bennett Falls, heading south to Boston.

Jack smiled and wrapped his arm around Keira's shoulder, pulling her close beside him. "Good visit," he said. "It's great to have old friends come see us here. You and Sarah had a good time together?"

"Yes."

"But what's with their girls? Maybe it's a good thing we never had children if that's what we'd have to deal with!"

Keira said nothing.

Arm-in-arm, they walked up the steps to the porch and back inside. Keira felt a small chill in spite of the heat inside the big house. Already she felt alone again, even with Jack's arm around her. She thought about how he was never home during the week. He didn't know the loneliness she felt eating dinner by herself every night in the vast echoing space of the house, sleeping alone while the cold wind howled outside. Jack was in Boston with friends, action, and excitement. She was alone, but she didn't want to spoil the good mood he was always in when he came back to Bennett Falls. She told him nothing of her emptiness.

Saturday morning dawned bright, with no wind but biting cold. Jack and Keira pulled out of their driveway and headed uphill on Concord Road, away from Bennett Falls. They drove less than a quarter mile, turned right onto Lake Street and began watching for the lake where Michelle had told Keira the town went skating. It was impossible to miss. A massive, dark wooden sign announced, "Clear Lake State Park." The frozen dirt parking lot was packed with cars and pickups. More were parked along the short road leading into the park. The lake was dotted with crowds of skaters.

They parked and went to one of the white benches placed on the ice just off the shore, laced up their stiff new skates, and pushed out onto the lake. Their first few strides were short and tentative; it had been years since either of them had skated. Then, feeling the old balance and rhythm coming back, Jack left Keira and swept away, with long, flowing strides circling swiftly out from the crowds of children and families onto the wide flat surface of the lake.

Keira watched him fly away, remembering one of their first dates skating on the outdoor rink on Boston Common. As she had then, she admired the easy grace he used to cover so much of the ice so quickly.

Jack circled twice, and then coasted back to Keira, beaming with happiness. "It's like riding a bike," he said. "It comes back in a moment. This is great!"

He and Keira began to skate together, slowly, holding gloved hands, his strides smooth, hers still tentative and tense. Around them, swarms of people skated: families, couples holding hands like Jack and Keira, little children stomping along on their skates, chattering excitedly like sparrows. Suddenly they were joined by a third skater, carrying a hockey stick, sliding swiftly up to them, stopping with a hiss of ice shavings.

"Jack! Keira! It's great to see you up here at the lake. I didn't know you skated," Jimmy Sanborn said, his face beneath a black stocking cap ruddy with the cold, matching his beard. He leaned on his stick, his hands under his chin, the blade of the stick on the ice.

Jack reached across to shake gloved hands.

"Yes. I love to skate," Jack said. "I've been skating since I was a little kid. I played hockey in high school."

"Really. How about you, Keira? Are you into skating too?"

"I like to skate, but I'm not as good as Jack. Sometimes we went skating together when we were in college in Boston, just for fun. But I'm not like him. I never played hockey or anything."

Jimmy nodded. "Ah, yes, you went to college. Did you play hockey in college, Jack?"

"No. I did okay in high school I guess, but I went to Boston College. Their hockey team is really good. Keira and I went to watch a lot of the games there, but I wasn't good enough to play at that level."

"Boston College." Jimmy nodded. "They're in Hockey East, right? We've had several of our Bennett Falls boys go on to play in Hockey East. A couple at UNH, one at Merrimack, I think one at Lowell, and we had one who played at Boston University. I remember he'd always come home and be down at The Sunrise, bragging about beating BC. You're right. That is top level college hockey."

"Yes, I miss it. I haven't really been able to play since high school. Keira and I both skated when we were younger, and we gave ourselves skates for Christmas, so, here we are."

"Well, you're becoming regular Bennett Falls residents then. Everyone comes up here on the weekends. My wife Lynn is over there with my daughter." He pointed to a woman on the edge of the crowd, watching a thin, adolescent girl circling fast on the ice. The girl pulled her arms lower, gathering herself, and leapt from the toe of her skate, turning twice, precisely, carefully in the air. She landed smoothly on an edge and swept her arms wide, head back, as she spun after her jump.

"That's my daughter Christine," Jimmy said proudly. "She's starting to do well in competitions."

Keira smiled, wishing she could do what the girl had done.

"Where's your son?" Jack asked.

"He's over there playing a little pick-up hockey with his buddies." Jimmy pointed to a group of boys away from the crowd. Sweaters and hats marked the goals on either end of an imagined rink. "He plays in a youth hockey league. They practice at six, three mornings a week and have games on Thursday nights. He'll probably be on the high school team in a couple of years. The high school plays Tuesday night and Saturdays."

"Where do they play?" Jack asked.

"There's an ice rink down behind the YMCA, off Manchester Road, right across from the high school. You should go down there sometime and watch the high school kids. They're pretty good."

"Maybe." Jack looked at Keira.

She nodded, smiling, and hugged him. "It would be like old times back in college, Jack. We could go to the hockey game and then grab a bite to eat someplace. It would be a date like in the old days."

"Yes. Tuesday I'll be in Boston, but maybe next Saturday."

Jimmy held his stick with both hands and turned to face Jack head-on.

"You know what? You're a hockey player. We have an old men's hockey thing we do on Sunday nights at six at the rink. We're not really old, I guess. But we're out of school and miss playing. We're just a bunch of guys who like to play hockey. We get together and slap the puck around, sometimes even have a pick-up game. There's maybe fifteen of us and we've even got two goalies. Come join us tomorrow night."

"I'd like that. Maybe I'll do it. Let me look for my pads and helmet. I'm pretty sure they're packed away at the house. I still have an old stick someplace too."

"Great! Come on down to the rink tomorrow evening at six."

"I sure will," Jack said.

"I'll come watch," Keira said. Then she pointed across the pond and asked, "What are all those little shacks out there on the ice?"

"Ice fishing," Jimmy explained. "They drill a hole through the ice, drop a line and then wait for a bite. It can be cold sitting there, so they build little houses out of scraps to keep out of the wind and stay warm inside."

Keira was intrigued. "How do they stay warm? Do they have little stoves inside the shacks?"

"Some might have camp stoves, but only to cook lunch while they're out there. Most don't. But if a couple of guys crowd into one of the little houses to share a beverage, they stay warm with the body heat."

"Interesting," Jack said. "But I think I'll stick to skating."

"That's fine. I wouldn't do it either. I don't have the patience for it. I guess they have fun with it. And down at the VFW, they have two betting pools set up."

"For who catches the most fish?" asked Keira.

Jimmy laughed. "No. One pool is for whose shack will be the last one standing come spring. That one's fun, because most of the guys come down late winter and salvage their shacks, drag them off the ice and truck them home, saving them for next winter. The ugly little things are made of scraps of wood and old blue tarps and bits of plastic. It's not like they're valuable, but they save them from year to year anyway. The last shack usually falls in when the ice starts to melt. That's the winner. The second pool is for when the ice will break up and the lake will clear. Overnight, sometime in early spring, the ice will thaw and wash away, past the dam, down the stream at the far end of the lake, and on out into the river."

Jack and Keira stood together on the ice, contemplating life in a town where, for excitement, people bet on when the ice would clear from a lake.

A stocky, bundled figure walked toward them from the village of ice shacks across the lake, heading into the crowds of skaters, aiming for Jimmy, Jack, and Keira. As he approached, they saw it was Peter Lacroix carrying a small plastic cooler. He stopped when he reached them.

"Afternoon, Jimmy. Jack. Mrs. Sullivan." Peter touched the bill of his grubby Bruins cap.

"How's the fishing?" Jimmy asked.

"Got a couple. Not a bad morning." Peter tipped open the cooler to show two gray-brown fish. They lay on top of several empty beer bottles.

"Nice. Good size," Jimmy said.

"Good enough. Michelle and I will have them for dinner, I expect."

"You pack them on beer bottles to keep them cool?" Keira asked.

Peter smiled, graciously. "No. The bottles are on top of some ice. The cooler keeps the fish cool. The bottles are empties I'm carrying out so the pond won't get littered. Never want to litter the pond."

Jack understood. "So you go out there and sit in your house all morning and drink beer. And when you've caught some fish, you go home? That's how it works?"

"That's about it. In the summer, I'd go out there in my boat and drink beer. And when I've caught a couple, I'd go home. It's pretty much the same, winter or summer."

Peter tapped the bill of his cap again and started to leave, heading for the parking lot. Jimmy called after him. "Hey Peter, we'll see you at the rink tomorrow? And guess who'll be joining us?"

Peter turned and stopped, waiting for the answer.

"If I can find my old pads and helmet, I'll be playing," Jack called.

Peter nodded, smiling, then turned and went on his way toward his pickup.

"He plays?" Jack asked. "He's old. He can still play?"

Jimmy replied, "Yes, he's… I don't know how old… in his sixties, maybe seventy. But he can still skate. He's in pretty good shape for an old guy. Don't let his age fool you. He can play."

Sunday evening, Keira drove, with Jack sitting in the passenger seat in his bulky hockey pads. Under his parka, he wore an old Boston College sweatshirt. They arrived at the rink a few minutes before six.

Inside, a Zamboni circled, laying a new surface on the ice. A group of men stood in their skates at the door to the ice, leaning on their sticks, waiting for their hour of ice time. Jimmy seemed to be the organizer and several of the players looked like men Jack remembered working on the Metcalfe House at one time or another. Peter Lacroix sat in the stands to one side, alone, adjusting his shin pads.

Michelle saw Jack and Keira and hurried over. "Welcome to the rink!" she said. "Peter told me you might be coming. Oh, this is going to be fun! Jack, you're probably one of the younger guys here."

"I'm not exactly young," said Jack, sitting to lace his skates. "I'm past forty. And I haven't skated for a few years."

Michelle dismissed the comment with a wave of her hand. "Oh, you'll do fine. Come on, Keira; let's go sit up in the stands." She led Keira to a seat several rows above center ice. A small crowd of women sat with them. From the few words they said, all of them seemed to have someone playing in the game. They greeted Keira with quiet nods.

The other men all appeared to know Jack. There was no introduction. Jimmy must have already told them the new man in town was joining their game. "What position do you play, Jack?" Jimmy asked.

"Forward. Left wing? Put me wherever you want."

"Left wing it is. I'm center. You're on my line."

The Zamboni roared off the ice, the players flooded out, and the door slammed behind them. Two goalies skated to either end of the rink, set the goals on steel pins, and began scuffing the ice in front of the nets. Jimmy directed Jack to play alongside him on the line for one of the teams. The other team donned yellow mesh bibs and organized itself with a few quick words among the players. Peter set up as a defenseman on the team opposing Jimmy and Jack's team. Two extra players skated to the bench and sat.

"If you get tired, just signal to the bench and one of the extras will change up with you on the fly," Jimmy explained. "We've been playing together so long we all kind of know how to make this work."

Jack nodded. "I'm ready. Let's go."

There was an extra man, older, with a thin white mustache and thick white hair hanging over his collar. He was dressed in a striped black-and-white shirt. He skated to center ice with a puck, slowed, stopped and bent between the two centers, ready to drop the puck. "This is our official," Jimmy explained to Jack. "He doesn't call many penalties. He just drops the puck and whistles offside and icing."

"His name is Emile and he's a pain in the ass," one of the players shouted.

Emile straightened from his stance. He looked at the player who had called him out. "This is a warning, Rodney," he barked, his whistle in his hand, pointing at the player. "One more word and I'll penalize you for offensive talking."

He turned back to center ice, looked at the two centers, and suddenly threw the puck to the ice between them.

Jack was instantly swept back into the chaotic mayhem of the game. The puck caromed off the boards and flipped from player to player, crossing the ice in sweeping runs from end to end. Shouts from players, the clack of the puck on the stick blades, the hiss of the skates cutting the ice, and the boom when the puck hit the boards echoed inside the vast space of the empty arena.

Jack found himself winded within seconds. But, a defenseman on his team corralled a wide shot on their goal, circled behind his net and started out of the zone. Instinctively, Jack fell into the pattern of the game, rehearsed years ago in endless days of practice. He started up the rink, weaving with the other forwards on his line, dropping the blade of his stick, clacking it on the ice, seeking the attention of the defenseman, offering a target. The defenseman fired the puck up, right onto Jack's blade.

At center ice, with the puck on his stick, Jack looked up and saw open ice all the way to the opponent's goal. He put his head down and dug hard, with short quick strokes of his skates, slashing across the ice, heading into the offensive zone.

Two strides after crossing the blue line, Jack felt, more than saw, just for a moment, the presence of another skater crowding closer. Then he was down, crashing on the ice, sliding, banging into the boards. He lay, sprawling, stunned. He heard the official blow his whistle.

Men skated up to where he lay. "You okay?" one of them asked.

"Yeah. I didn't see the hit coming. I'm fine." Jack rolled to his back and sat up.

"I didn't mean to hit you that hard. I thought you saw me and were ready for it. You had your head down."

Jack looked up to see Peter. "Yeah. You're right. My head was down," Jack said. "I should have been ready."

Peter reached down with his padded glove. "Let me give you a hand."

He pulled Jack to his feet and wrapped an arm around his shoulder. "I hear you thought I'm too old to play," Peter said quietly. Only Jack heard him.

"Yeah. I might have said that. Now I know better."

"You're okay?"

"I'm fine."

Peter turned Jack to face him, spinning him carefully on his skates. "Yes, my friend. You're fine. Welcome to Bennett Falls." Peter cuffed him softly on the shoulder with his glove, gave him a wink, and skated away backwards before wheeling and gliding back to his position.

Emile blew his whistle and raised his hand. "Lacroix. Eighteen-second penalty for cross checking. Released for good behavior with time served."

Jimmy skated alongside Jack as they set up for the faceoff. "Do you need a minute? You want to let one of the other guys take a shift?"

"No. I'm fine. I had a minute while I was down there napping on the ice."

"Atta boy. Let's go." Jimmy slid away, ready for the faceoff. Two players, one from each team, swapped with the players who had been on the bench.

When Keira saw the hit, she dashed down the steps to the glass, frantic, worried that Jack was hurt. Michelle was a step behind, then by her side. When Jack sat up, both women relaxed.

"Peter's always been a hard player," Michelle said. "You should have seen him when he was younger. Do you think Jack's okay?"

Keira watched him skating, first with Peter, then with Jimmy. "Yes. He looks like he's fine."

"Looks like it. Men have ways of settling these things. I think Peter just initiated your husband into Bennett Falls. They'll be all right."

When their hour of ice time ended and the Zamboni was back, the men skated off and met their wives and girlfriends. They switched to sneakers or boots and dropped skates, pads, gloves, and helmets into oversized duffle bags. Jack, still a newcomer, was unfamiliar with the way they did things. He had worn his pads to the rink rather than packing them in a bag, so he left still wearing his bulky pads. Then, rank with sweat, wet and steaming inside their Carhartt coats and down-filled parkas, the crowd caravanned past the Common to the VFW for Sunday evening dinner: burgers and beer.

CHAPTER
Twenty

Keira parked at the curb on the shallow traces of soft, powdered snow, stained tan by sand. Between the snowbanks, the pavement was flat, dull black, streaked with road salt. She pushed out of the car door into the wind and walked up Main Street, leaning into the brutal cold, her face aching, her eyes watering. It was a relief when she came through the door to the warmth of the New Hampshire Artisan Craft store. She stamped the dry, caked snow off her laced boots, took off her parka and inhaled. The store smelled faintly of potpourri. Display cases had been moved to the middle of the store, exposing the walls. Michelle Lacroix and Lana Briggs sat on rail-back chairs by the big window at the back of the store overlooking the icy river. They both held paper cups of coffee from The Sunrise.

Peter Lacroix leaned against one of the glass cases, fidgeting, clearly out of his natural element in the scented feminine environment of quilts, pottery, wall hangings and other crafts.

"Morning, Mrs. Sullivan," Peter said, touching the bill of his smudged cap. He looked at his wife and Lana. "You're all set? Anything else you need me to move before you get started?"

"No. Thank you, my love," Michelle replied. "I think we can take it from here. I'll call after lunch. Maybe you could come help us move all the tables and cases back?"

"Sure thing." He kissed his wife, zipped his coat and strode out the door, hunching his shoulders, fighting the wind.

Michelle turned to Keira. "You're a tea drinker, right? Here you go," she said, handing her a paper cup. "There's some honey in that jar there by the cash register, and a spoon."

"Thanks," Keira said. "How did you know I like tea, not coffee?"

"I didn't. I picked up coffee down at The Sunrise this morning, and when I mentioned to Debbie that you were coming in, she told me. So, I got you tea."

"Debbie's the waitress there? I'm impressed she remembered. I only went there once."

"Debbie's the owner. She doesn't miss anything. And you remember my friend Lana Briggs?"

"Yes, we met at the parade. You were there with your husband."

Lana smiled. "Yes. My Warren. He's harmless."

Keira nodded, uncomfortable with the response. She stirred some of the honey into her tea. "Oh, he seemed pleasant enough. Just not particularly talkative."

"He can be a bother sometimes," Lana fussed. "He doesn't handle change well. Or strangers and newcomers to town. Lord love him, he does go on about things. He's been that way for years. First it was Amos Sanborn building all those new houses. Then it was the new schools. Then the ice rink and the new station for the police and the fire department. He thinks it's all a waste of money, raising taxes. Now he's dead set against your bed and breakfast."

Keira frowned, puzzled. "Why wouldn't he want us to run a bed and breakfast? We're on the agenda at the town meeting on a Monday night in a couple of weeks to get approval for our license to open for business."

Michelle stood and gave her a hug. "Don't you worry about a thing.

Lana's husband is all alone on this. You won't have any trouble."

"But why would he be opposed to it?"

"He's against anything that everyone else in town's for," Lana said. "He's just contrary. I try to talk to him. So do his friends. Andrew Holmes. Debbie down at The Sunrise. Amos Sanborn, the head of the Town Council. I think he just likes being against everything. I'm sorry. You shouldn't have to put up with his nonsense. It's enough that I do."

Michelle interceded, resting a comforting hand on Keira's arm. "We'll take care of it. One loud voice, one naysayer won't get in your way on Monday."

"I'll need help from someone. The town meeting is essential for our business. Jack's not going down to Boston till Tuesday morning after the town meeting, so he can go to the meeting and plead our case. We probably should have gotten the license months ago, but this is the first town meeting since we got settled in here."

"Well, expect my Warren to be there making a fool of himself about this. Just let him talk and understand that what he says won't make a difference. It never has before and it won't now. It's just what he does. I apologize for him. But I do love him, the old fool."

"That's right." Michelle concluded the uncomfortable conversation. "Not to worry, Keira. Now. About today. We're going to paint the walls and all the trim. I've already moved the crafts upstairs out of the way, and Peter pushed the cases away from the walls. Lunch is on me if we finish by noon. Then I'll hunt down Peter and bring him back in to move everything back."

Dressed in worn, old clothes for painting, the women set to work. New spotlight bulbs in the light fixtures made the bare walls glow under a new coat of pearl-gray paint. They added glossy white trim on the baseboards, chair rail, and doors. Quiet country rock music played on the radio. They talked little as they worked and were cleaning up shortly before noon. They washed the brushes and rollers and threw the rags in trash bags.

Then they headed down to The Old Mill for lunch.

"Sit anywhere you'd like," the hostess said. "It's Saturday, but we're not busy till the evening. And you get your usual discount, Michelle."

They sat at the table by the fireplace and looked down on the icy river. Faintly, through the glass, they could hear the roar of the tumbling water that rushed over the falls, even in the bitter cold. The black rocks that lined the river were shiny with ice, and branches of overhanging trees were glazed white. Inside by the fire, they were warm. They all ordered soup.

"Tell me more about the town meeting," said Keira. "What should I expect on Monday?"

Lana smiled and chuckled. "I don't know about Boston politics, but I can tell you what happens here. Everybody knows everybody else, and everybody knows what each other believe in and what they'll say. For us old-timers, it's all very predictable."

"It's not at all predictable for me." Keira twisted a napkin with both hands. "I understand how things work in Boston. The joke down there is that next to the Red Sox, politics is the number one spectator sport. The legislature there is heavily Democratic, but sometimes the governor is a Republican. That can be interesting. And then there's the mayor of Boston. He's usually got friends in every bar in town."

Michelle nodded. "That's a lot like how it works here. The VFW and The Sunrise are where decisions are made. Then we hold the town meeting in the cafetorium at the high school. Everybody in town goes. It's our mid-winter entertainment. The meeting's not much more than a formality."

"Cafetorium? What's that?"

"It's the biggest room in town," Michelle explained. "It's a combination cafeteria, gym, and auditorium. During the school day, they have roll-out tables with seats attached, and the kids eat their lunches there. And there are basketball hoops that drop from the ceiling after school and the floor is marked for them to play basketball. When there's a game, they roll the tables away and pull bleachers from the walls for the spectators."

Lana interrupted. "Not that basketball is much of a sport here. Any kid who's a good athlete plays hockey."

Michelle continued. "Yes. And at the end of the room there's a stage where they put the band for concerts and do the school plays. The Town Council will be up there at a table on the stage. Everyone else will be in the bleachers and in rows of folding chairs on the floor. There'll be a center aisle and a microphone. If you want to comment on anything, like when you want to state your case for the license for the bed and breakfast, you go up and wait your turn and go to the microphone and talk."

"Jack will probably do that," Keira said. "I'm not very good at speaking in front of a crowd. It makes me uncomfortable and nervous."

"That's okay," said Michelle. "Some people in town probably still think the man should run the business. I got a bit of push back when I wanted to open my craft store. But that was a long time ago. Most people have gotten past that now."

"How do you think the town will feel about us wanting to run a bed and breakfast?"

"Most people will be all for it. It'll bring tourists and revenue, and that's good. A very few won't support it because it will make the town too commercial."

"Like my Warren." Lana shook her head with a resigned smile.

"Yes, like Warren and one or two others," continued Michelle. "But Amos Sanborn is the head of the Town Council. People follow his lead. The Town Council does what he wants. So, after everyone has their say about Jack's proposal, the Town Council will vote on it."

"That's it?" Keira asked. "They hear from Jack and a few people in town, and then they decide the fate of our business?"

"Yes. That's how it works. There's five on the council. You need three votes for it to pass. Don't be upset if it's not a unanimous vote. There's always one who'll dissent just to show everyone they've thought it through."

"Probably Wilbur Jackson. That's what he does." Lana laughed again.

"He's almost as much of a bother as my Warren."

"Probably Wilbur," Michelle agreed. "He's the chief of our volunteer fire department. Some people say he shouldn't even be on the Town Council since he's on the town payroll, but he keeps getting elected for another term. He recuses himself whenever they vote on the fire department budget or on buying a new truck. He's a good man, though, and the only reason he dissents is to make it look like every issue has two sides that the council is considering. It doesn't make sense. Everyone knows what's going on."

Keira only wanted the approval. "Okay. But are you sure that's how the vote will go?" she asked. "I'd hate to have invested all our money and then not be able to open."

Lana reached over and took Keira's hand. Michelle took her other hand. "Don't you worry," Michelle said. "I expect the vote will be four to one. Amos likes the idea. Jimmy Sanborn's his grandson. And Amos is all for growing the town. So he'll be for awarding your license. And he'll bring along most of the rest of the council."

"And Wilbur will vote 'nay' and get a little applause from three or four people, including Warren," Lana added.

"Then you'll go into the town hall on Tuesday, pay a small fee for the paperwork, and you'll be ready for business."

"That's all there is to it?" Keira asked.

"That's it. It's so predictable it's almost boring," Michelle said.

Lana agreed. "That's right. But it's the middle of the winter and there's nothing good on television. So, the whole town will be there."

CHAPTER
Twenty-One
Late February
Monday

Jack and Keira arrived at the cafetorium at quarter to seven, fifteen minutes before the meeting was scheduled to start. The room was packed. Bleachers were pulled out from the wall on either side of the wide gymnasium and ranks of folding chairs were aligned in the middle of the room along a center aisle. People filled every available seat. Noise swirled around them, with animated conversations among old friends and neighbors, most of whom Jack and Keira had never met. They found a place to stand along the back wall near the double doors to the lobby.

Someone along the aisle stood and came to them. "You're Jack Sullivan?" the stranger asked. "And Keira Sullivan? The folks with the bed and breakfast at the old Metcalfe place up the hill on Concord Road?"

"Yes," Jack replied.

"I'm Joe Stanley. I've done a bit of work up at your house. You shouldn't have to be standing back here if you're going to be speaking. Come on up and take my seats. My wife and I'll stand." The stranger led them up the aisle. His wife stood and surrendered her seat. Jack and Keira settled in, unzipping their coats.

"Thank you," Jack said. "I thought the meeting didn't start until seven. I guess we're late."

"Oh, you're not late, but everyone comes early to be sure they get a good seat. This is the place to be on a winter night."

"Well, I appreciate it," Jack said.

"Not a problem," the stranger said. "I saw you come in and figured it's what I should do." The man and his wife walked to the back.

Amos Sanborn, three other men, and a woman stood chatting in a huddle behind a table on the stage. Amos and the three men had on white shirts, neckties, and sport jackets. The woman wore slacks with a blazer over a turtleneck sweater. Amos and one of the other men appeared to be older, possibly in their seventies. The other two men and the woman were middle-aged.

Promptly, when the big clock mounted on the wall above the stage clicked over to one minute before seven, they all took seats at the table, with Amos in the middle.

Keira whispered to Jack, "That's Amos Sanborn in the middle. He's the head of the town council. Michelle and Lana told me he runs the show. They said only one member of the council might not support us and that will be Wilbur Jackson. That must be him on the far right end of the table, the other older man. They said he's not necessarily against us getting the license, it's just his role to dissent."

Jack remembered Amos Sanborn from the speeches at the Veteran's Day parade. Jack looked to the end of the table where the other older, brawny white-haired man sat, shuffling a thin stack of papers.

As the wall clock ticked seven, Amos banged his gavel three times and the room slowly became quiet, conversations muttering into silence.

Amos Sanborn stood, followed by the others at the table. "Please stand and join me in the pledge to our flag," intoned Amos. Everyone in the packed auditorium stood, then Amos began the pledge of allegiance, followed by a rumble of voices echoing in the cafetorium.

When it ended, Amos leaned to his microphone and spoke again. "You may be seated." The room became hushed again.

"The town meeting is hereby in session," Amos Sanborn announced into his microphone. "We have three items on our agenda for this meeting. We will take up the budget and one other issue on the school board agenda at a closed meeting next week. As we always do with the open town meeting, interested parties will bring their requests before the council in front of the town. We on the town council already have your written requests and we've looked them over to prepare for the meeting. After each of you presents your case, we'll open the microphone for general discussion from the town as a whole. Finally, the council will vote."

Amos paused and looked to his left and right at the other members of the town council. They sat with their papers, solemnly readying themselves for their work. Wilbur nodded to Amos. Amos returned the nod quickly and turned back to his microphone. "All right then. Let's start with the highway department. Could a representative from the highway department please come forward?"

A lanky bearded man in a heavy, gray wool sweater came down the aisle to the microphone. "Good evening," he began. "You all know me. For the record, I'm Michael Smith, head of the highway department." He looked down and started reading from a piece of paper. "We're requesting a flashing traffic light be erected at the intersection of School Street and Washington Street. It's in the proposed budget, and I know you'll be debating that next week, but first, we need your approval to put the light in. That intersection gets really busy when schools are opening in the morning and again when the schools let out in the afternoon. It blocks traffic up Washington Street past the Common. Also, the driveway into the YMCA and the rink are there, right across the street, and it gets really busy when there's a hockey game. We would have the light set to flash most of the time. Flashing yellow for the Washington Street, or Manchester Road as we call it when it leaves town, and flashing red for cars coming out of the Y, or off School Street. Then when the school is opening and letting out, it would switch to a regular traffic light to regulate the traffic flow. Thank you." He turned and went back up the aisle to his seat.

"Is there any discussion?" Amos asked.

A police officer in uniform came to the microphone. "I'm Tom Henderson, police chief. I'd like to endorse this motion from Michael, um, from the highway department. That's a busy, dangerous intersection at the times he mentioned. We station a policeman and a car there every day when the schools are opening and closing, and we have an officer there at all the hockey games. The light would mitigate that need. We'd probably still put an officer there when there's a game, but it would straighten things out regarding the schools. I support the idea."

Chief Henderson returned to his seat.

"Is there any further discussion from the town?" Amos asked.

The question was met with silence. No one approached the microphone.

Amos turned and looked up and down the table at the other town council members. "Is there any discussion here on the council?"

Wilbur Jackson raised his hand and pulled his microphone close. After a moment, clicking the switch to turn the microphone on, he said, "There will be a considerable expense in paying to install the light. And this will be the first traffic light ever in Bennett Falls. But I believe this expense will be offset by the pay we'll save by having a police officer stationed elsewhere during the school days. It could mean we don't have to hire an additional officer. We'll work through the budget next week anyway. I support this proposal."

A surprised murmur rumbled through the cafetorium. Wilbur never, ever supported anything that necessitated spending money or raising taxes unless it had to do with the Volunteer Fire Department. When Fire Department purchases came up, he made his position known on those topics down at the VFW and The Sunrise, but he recused himself from those discussions at the town meeting.

"Any further discussion before we vote?" Amos asked. The town council sat quietly, ready. "Well, then. I don't think we need to go through a roll-call vote. The proposal is to erect a traffic light at the intersection of School Street and Washington Street. All in favor?"

A chorus of ayes rose from all the Town Council members. Amos banged his gavel. "The proposal is accepted."

Keira leaned over and whispered, "I hope our proposal passes that easily."

The members of the town council shuffled their papers. Amos spoke again. "Our second piece of business is a request to build four new houses in a new development off Woodland Road, up the hill from French Town. The proposal is to add a street up there and build the new houses."

A trim gentleman in a suit and tie came to the microphone and adjusted his glasses. "I apologize for taking your time tonight," he began. "I'm Richard Weeks from Concord, and I represent New Hampshire Property Development, the company that planned to build the houses. I don't believe we're ready at this time to go forward with the development. I've spoken in private with Mr. Sanborn and Mr. Jackson and Ms. Chambers from the Town Council about the matter. I understand we need to run some more tests on the land, drainage and such, and we need to get approval just for the new street before we can start with the houses. So we're withdrawing our proposal at this time."

The council shifted in their seats, clearly pleased with the decision. "I believe that is a wise decision," Amos said. "Come back when your ducks are in a row. I expect everyone in town knows where I stand on development of the town. But you need to do your homework first. Thank you."

The developer, dismissed, turned and walked to the back of the cafetorium. He pulled on his overcoat and went out the door into the cold. There was scattered applause when he left.

"Now for our final piece of business this evening," Amos said. "We have a proposal for a license to run a new business up at the old Metcalf House on Concord Road. Do we have a representative for the Metcalfe House?"

Jack raised his hand. He stood, ready to approach the microphone. "Good luck," Keira whispered, patting his arm as he started forward. He gave her a taut, nervous smile.

Jack had thought about how he wanted to look when he went to the meeting. His plan was to appear business-like, but not too "Boston," not too sleek or sophisticated. He had decided on a casual sport jacket and a plain striped necktie. It really didn't matter. Some of the people in the cafetorium already knew Jack and Keira. The rest had seen him around town, in the supermarket, down at The Sunrise, or even skating on Clear Lake a few weeks earlier. No matter what he wore, the residents of Bennett Falls had already made up their minds about the Sullivans and about their plans for the Metcalfe House.

He began. "My name is Jack Sullivan. It's an honor to be here before you and presenting my proposal for the Metcalfe House. I expect some of you already know my plans. I got the building permit to refurbish the house and Jimmy Sanborn has been working up there for several months fixing the place up to be a bed and breakfast. We now have seven guest rooms, each with its own private bath. We have a new kitchen and plenty of common space on the first floor for dining and general relaxing. Maybe I should have taken care of this when we started work on it, but there wasn't a town meeting until shortly after we bought the place. Anyhow, it's a beautiful old house and we would like to get a business license to run it as a bed and breakfast. Thank you"

Jack returned to his seat. Silence enveloped the room, everyone anticipating the drama they had all come to see.

"Is there any discussion?" Amos asked, knowing what would follow.

A line formed at the microphone.

Jimmy Sanborn spoke first. "I doubt that most of you have had an opportunity to see what Jack has done with the Metcalfe House. I have, and so have the men who've worked with me. It's beautiful. Every one of the guest rooms is a treasure. The house sat empty for some time and needed refurbishment. Now the whole house has been beautifully restored."

A heckler from the back of the room interrupted. "You say it's beautiful? Of course. You did the work. What else would you say?" A brief laugh from a few people followed the comment. Amos banged his gavel once. The room went silent again. "Go on, Jimmy," Amos said to his grandson.

"Thanks. Yes, I might be a bit biased, seeing as I did the work. But you should see the place." He turned, looking back to where Jack and Keira sat. "Jack, once you get the license, you should hold an open house for the town so people can come up and see what you've done with it."

Jack nodded and gave a quick wave of acknowledgement. Jimmy turned back to his grandfather and the other council members. "At any rate, what we've done up there has turned an old abandoned house, one of some historical significance to Bennett Falls, into a real asset to our community. I certainly can't voice enough support for Mr. Sullivan's proposal to open it as a bed and breakfast."

Jimmy returned to his seat. Next up was Warren Briggs. "Good evening Amos," he began. "Good evening," he repeated, nodding to each of the other Town Council members, one by one. They waited, knowing where Warren would likely go with his time at the microphone.

"This whole situation up there at the Metcalfe House should concern everyone in Bennett Falls. If Mr. Sullivan comes up here from Boston and opens a fancy bed and breakfast with seven rooms for his guests, well, that'll lure plenty of people to our quiet little town. If it's two people in each room, if they come up as couples, which is what I expect will likely happen, that adds fourteen more people crowding our town, and seven more cars clogging our streets. Every day there'll be a traffic jam there at the covered bridge. And next year we'll all be back here with the highway department wanting to add a second traffic light there. And we'll need to add more police. Taxes will go up. It's the beginning of the end for our way of life here in Bennett Falls. As if all the new houses Amos built up there off School Street weren't enough. It's because of that bunch of new houses that we just approved that new traffic light. If we allow this new bed and breakfast place, we may never again see the Bennett Falls where we all grew up. Think about that. Vote to approve this nonsense at the risk of losing everything we love about our little town. Thank you."

Warren took a moment more at the microphone without speaking, looking each member of the Town Council in the eyes before he turned and slowly walked back to his seat. His speech was rewarded with thin applause scattered around the big room.

Andrew Holmes stepped forward. Someone in the crowded cafetorium called out. "Oh Lord, spare us! Andrew's going to tell one of his stories. Debbie, I'm going to need a cup of coffee."

The remark was met with laughter. Again, Amos banged his gavel. Pointing with the gavel to the heckler, he said, "If you care to speak, please get in line at the microphone and wait your turn."

Andrew started, speaking solemnly, quietly. "Good evening, Mr. Sanborn and other members of the council. My name is Andrew Holmes, and my house is right down the hill from the Metcalfe House, there at the intersection with River Road at the covered bridge. I guess everyone in town knows that Warren and I are old friends. The best of friends. But he and I disagree on this. And apparently, some people in town recognize me for the stories I occasionally tell."

"Occasionally?" The shout was ignored. People wanted to hear Andrew.

"But I'm not here for story time. I want to address this business proposal from Mr. Sullivan. Concord Road heading out of town is a wide, well-traveled road. Seven more cars won't make a difference. And if fourteen more people come to town, tourists, staying up at the Metcalfe place, I won't mind. They'll pump a little fresh money into our town's economy. And I've met the Sullivans several times. They're good people who bring a new perspective to our town. I'm fine with their running a bed and breakfast up the hill from my house. I support their request."

Andrew returned to his seat amid more applause.

Two more speakers voiced their support for Jack's request for a license. They cited the value tourists would bring to the town's economy and how little the bed and breakfast would intrude on the quiet life of Bennett Falls.

Peter Lacroix, the last person in line to speak, stood, red in the face, anxious, and didn't waste time. He went right into what he wanted to say. "I spent a lot of time working up at the house, doing the plumbing. I can tell you this; it's a beautiful old house. And I agree with Andrew. Jack and Mrs. Sullivan are good people. I support their proposal."

He turned from the microphone, head down, still flushed, beads of sweat on his forehead, and hurried back to his seat next to Michelle. The Town Council waited till Peter took his seat after his short speech. Amos gave one last call to the assembled citizens. "Does anyone else have anything to say about the proposal to open the Metcalfe House as a bed and breakfast?"

In a back corner of the cafetorium, an old man stood and began slowly shuffling down the aisle toward the microphone.

"Oh God," someone said loudly enough to be heard throughout the cafetorium. "It's Harold Wheeler. Every meeting he's got to have his say."

A different voice called. "This is democracy. He paid his taxes and he has a right to speak."

Harold was an old man of an undetermined age. His gray hair hung to his collar. To prepare for his address at the town meeting, he was cleanly, freshly shaven though he retained a drooping mustache. He wore a plaid shirt and faded jeans held up by leather suspenders bracketing his belly. For the occasion of speaking at the town meeting, he had added an out-of-fashion wide striped necktie to the plaid flannel. He paused at the microphone checking to his right, behind the Town Council members on the stage, where a small television camera was situated on a tripod. The rumor around town said that whenever he spoke at the town meetings, Harold used an old video recorder back at his house to preserve the public access television community service broadcasts of town meetings.

According to the town's speculation, he had a box full of old tapes chronicling his many times appearing before the Town Council.

He began, speaking in a deep, resonant actor's voice, taking his time, pausing after each phrase, reading from a folded paper he had pulled from the pocket of the jeans. "Good evening. My name is Harold Wheeler and I live on Woodland Road about a half mile west of the Grange Hall. I've lived in Bennett Falls more years than most of you have been alive, so I know what this town is all about. Bennett Falls is a small town. Or it was. It's getting bigger every day. Now, the way I see it, bigger isn't necessarily better. And it's not necessarily worse either. It's just bigger. And I've seen what happens when a town gets too big. I've been all over. I've been to our state capital in Concord. I've been to Manchester. I've been to Nashua too, and don't even ask about what things are like in Nashua."

Harold paused, consulting his paper. The town waited.

"I've been to Boston. I went to a Red Sox game there once and I've gone to the Garden to see the Bruins play twice. Both times I won the Bruins tickets in the lottery at the Grange. Back in high school, at the old school where they now have all the town offices, they took my class down to Boston to see the Freedom Trail. So I know what it's like in a big city."

Harold paused again to catch his breath. The town sat waiting for more.

He rambled on. "Now, Mr. Sullivan and his wife come here from Boston. The Boston way of life might suit him. So maybe he doesn't see anything wrong with moving to our little town and fixing up the old Metcalfe place and opening it for business as an inn. Seven more hotel rooms in a place like Boston might not matter. But this isn't Boston. I hope it never gets to be that way. But it is only seven rooms. So that's only a handful of visitors. If they even come. Why would they come to Bennett Falls for their vacation? Mr. Sullivan can open the old place as a business and it might not even be a success. Maybe nobody will come."

Harold stopped a third time and surveyed the whole room, first the town council in front of him, and then turning, he scanned the audience.

"Let's give him his license. If it works out, good. He'll make a little money, and the few people who stay at the Metcalfe House might spend a few dollars in Bennett Falls. And if it doesn't work? So be it. That's his problem, not ours. So I say, give him the license."

Harold looked into the camera, saluted, and returned to his seat. The citizens of Bennett Falls sat silent and stunned. Harold Wheeler never agreed to anything new.

Amos surveyed the gathered town and asked again. "Is there any further discussion?" More silence. "Well then, let's vote. I suggest we do a roll call for this vote." He looked at the other members of the Town Council for assent. They all nodded. He started with the councilor on the far left side of the stage. "Aye." Then Ms. Chambers, the woman on the council. "Aye."

Amos' turn came next. He took a moment, letting the suspense build. "I vote Aye." Three votes. The Sullivan's request for a license had passed. Jack sank in his seat for a moment, releasing the tension he had felt for days. Keira hugged him, her head on his shoulder, crying quietly. Scattered applause echoed in the cafetorium.

Amos continued with the fourth councilor. "Aye."

Finally, he came to Wilbur Jackson in the seat at the end of the Town Council table. "Nay."

Amos and Wilbur nodded to each other. Amos remained deadpan but his face betrayed a slight smile. "Mr. Sullivan, your proposal is accepted by a vote of four to one. You have two weeks to pick up your license at the town offices. Thank you everyone. There's no further business. The town meeting is adjourned."

Jack and Keira left the meeting, exhilarated, and joined the traffic jam leaving the school parking lot. They drove in silence back by the town common and through the covered bridge. As they turned in the driveway of The Metcalfe House, Jack finally spoke. "We got approved! We're on our way! Nothing can stop us now!"

CHAPTER
Twenty-Two
Tuesday-Wednesday

Jack left for Boston mid-morning on Tuesday after stopping by the town offices to pick up the business license for the bed and breakfast.

Keira settled in for the week ahead, reminding herself that Jack's Boston work would end in early March, just two weeks away. She missed him terribly and stayed busy all day so she wouldn't think about him. When she did, she counted the days until he would be home. She also tried to estimate how many days would pass before the bed and breakfast was open for business and guests were a part of her life.

Now that they had the license, they were ready to open the Metcalfe House. She began to finish their website, preparing it to take requests to book dates for visitors in each of the seven rooms. She loaded photographs of each room, each carefully framed to show the most romantic aspects of the decor. Pictures of the dining room, the living room, the parlor, and the exterior of the house were already loaded on the website. The exterior shots had been taken in late summer when the gardens were still in bloom and in the fall with the foliage in full flaming color. It might be possible, she decided, to start accepting guests as soon as April.

Emotionally drained after the town meeting and anxious for the opening, Keira fell asleep that night, exhausted. She woke at dawn on Wednesday with pale light sifting into the bedroom past the curtain. The house was silent, the same silence she had heard on Thanksgiving when the first fast snowstorm had blown across Bennett Falls. That day, a plow had rumbled up the hill on Concord Road. This morning she heard the plow again. When Keira peeked out through the curtains, she saw she was right. The silence was because, aside from the plow, no trucks grinded up the hill. No cars were out either. Nothing moved but the swaying boughs of the snow-laden pines that ringed the yard. The snow fell hard, blowing and drifting against her car and the hedges. She realized she wouldn't be leaving the house that day and had no reason to get up. She went back to bed.

An hour later she was woken again by a grating noise outside the house. Pulling on her robe and slippers, Keira hurried to the living room and looked out. Jimmy Sanborn's truck, fitted with a plow blade, was plowing the driveway and the turning circle in front of the house, grinding over the gravel. Keira pulled her robe close and stepped onto the porch, careful to avoid the thin dusting of snow near the edge. She waved, catching Jimmy's eye. He waved back and continued backing and plowing, backing and plowing.

Keira returned to the house and put on a pot of water for her tea. Then she filled the coffee maker and started that as well. With the water started, she dressed hurriedly in a turtleneck, jeans, and wool socks.

As Keira was pouring her tea, Jimmy stopped his truck, wallowed through knee-deep snow from the plowed driveway to the back steps, and came to the kitchen door, pausing to stomp the snow off his boots on the back porch. Keira opened the door. "Come in and warm up. Would you like some coffee?"

"That would be great. But I can't stay. Lots of work to do on a day like this."

"You have a plow on your truck," Keira said, noting the obvious.

"Yes. A lot of us do. I have a few folks around town I plow for. I got an early start this morning, out before six. I do a bunch of my neighbors over in Sanbornville where I live and a couple of others. I was right down the hill taking care of Andrew Holmes' place and figured I'd come up and see how you were doing. Jack's down in Boston?"

"Yes. He picked up our business license yesterday and headed out. He'll be home probably tomorrow, Thursday night. Maybe Friday."

"You haven't got anybody to take care of the drive for you?"

"No. Back in Boston either Jack, or I, or both of us would shovel out the driveway, but it wasn't that long. I guess we hadn't thought about how long the drive is here."

"You're going to need somebody. The drive's not too long, but with that turn around circle in front… You can't shovel out a place like this. Certainly not when a big Nor'easter comes through like today. You need to stay ahead of the storm. It doesn't often happen, but if you get a couple of feet of snow and you don't take care of it, before you know it another storm comes in and you'll be stuck for the rest of the winter."

Keira nodded, folding her arms against the chill. "I guess we've both been so busy with the house we never realized…" For a moment her voice trailed off as she thought about her situation, isolated without Jack for the rest of the winter. "Listen, Jimmy. You've been so good to both me and Jack, advising us on how things work here in New Hampshire. Since we need a man to plow for us. Could you do it?"

"Sure. I'd be happy to. We can talk about my rate when Jack is home. The way I work it is this. I come whenever we get more than about four inches. With a storm like this, I'll probably need to plow a second time later today after the snow stops, just to clean things up a bit. You take care of the walks and steps unless you want me to do that too. I shovel Andrew Holmes' steps. He's old."

Keira nodded. "That sounds fine. I really appreciate your help. I think I can handle the steps. I dreaded digging out the whole driveway, and we don't have a plow."

"You do now." Jimmy took a sip of his coffee. "You've got me. I'll plow you out this time for free. By the way, I hear my fireplace guy came and installed the woodstove for you."

"Yes, a week ago. I haven't lit it yet. Maybe I'll wait till Jack gets home."

Jimmy smiled, recalling Jack talking about how a wood stove might create a romantic atmosphere for their guests. He took another sip of his coffee. "Mm. This is good coffee."

"Starbuck's," said Keira. "I expected they would sell it down at the Stop and Shop in the plaza past the high school, but I haven't seen it there. I stocked up the last time I visited Boston."

"There's a Dunkin Donuts there." He took another sip. "Well, this is good. I like a strong cup of coffee and this is the way I like it."

"You usually get your coffee down at The Sunrise Café, right? Jack and I went there once."

"Yeah. The Sunrise is a good place. Debbie takes good care of me."

"It sounds like everyone in town has breakfast there."

"True. It's usually busy. Debbie saves a spot for me if she knows I'm coming in. There are a bunch of regulars there most days. Everyone knows each other."

"Jack and I'll probably stop down there from time to time, but when we start having guests here, I'll be cooking breakfast and eating here in the morning."

"Yeah. Don't you hate it when work gets in the way of having a good time?" Jimmy laughed.

Keira thought of Jack working in Boston while she took care of things in Bennett Falls. "Yes, never good when work gets in the way of fun."

Jimmy tipped back the last of his coffee. "Speaking of work," he said, "I've got to run. I've got to take care of a couple of more driveways over in Frenchtown and I do the parking lot up at the Mill. I'll come back for one more run at your driveway this afternoon. When did you say you expect

Jack to be back?"

"Friday probably. Maybe Thursday night after work. I really miss him when he's away. But he'll be finished with his job down there in a couple of weeks."

"I'll try to stop by again Friday when you're both home to talk about my plowing for you folks." Jimmy paused at the back door, zipping his parka, pulling his wool cap down to his eyebrows. "Thanks for the break and the coffee. You have a good day, Keira. Now back to work."

Back in his truck, he circled the driveway, giving one final quick pass with the plow to the turnaround. Then he was gone, rumbling down the hill toward the covered bridge.

As she watched his truck go, the empty, quiet house closed around her again and the loneliness sank in. The driveway was open and the big town plows had cleared the Concord Road. She was free to leave, but where could she go in the storm? It was still snowing hard and already new snow had accumulated on the drive Jimmy had just finished plowing. She fixed a muffin for breakfast, poured a second cup of tea, and called Jack.

He answered. "Hi. Everything okay up there? Do we have any snow yet? The storm dropped about six inches here in Boston, but it seems to be letting up. How are you doing?"

"I'm fine. We probably have eighteen inches, maybe two feet. It's hard to tell because it's drifted so much with the wind. Jimmy stopped by and plowed us out."

"Oh. That's good. I'd been meaning to find a guy to plow for us."

"Jimmy said he'd take care of it. He'll come up and meet with us Friday to talk about what he'll charge. I don't know what it'll cost. But I told him yes."

"Good. If his rate is as reasonable as what he charged for the work he did on the house, we should be okay. He did a good job?"

"Yes. He said he'll swing by this afternoon to plow us again."

"Why? Once isn't enough?"

"It's still snowing hard outside. He says he only comes when there's more than four inches, but it looks like we could have more than that much new snow by this afternoon."

"Okay. I guess. But plowing twice for one storm?"

"Ask him about it when you're here on Friday."

"I will. Hey, I'm glad you called. I was thinking about you up there with the snowstorm and all. Just a little worried."

"I'm fine." Then she thought about how alone she felt. "I miss you, Jack. I wish you were here. It's hard being alone here."

"You'll be fine. Enjoy the day. I bet it's beautiful with all the fresh snow."

"You don't know what it's like. It would be okay if we were together in this. But it's awful being alone in a storm like this."

"You're fine. I'll be home Thursday night. I've got to go."

After he hung up, Keira sat quietly, looking out the window at her car, swamped with drifted snow. It was snowing less heavily now, and the wind had abated. She sighed, finished her tea, and bundled into her parka and boots. Time to dig out her car and clear the walks and steps. The path broken through the deep snow where Jimmy had labored from the plowed driveway to the kitchen back door gave a hint at the work she had to do. Out she went, picking the snow shovel out of the closet on the back porch.

CHAPTER
Twenty-Three
Wednesday

The snow stopped at lunch time. Several inches of light, fluffy snow had accumulated since Jimmy plowed the driveway. A bitter, breezy, bright afternoon followed, thin cumulus clouds scudding across the pale sky, racing east. Keira had cleared the steps and walks. Her work was done. She changed into dry clothes and grilled a cheese sandwich for lunch. Mid-afternoon she heard a knock on the front door. Expecting it might be Jimmy since he had plowed again just an hour earlier, she went to the door.

Instead, Michelle and Lana were there, beaming, their hands wrapped inside their coats.

"Michelle stopped over to see me," said Lana. "We like to walk together in the mornings, but not in this weather. So once she dug out her house, she came over. She said Jimmy told her he took care of your driveway. And we figured if Jack was away, you could use the company."

"How have you weathered our storm?" Michelle asked.

"I'm doing well! It's very peaceful and quiet. And so beautiful with the fresh snow. Please, come in. I'm glad you came by. I'll make some coffee."

"Oh, that won't be necessary." Michelle grinned as she pulled a bottle of white wine from inside her parka. "We brought something to share." She handed the bottle to Keira.

Keira laughed. "Perfect!"

"There's more," Lana added. Her left hand came out of her parka holding a gray and white striped kitten. "I brought all her supplies." She handed the kitten to Michelle and picked up a big plastic tub filled with two bags and a smaller plastic dish. "The big tub is a litter box. The small one is for her food. You'll need to supply water, but here's cat food and kitty litter. Food in; poop out. This little one is already litter box trained."

Michelle said, "You mentioned you're lonely when Jack's in Boston. And you told me once you love cats. We figured a kitten might help."

Keira took the little cat. "She's adorable! Where did you get her?" The kitten snuggled up to Keira's neck, wiggling in her hands.

Lana said, "We have a few cats hanging around my farm. Barn cats, sometimes sneaking inside the house, though Warren doesn't care for cats in the house. One of our cats had kittens. And we thought you could use a friend here when Jack's away."

"What's her name? She is a girl, right?"

"Yes, she's a little girl. You'll need to take her to a vet in a month or so unless you want more kittens. I haven't named her. What do you think her name is? She's your cat now."

Keira held the kitten away from her, looking into the little blue eyes and the striped gray face. The kitten purred, rumbling loudly and wriggling. "Smoky. She looks like smoke. I'll call her Smoky," Keira declared, setting the kitten on the floor. Smoky began to explore the house, tentative steps, sniffing and inspecting everything. A puff of warm air came out of the heating grate next to the wall and the kitten jumped, startled.

They set up the litter box in a closet off the kitchen, leaving the door ajar. Keira poured food in the bowl and set it on the kitchen floor. Smoky prowled, watching what they were doing. Then she slipped into the open closet door. They heard scratching and sifting of litter. A moment later

Smoky emerged, trotted to her food bowl and nibbled. Keira set down a dish of water and the kitten drank.

"Settled in already," Lana laughed.

"Now about this wine…" Michelle said.

Keira pulled the cork, poured three glasses of wine and led her guests to the parlor. Smoky galloped after them and, when they were all seated, she jumped and clambered onto the sofa, curling on Keira's lap.

"Smoky's already picked you," Lana said. "She knows you're her human."

"This is so nice of you. Thank you for looking out for me. Not many people in town know me. But you two are special. I love it."

Michelle smiled. "I told you how things would go at the town meeting. Even old Harold Wheeler accepted you. You've got a lot of friends here in Bennett Falls. We're not the only ones."

"Everyone but my Warren," Lana said. "He'll never change. Don't worry about him. He's my burden."

"I'm curious," Keira queried. "I had friends back in Boston. I still do. But we've all become such good friends. You're probably the closest friends I've got here. Why? What made you decide to accept me like this?"

"I don't know," Michelle said. "Lana and I go back together longer than time. But you fit right in that first day you came in my store. I like you."

"We both do," Lana said. "You're a good person. Maybe we just want a new friend with new ideas, not stuck in the old ways. The town would never change if we left it to itself. Sure, you're a bit younger than us, but we're all still just women trying to manage our husbands. We share that."

"That's true," Michelle agreed. "I've got my Peter. I love him but he can be a handful at times. And Lana's got Warren. Need I say more? And you've got Jack, who's never home. We've all got something."

Keira raised her glass of wine. "Here's to husbands. Can't live with them, can't live without them!"

Lana agreed. "Well said. It's an old saying, but so true." Lana was the first to clink her glass with Keira's, followed by Michelle.

Keira spoke, becoming thoughtful. "One of the nicest things about Bennett Falls is moments like right now. It feels very serene. Part of it is the quiet after the snowstorm. But part of it is that it slows everything. Nothing ever seems to happen here. Back home in Boston, everybody's rushing. There's always something going on, my commute every morning and again at night, things happening at work, noise, chaos. A lot of drama. Part of the charm of Bennett Falls is that the pace here is so slow."

Lana laughed. "Huh! Nothing ever happens here? There's always something. Maybe you don't see it up here on the hill in your big old house. There's plenty of drama going on in town. Too much maybe, sometimes!"

"You'll get into the mix once you've been here a while," Michelle said. "Jack's already into it a bit with playing in the hockey games. You know what? Once the weather warms up, you should come walking in the mornings with Lana and me. We meet by the bridge at eight every day."

"I'd enjoy that. As long as I don't have guests staying here who would need me to be around cooking breakfast and everything."

"We could meet a bit later in the morning or in the evening if that would work better for you," suggested Lana.

"We'll have to work around my schedule at the store and your schedule here at Metcalfe House," Michelle said. "I usually open the store before ten. We have a month to figure it out. We won't be walking until maybe April when the snow's gone."

"We'll make it work," said Lana. "For years, it's been just the two of us against the world. Now we've got three."

Keira smiled, warmed by her two new friends. She thought of Sarah, her Boston friend, a woman her own age who shared so much with her. She'd hoped she'd meet a friend of a like age in Bennett Falls, but there was no reason her two friends in the town couldn't be older. They all seemed to share so much, to fit so well together. On her lap, Smoky slept, curled, purring loudly.

CHAPTER

Twenty-Four

Wednesday Night

After Michelle and Lana left, Keira finished straightening the house and cooked a light dinner. Smoky followed her wherever she went, like a tiny ghost. In the evening, Keira felt the quiet house turning chilly. Outside, the wind moaned. Even with the new furnace, she knew nights like this could become cold in the huge house. She decided to try out the new wood stove in the living room.

Keira went to the woodpile by the driveway and pulled thin, split logs from the plow-piled snowbank. She brought the wood in the house, greeted at the door by Smoky mewing the whole time. Keira assembled a teepee of wood over crumpled newspaper. She had read in the manual that came with the woodstove how to start a fire. She checked the vents on the stove and lit the paper.

The paper flared, burned, scorching the snow-dampened firewood. Keira waited, watching as the flames flickered and settled down to smoldering ashes. Smoky meowed again. Keira crumpled more newspaper, rebuilt the fire, and tried again. This time the blaze took and after a few minutes watching the flames, Keira added thicker logs, shut the doors on the woodstove, and settled in with a book on the sofa. Smoky nestled on her lap, asleep. Warmth radiated from the stove.

Keira replenished the fire with two more logs and read some more. Finally, late in the evening, she watched the fire with the stove doors open and a screen protecting the opening. The last logs popped and burned out, settling softly, sending a cascade of sparks up the chimney. When there was nothing left but smoldering ash, Keira closed the woodstove doors and went to bed. Smoky curled beside her on the pillow. The kitten wasn't Jack, but she was a comforting companion. They both fell asleep quickly after the hard day of snow shoveling and fire building.

Keira woke, startled and frightened.

A screaming noise echoed from beyond the kitchen, from the main part of the house. Smoky scrambled off the bed and hid under it. Keira grabbed her robe and her phone and ran to the living room. The smoke alarm blared upstairs, and now on the first floor, it howled and flashed. In the shadowed, moonlit room, thin traces of smoke trailed down the stairs, pooling and snaking across the ceiling to the alarm. *Oh God! Oh no!* She dialed 911.

"911. What is your emergency?" said a woman in a matter-of-fact, calm voice.

"My house is on fire. My smoke alarm is going off and there's smoke!" Keira shouted, plugging one ear with her fingers against the shriek of the alarms.

"Where are you? What is your address?"

"The Metcalfe House in Bennett Falls. On Concord Road, up the hill from the covered bridge."

"I'm dispatching the fire department and the police. Are you in a safe place?"

"I'm in the living room. Oh, dear God, the smoke is thick!"

"Please ma'am. Stay calm but leave the house quickly. Stay on the phone with me but get outside right now."

Keira ran to her bedroom, dropped her robe, and pulled on her snow boots over her bare feet. She grabbed her parka from the kitchen closet and ran out the kitchen door onto the porch. Brutal cold hit her. Desperate and frantic, she turned, ran back inside, and grabbed a sweatshirt and her purse with her car keys. *Did I forget something? I don't know. There's no time! I've got to get out!*

Outside, she laid the parka on the hood of her car, pulled the sweatshirt on over her nightgown, and wrestled back into the parka, zipping it. Her legs were still bare.

Down the hill in Bennett Falls, sirens wailed. The voice of the 911 dispatcher called to her. "Ma'am? Ma'am? Are you still there?"

"Yes. I grabbed my coat and boots and I'm outside." A glow lit the third-floor bedroom windows.

"That's good. The fire department is on the way. Move as far from the house as possible and be prepared to tell the firefighters what you can to help them. Otherwise, give them room to work."

"Okay." Keira felt her voice shaking as she watched the glow in the third-floor windows brighten, flaring suddenly. She started to cry. "Oh God!" she screamed.

"Stay on the phone with me," said the dispatcher, comforting. "I'm with you. What is your name?"

"Keira. Keira Sullivan. My husband and I own the house."

"Your husband is out of the house?"

"Yes. He's in Boston. Oh God, this is going to kill him. We were ready to open the B&B!"

"The important thing is both of you are safe."

The first fire truck swung into the plowed driveway, lights flashing, bouncing red off the snow and the front of the house. Men in heavy coats, helmets, and big boots ran onto the porch. Others could be seen working out on Concord Road, digging in the snowbank for the hydrant. Keira chased the firefighters onto the porch. "The front door is locked. Do you need to get inside? I've got the key."

"Yes. But give us the keys. We'll unlock it."

Keira handed the man the keys. He unlocked the door and tossed the keys back to her. "Thanks. Now, Mrs. Sullivan, could you please get off the porch. We need to go in, but you need to stay safe."

Keira did as she was told, huddling near her car away from the house on the far end of the driveway. She watched the fireman crack the door open and heard a whoosh of air. A cold breeze rushed past her toward the open door followed by new warmth emanating from her house.

A second fire truck pulled into the driveway, its siren wailing, and winding down. More firefighters appeared. Pickup trucks lined the road at the driveway entrance. Many of the new firefighters wore basic work clothes, jeans, parkas, heavy gloves. They lacked the gear the first firemen wore, but they seemed to know what they were doing, working in coordination with the regular firemen.

"Are you still there, Keira?" the dispatcher asked.

"Yes."

"You okay?"

"No. My house is on fire."

"Yes, it is. But the fire department is there and you're safe. Right?"

"Yes."

"I'll stay on the phone with you. Please stay out of the way and safe, Keira."

"I will." Keira had stopped crying. She no longer felt the hammering cold air or the draft of heat that had washed over her when the firemen opened the front door. She felt only numb, her ears ringing. She was nauseous.

Several firefighters strung hoses off the road onto her driveway. Other firefighters threw up a long ladder from the second truck against the side of the house next to the chimney. One man climbed the ladder with a hose. When he reached the top of the chimney, he released water from the hose, pouring down inside the chimney. Keira assumed it was water, though it could have been foam or some other chemical.

"Oh, God!" Keira screamed, imagining the torrent of water flooding out of the chimney through the new wood stove into the parlor and living room. All the antiques and the oriental rugs, everything they had just bought would be ruined.

"Are you okay, Keira?" asked the dispatcher.

"Yes. But they're flooding the house. My furniture will be ruined."

"That may be true. But maybe they'll save the house. Stay clear and let them do their job."

"I am. Oh, God!"

Keira felt an arm around her shoulder. She turned. It was Michelle. Keira fell into her arms, sobbing. Michelle held her, patting her back, soothing her, saying nothing. Keira held on tight, burying her face in her friend's coat, her body shaking.

After a minute, Keira eased back and said to the dispatcher. "One of my friends just got here. I'm okay with her. Thank you so much for staying with me. You've been wonderful." She hung up.

"Was that Jack?" Michelle asked.

"No. The 911 operator."

"Oh. That's good. I got here as fast as I could. But I wanted to give the firefighters their space to work."

Keira pulled back a bit farther, looking Michelle in the eyes. "How did you know? I'm so glad you came, but how did you know?"

"Peter's one of the volunteers. He told me where the fire was as he rushed out the door. Of course I came. I had to come."

"Oh. Peter's here?"

"Yes. Somewhere." Keira and Michelle looked for him among the crowd of firefighters milling about the yard, going in and out of the open front door. The frenzied pace of activity when the first truck arrived seemed to have abated. But the glare of spotlights still lit the snow-covered yard and the face of the house. Red light still pulsed from the trucks. The man on the ladder still held the hose, but he didn't seem to be flooding the chimney anymore.

They saw Peter walking toward them, dressed in his everyday work clothes. He came up and gave Keira an awkward hug, one thick arm around her shoulders. "Jeez, I'm sorry. I think we may have saved the house, but there'll be a lot of damage to fix up."

Keira nodded. She shivered, partly from the cold, partly from the shock.

Peter continued. "At least you got out and you're safe. And Jack's in Boston?"

"Yes."

"So, everyone's safe. Nobody inside, right?"

"Right." Then Keira and Michelle both remembered. "Oh, God! Smoky!" Keira screamed.

"Smoky?" asked Peter.

"She just got a new kitten," Michelle explained.

"It's not out here with you?" Peter asked.

Keira shook her head. "I think she hid under my bed."

"I'm on it." Peter turned and ran to the porch. He was in the door, into the shifting, thick wall of smoke.

Wilbur Jackson, the Volunteer Fire Chief rushed over. "What happened? Peter ran back in there? We've just about got things under control, but I wanted everyone out while we pump the water into the house."

"My kitten's still inside. He went in for her."

"It's just a cat. It's not safe in there. He hasn't got an oxygen tank."

Now it was Michelle's turn to worry. "Oh, God, dear Peter." Keira hugged Michelle.

Wilbur shouted. "Who's got oxygen? We need someone to hustle back in there and drag Peter out."

Jimmy Sanborn stood nearby in firefighter gear, and he was the quickest to respond. "I've got my mask. I'll get him."

He slapped his oxygen mask on, leaped the steps two at a time, and bolted through the door. Endless seconds passed. At last, Jimmy appeared through the thinning waves of smoke. Peter's arms were draped over

Jimmy's shoulders like the straps of a backpack. Jimmy's mask covered Peter's face, but after a moment, Jimmy took it back, breathing deeply. Peter's limp body slumped against Jimmy and dragged behind. Jimmy pulled him down the steps onto the driveway. Michelle rushed toward Peter, but a wall of firefighters surrounded him, feeding him oxygen, blocking her path. Keira stayed beside Michelle, clinging to her. For the moment, Keira forgot her own dire situation.

Jimmy pushed through the crowd of firefighters to Keira, holding out a wet, bedraggled, soot-covered kitten. "This is yours? Peter had him tucked inside his coat."

Keira cried, taking Smoky. The kitten burrowed under her parka, terrified, soundless, snuggling against the warmth of her body.

In the stark light from the trucks, Peter sat up slowly, his face streaked with black above his dark beard, carefully taking deep, slow breaths through the oxygen mask. Michelle sat on the ground next to him. Peter took the mask away for a moment and looked at her with bloodshot, tired eyes. He coughed, gagged, and pulled the oxygen mask over his face again, breathing deeply, wheezing.

Overcome, Keira slumped first to her knees on the snowy ground. Then sagging, she fell sideways, sitting. Finally, she sprawled, fetal, curled on the frozen driveway, her bare legs pale beneath her nightgown. Alone on the snow, she clutched her tiny kitten and silently wept, her shoulders shaking in her parka.

Keira heard Wilbur Jackson say, "We need to get Peter to the hospital down in Manchester to make sure he's okay."

"I'm going with him." Michelle's voice wobbled.

She was aware of Michelle leaving, but she felt new arms embrace her, pulling her up. Then Keira saw only blackness.

PART
Two

CHAPTER
Twenty-Five
Late Winter
Thursday Morning

Keira woke slowly, imagining a horrible dream in which The Metcalfe House burned down around her. *It was just a dream, right? My house can't be gone.*

As she stumbled awake, she became aware of the smell of smoke in her tangled hair. She opened her eyes, disoriented, and saw an unfamiliar, small bedroom. The bed seemed tiny, not her own queen-size bed. Two short, golden trophies sat on the dresser, both of girls: one an ice-hockey player, the other a softball player. There was a small vase with silk flowers on the bedside table. Three posters hung on the wall: a picture of a teen rock star Keira didn't recognize, a poster for Les Miserables, and a team picture of the US National Women's Soccer team.

Seeing that she was awake, Smoky crawled over the covers to Keira. The kitten was filthy, her fur matted. She mewed, snuggled against Keira's chin, and started to purr.

Keira held the kitten and stood up from the bed. Her nightgown, like her hair, smelled of smoke. She saw her sweatshirt on the floor, picked it up and sniffed. It, too, was smoky. Keira opened the door and peered into a hallway and down a narrow flight of stairs. "Hello? Is anyone here?"

Lana appeared at the foot of the stairs. "Oh, good. You're awake. How are you feeling?"

"I don't know. Okay, I guess. Where am I?"

Lana started up the stairs to meet Keira. "Michelle's house. I put you in her daughter's bedroom. I figured Michelle wouldn't mind, and it was better than taking you home to my house and Warren."

Keira went down the stairs, holding Smoky, meeting Lana halfway. "My house burned down, right? It all seems like a bad dream."

Lana led Keira, an arm around her shoulders, through the cramped living room into the kitchen, seating her at the table. "Yes, there was a fire. I think the house is still standing, but I don't know how damaged it is. What matters is that you got out and you're okay."

Keira put Smoky on the floor and looked around. "I don't know what to do. I don't know how to start to piece everything back together. My mind is all over the place."

Lana set a dish of water on the floor for Smoky then joined Keira at the table. "Let's take it one small step at a time," she said. "I know you're a tea drinker, but Michelle doesn't have any. Would you like some coffee? Maybe a Danish for breakfast?"

"That sounds good. How did I get here? I don't remember much after Peter came out of the house with Jimmy and the kitten."

"That's when I got there. You were on the ground, in shock, I guess. They were loading Peter into the ambulance and Michelle was going to follow the ambulance to the hospital in Manchester. I picked you up and brought you here. You were out of touch the whole way. The firemen were still working at your house when we left."

"Michelle's not here?"

"No. She spent the night in the hospital with Peter. I talked to her this morning on the phone. They might be coming home this afternoon."

Lana got up and returned to the table with a cup and a plate with the Danish. From where Keira sat, Michelle's house seemed much smaller than the open spaces and lavish rooms of the Metcalfe House. It was an unaccustomed feeling—confining and claustrophobic. It reminded her of the starter house in Quincy, where she and Jack had lived until their move to New Hampshire. Still, the sunshine made the morning bright, such a contrast with the horror and the chaos at the Metcalfe House the night before. It seemed incongruous for the morning to be so cheery when right up the hill a house had been destroyed hours earlier.

Keira took a bite of Danish and a sip of coffee. She couldn't focus. "I need to do something," she said. "Oh my God, I haven't even told Jack! I was so busy just getting out of the house last night I never called him."

"It's taken care of. I saw your purse and your phone on the ground and brought them with you last night. I found Jack's number on your phone and called him first thing this morning to let him know what happened and that you're safe. He's on his way."

"Thanks for calling him. How did he react when you told him?"

"He was upset, of course. Mostly worried about you. I called him a bit after seven, hoping he'd be awake. He said he'd be here as soon as he could."

"He was coming home today or tomorrow anyway. What time is it?"

"Almost nine. You slept in."

"He should be here soon, then. Oh. Look at me. I'm a mess, all smoky and dirty. I need a shower. And I don't have any clothes that aren't dirty and smoky."

"I'm way ahead of you," Lana said. "I checked Michelle's closet. She and I borrow clothes from each other now and then, so it's not a big deal for me to go through her things. You're taller than us, but I dug out a pair of loose jeans and a baggy sweater for you. Your sweatshirt is filthy and smoky, so take the sweater for today. I got you a pair of socks, but no underwear. At least you've got something to wear."

Dressed only in her nightgown, Keira shivered. Her bare feet were cold on the tile floor. "Let me get showered then. Where are the clothes?"

"On the sink in the bathroom, with a towel. Top of the stairs and straight ahead."

Keira went for her shower. Smoky hopped up the stairs behind her.

Feeling better after the shower, Keira sat again at the kitchen table with Lana, sipping a second cup of coffee rather than her usual tea. She set the cup down and went to work, swabbing the soot off Smoky with a damp cloth. When the kitten was clean, Keira put her on the floor. It made her feel better to be clean and neat. The sweater was too big, the jeans too short, but she was dressed. Aside from the wool socks, her feet were still bare, but she saw her snow boots by the kitchen door. Her parka hung on a coat rack by the front door next to her filthy sweatshirt.

"I called Jack while you were in the shower," Lana said. "He's almost here."

"Good. I need to see him." Keira looked out the window, on the edge of tears, hoping he'd already arrived. He hadn't. Seeing the bright winter morning, the sky pale blue, a light breeze blowing, and sunshine melting the snow, the terror from last night loomed in her mind. She recalled the smoke, the screaming alarm, and the flashing lights as the trucks arrived. She remembered the fireman pouring water down her chimney and wondered what was left inside the house today. She thought of Peter dashing in the house to save Smoky and then Jimmy chasing behind to save Peter. She worried how Jack would react when he saw what remained of their house.

Lana reached over and placed her hand on Keira's. "You're remembering everything, aren't you?"

"Yes. Jack and I'll need to go up to the house to see what's left of the place. We were so close to opening. We got the license on Tuesday. What day is today?"

"Thursday morning. A lot has changed in a hurry."

They saw Jack's SUV slow and stop in front of the house. Keira and Lana went to the door. Jack jumped out of the car in a moment and bounded up the short, shoveled path to Keira. They held each other, desperate, breathing deeply.

"You're okay?" he asked.

"Yes. I'm alive anyway. Unhurt, thank God. I don't know about the house."

"We've got insurance. We can take care of that. I was so worried about you when Lana told me what happened."

"Come inside. This is Michelle's house. I slept here last night."

They went in and sat again at the kitchen table.

Jack seemed puzzled. "Lana's here, but if this is Michelle's house, where's Michelle? And Peter?"

"They took Peter to the hospital in Manchester for smoke inhalation," Lana answered. "Michelle's with him."

"But this is their house?"

"Yes," Keira said. "Lana brought me here instead of back to her house and Warren."

"I thought it for the best." Lana gave a wry smile.

"Understood," Jack said with a quick chuckle. It felt good to laugh for a moment with everything else that had happened. "How's Peter?"

"He's still in Manchester, but if everything goes according to the plan, he'll be out and home this afternoon."

"That's good. He was one of the firefighters?"

"Yes. He's been on the volunteers most of his life."

Smoky jumped up, digging tiny claws into Jack's jeans, climbing onto his lap. "Now, who's this?" Jack asked. "Michelle has a kitten?"

Keira smiled. "No. That's Smoky. She's our little cat. She came to live with us yesterday."

Jack stroked Smoky's head. "Appropriate name. Smoky." Smoky purred.

Keira laughed. "Appropriate maybe, but I hope she's not an omen. She comes to live with us and the house catches fire."

"Don't even think that," Lana said. "You can't blame the kitten. Nobody's to blame. It was a chimney fire."

"I suppose we need to go up and see what's left of the house." Jack stood.

Keira stood as well and hugged Lana. "I don't know how I would have gotten through last night without you and Michelle. Or this morning. Thank you."

"Happy to help. Michelle told me to tell you that if you two need a place for a few days… if you can't stay at your house, you're welcome here. She leaves the door unlocked, so just let yourselves in if she's not here. You've got both of our phone numbers? Call and let us know how you're doing. I'm going home to rest. I've been up most of the night."

Keira gathered her filthy clothes, rolling them in a ball. She pulled on her boots over her borrowed socks, shrugged into her parka, took her purse and phone, and grabbed the bundle of smoky clothes. Carrying Smoky, she followed Jack to his car. Lana waved goodbye and closed the front door of Michelle's house.

In the car, Jack said, "Your coat smells like smoke. And where did you get those clothes?"

"They're Michelle's. Lana lent them to me." Keira smiled suddenly, mischievously, and attempted to lighten the moment. "But I don't have any underwear. I'm going commando this morning."

Jack looked at her, unsmiling. "I'm not in the mood. Our house is gone. Remember?"

"Of course." Keira slumped in her seat, angry. "Yes, I know the house is gone. I was there when it burned. You weren't."

"What happened? How did our house catch fire?"

"I don't know. Lana said it was a chimney fire. I lit the woodstove, and everything seemed fine. The fire had burned out before I went to bed. Then

I woke up with the alarm blaring and smoke coming from upstairs."

"Why did you light the woodstove? You didn't need that."

"It was a cold night. It seemed like a nice thing to do."

Jack shook his head in silence.

As they turned into the driveway, nothing appeared to be out of the ordinary except that there were two pickup trucks parked and the front door stood ajar. Jack recognized one of the trucks belonging to Jimmy Sanborn but not the second truck.

"At least the place is still standing," he said. "I was afraid it burned to the ground."

They got out of Jack's SUV and started toward the house. Keira held Smoky, but seeing the house, the kitten mewed once and burrowed deep inside Keira's coat.

Closer to the house, it was evident that things were no longer normal. The deep snow around the house was tramped down by hundreds of footprints and there were big tire tracks on the driveway. The front door was open, blocked by a thick patch of ice, a rough sheet that flowed across the porch and down the steps to the gravel walk. Now, in the early spring sun, it glistened wet. A spreading puddle surrounded the end of the ice where it met the driveway.

Jack and Keira climbed the steps carefully on the ice, holding the rail. They tiptoed across the frozen porch and pushed through the front door. Inside the parlor, the stench of smoke was strong, but not as overwhelming as Keira had feared. Jack put his hand over his nose and looked around the room. Nothing was out of place. The doors of the woodstove were ajar, knocked open by the torrent of water that had poured down the chimney. Charred rubble filled the woodstove. A delta of sodden ash spread from the stove across the hearth, the polished wood floor, and onto the rug. The soaked rug was filthy and littered with bits of burnt wood. In the hall by the front door, a glaze of ice coated the oriental hall runner. The stairs were stained and wet. The wall along the staircase also looked damp.

"Hello?" Jack called. "Jimmy, are you here?"

Voices and footsteps came from the second-floor hall. "Jack, is that you?" Jimmy appeared on the steps, followed by Wilbur Jackson.

At the foot of the stairs, Jimmy went to Jack and put his hand on his shoulder. "This is a bitch. Glad you could return so quickly." Then he turned to Keira. "How are you? I can't imagine what it must have been like for you being here alone through the whole thing last night. Did you get any sleep?"

"Yes. Lana took me to Michelle's house."

"Good. You've got two good friends there, looking out for you."

Wilbur stepped forward and shook Jack's hand. "Wilbur Jackson. I'm the Fire Chief. I stayed at the house through the night, making sure the fire was out. I've been looking over the damage with Jimmy this morning."

Jack sighed. "How bad is it? We just got our license to open. How long will it take to fix everything?"

Wilbur took a deep breath. "I don't expect you'll be open for a while. But it's not as bad as you might think. For the most part, the fire was contained in the chimney. It started to break through on the third floor, right about when we got here with the trucks and the firefighters, so there's some damage up there. And there's smoke and water damage upstairs and here on the stairs as well."

Jimmy interrupted. "The good news is that structurally the house appears to be fine. Sometimes when chimney fires get out of hand, the whole place needs to be torn down. I don't think that's the case here."

"It doesn't look like we have structural damage, but that needs to be confirmed with the State Fire Marshal," Wilbur cautioned. "He'll be out first thing tomorrow morning to look at things."

"Can we stay here?" Jack asked.

"Technically, no," Wilbur stated. "Not until the State Marshal says it's okay. But you own the place. The apartment out back sustained no damage."

Jimmy nodded. "The heat's on. I checked the thermostats this morning and turned them off on the top two floors. I'll see about turning off the water up there this afternoon. I may have to do that myself because Peter's still down at the hospital in Manchester."

"I can probably take care of the water," Jack said.

"Let me do it," Jimmy said. "I know where the valve is for the top two floors. And yes, there's running water in the kitchen and your apartment. You have electricity, and the smoke isn't noticeable back there. But you'll need to clear that ice so you can close the front door."

Wilbur concluded, "So, no. Legally, you can't stay here until the state says it's okay. But what you decide to do is up to you. I'm leaving in a few minutes to go home and sleep. It appears to be safe. Just be dressed and outside by eight tomorrow morning, before the man from the state gets here."

"I can't do anything today about the smoke and water damage," Jimmy said. "But I know someone who can take care of that."

"What do you think we'll have to do to repair all the damage?" Jack asked.

"It's too soon to say," Jimmy said. "Definitely a new chimney. And probably a lot of rebuilding on the third floor. We'll see about the roof. The rest, if we're lucky, will be cosmetic work."

"I'll call my insurance agent today and see how soon he can come check the place out. Let's get ahead of this whole situation and talk about what we need to do." Jack, hands on his hips, looked around the parlor at the debris. He flipped a light switch and the chandelier in the middle of the room lit, glaring, showing the grimy, sooty reality of their home.

"Take a look around," Jimmy said. "I'll stop by in a bit to shut off the water upstairs. Leave the door unlocked if you go out. I'll meet you here tomorrow at nine to start planning the next steps."

"That's good," Jack said. "Thank you both."

"I'll be here by eight, waiting for the man from the state," Wilbur said. Deadpan, he added, "Be sure you're here bright and early tomorrow as well. Now, I'm going to grab a quick bite at The Sunrise and then go home and catch up on last night's sleep."

"I'll swing by The Sunrise with you," Jimmy said.

Wilbur and Jimmy tiptoed carefully over the icy porch, down the steps to their trucks. Inside Keira's coat, Smoky squirmed. Keira set the kitten on the floor and Smoky ran to the kitchen closet and slipped inside.

Grimly, Jack said, "Let's start and see how bad it is. Then we've got to get this ice out of the parlor and close the door. That'll be about all we can do until after the insurance company inspects the damage."

"I need you right now." Keira went to Jack and pulled him to her. "But first things first. Let me change into some of my own clothes." She passed through the kitchen to their apartment. Smoky was out of the closet, already gobbling cat food from her bowl.

CHAPTER
Twenty-Seven
Thursday

Too much was happening inside The Sunrise for anyone to notice when the bell tinkled above the door. Jimmy and Wilbur walked into a scene reminiscent of the start of an old western barroom brawl. Shouts reverberated throughout the usually cheery restaurant. Chairs scraped on the wood floor, angry men crowded between the tables, standing and pushing, pointing fingers. Of all the regular patrons, only Warren and Andrew remained seated, an unfinished cribbage game on the table between them.

Debbie leaned against the counter, arms crossed, waiting for the storm in her café to abate. She caught the attention of Jimmy and Wilbur, raised her hand and silently shook her head for them to wait.

"You wanted this!" Rodney, a dark whiskered man, shouted derisively. "Winter's a slow season for a carpenter, so you're probably happy the place burned down. Now you'll have some work rebuilding it."

"What are you saying?" Brian, Rodney's long-time adversary, shouted. "That I set the Metcalfe House on fire to get some work?"

For years, Rodney and Brian had been frequent foes in fights like this, ever since they were in high school.

"I wouldn't be surprised. Fires don't just start themselves."

Men stepped between the two, keeping them separated. But there were murmurs of agreement. "Maybe Rodney's right. Maybe Brian didn't light it. But something happened. Something went wrong."

"Maybe that guy Jack lit it to collect insurance money," Rodney speculated.

"Be serious. Jack Sullivan just went to the town office a couple of days ago to get his license to open the place."

"Well, somebody must have started it."

"Maybe it was you, Warren," Rodney said, turning toward the table where Warren and Andrew sat. "You're always bitching about it, saying how you'll do anything to keep it from opening. Maybe you tried to burn it down now that he's got the license."

Warren stood as quickly as his arthritis allowed, banging into the table, spilling his coffee, scattering the cards on the floor. "Whoa! I said I didn't want that Sullivan fellow to open a bed and breakfast. But I'd never burn another man's house down. Don't you start with that kind of talk!"

Andrew reached across and gently steered Warren back into his seat. Warren sat, but he hunched forward, his feet planted wide apart, red in the face, catching his breath, staring at Rodney wide-eyed. His fists were clenched.

"Then maybe Peter did it," Rodney shouted. "He's probably made more money out of that house than anyone except Jimmy Sanborn."

"What?" A customer laughed, shaking his head. "You're saying Peter Lacroix went up there, lit the house on fire, and then got sent to the hospital for smoke inhalation from fighting the fire he set? You're crazy!"

"Well, then, maybe Jimmy Sanborn set it," Rodney carried on. "He's going to get the most money out of the rebuild. If Sullivan decides to stay and rebuild. And who knows what else has been going on? Jimmy's sure been spending a lot of time up there with the Sullivan woman while her husband's in Boston. Who knows what that's all about?"

"Enough!" Jimmy's shout stunned the patrons of the café. He strode slowly to the center of the room, stopped, his arms loose and swinging, and looked silently around, finally locking his eyes on the loudmouth Rodney, with all his accusations and conspiracies. Jimmy Sanborn was not a man to be trifled with. He was known to be able to hold his own, whether on the hockey rink ice, in his business dealings, or in any situation anywhere in town.

"You suggest that I might have burned The Metcalfe House? And you start a rumor that I might be fooling around with Keira Sullivan?"

Jimmy stopped and waited to see if Rodney would respond. Rodney didn't. He looked away and down at the floor like a scolded child.

"Wilbur and I were just up at the house, looking over the damage. Jack and Keira Sullivan are there now. They're both good people. Good friends. While you're all down here going on about it, they're up there checking things out. They might have lost their home. People could have died last night. Peter Lacroix's in the hospital down in Manchester. And you're here talking like this, making jokes and starting rumors?"

Jimmy stopped again and surveyed the room. Everyone waited. The Sunrise was silent. "The place will need some work, but it doesn't look too bad. If Jack decides to fix it up again, I expect he'll want to work with me. And…" Jimmy paused and looked directly at Rodney, the rumor monger. "I expect I'll be talking to *some* of you about helping out with more work up there in the next few months. Jack and Keira will need our support." Again, Jimmy paused and looked hard at the one loudmouth. "And I'll need *some* of you to lend a hand up there."

Jimmy took a step back, a signal that he'd had his say. Everyone took a deep breath. Feet shuffled beneath tables.

Wilbur Jackson took his turn, speaking slowly, calmly but with authority in his deep voice. "Let me put an end to your rumors, Rodney. It was a chimney fire. That's all. Not arson. The woodstove may have started it and if the chimney hadn't been used for a few years, who knows what might have been up in the flue and caught fire. It was an accident, one of those unfortunate things, but nobody's to blame. I don't want to hear any more of this talk. We don't need these rumors flying around town."

Andrew stood up and rested his hand on a still-fuming Warren's shoulder. "I'd like to say a few words if I could," he began. People turned to hear what Andrew had to offer.

"Oh, God. Here comes one of his stories." Nervous snickers followed the remark.

Andrew looked stone-faced at the man who had joked. At least it wasn't Rodney. "No," Andrew said placidly. "This is not a time for any of my stories. Not a time for jokes. The Sullivan's house burned last night. A few of you were probably there fighting the fire, so you know how bad a thing like this is. Like Jimmy said, these are good people who could have lost their home and their business. If you want to respond, I say we do it by coming together as a community to see how we can help them. They're new in town, but they're our neighbors. We need to support them with whatever help they might need."

Billy slipped out of the kitchen, one of his rare sorties into the dining area. "I agree with Andrew," he said. "Debbie and I were talking about things this morning and here's what we're going to do."

He was uncomfortable speaking in front of the crowd, looking at the floor as he spoke, swaying from foot to foot. He stopped, looked out straight at the customers, and held up a clear plastic gallon jug that might have once held some kind of condiment. Stammering, he went on. "I cleaned up this old jar rather than throwing it out and stuck a label on it." He showed the jar to the crowded room, turning so that everyone got a good look. The label had a photograph of the Metcalfe House that Billy had lifted from the internet. Beneath the picture, Billy had lettered in bold black marker using careful penmanship, "Metcalfe House Fund".

Billy finished by saying, "I'm putting this here on the counter by the cash register." He set it down with a hollow thud. "Anybody that wants to help can drop their change in here. Debbie and I will see that the money goes to help rebuild the place." Billy nodded to the crowd and retreated to the haven of his kitchen.

Debbie reached under the counter and took a small stack of bills and a handful of coins out of a cardboard box. "Here's this morning's tip money. It's not much, but it's a start." She held it up for everyone to see. Then she folded the bills and dropped all the money into the big jar, the change rattling as it poured from the box.

Without a word, Andrew walked up, reached in his wallet and dropped a bill in the jar. Wilbur Jackson was next. Then Jimmy Sanborn. Big bills and small followed from most of the patrons of The Sunrise. Finally, the loudmouth Rodney came forward. He looked contritely at Jimmy and dropped a rolled bill in the jar. Jimmy looked at him, unsmiling, and said nothing.

Warren reached down and gathered the playing cards from the floor. He straightened them, tapping the worn deck on the tabletop, and set them next to the unpolished wood cribbage board. The pegs were old, burnt, wooden matchsticks.

Andrew sat back down. "After all this? We're going to finish the game?"

"Nah," said Warren. "I've had enough for one morning. I think I'll be heading home. See where Lana is and what she's up to."

"Afraid I might skunk you if we played it out?" Andrew smiled.

"No. Just time to move on."

Warren stood and pulled himself into his coat. Then he shuffled slowly toward the door, detouring around the tables to pass by the jar at the register. Casually, hoping nobody would notice, he dropped a bill in the jar. Everyone noticed, but nobody said a word. Then, quietly, Warren walked out alone into the bright day, sun gleaming off the snow, the bell ringing above the door as he left.

CHAPTER

Twenty-Eight

Thursday

Keira changed into her clothes: jeans, a sweatshirt and sneakers. She found Jack in the front hall, holding a snow shovel and surveying the ice-coated carpet. He took a deep breath and began hacking at the ice with the shovel.

"Stop!" Keira rushed to him and grabbed the shovel. "You'll cut the carpet and scratch the floor."

"What do you want me to do? Just leave the ice here blocking the door? I've got to do something to clean up this mess."

Keira said nothing. She pushed Jack aside, dropped the shovel, and grabbed an end of the hall runner. She shook it once, like cracking a whip, loosening it from the floor. Pebbles of ice scattered across the polished planks, and the rug was free. She elbowed the front door open, held it with her hip and backed out, dragging the carpet onto the porch. Outside, she draped the rug over the porch railing. With the ice gone from the doorway, she went inside and closed the front door.

Jack started in. "Fine. Now, what about the wet stairs? And what are you going to do about the third floor where the fire did the most damage?"

Keira, irritated, stood with hands on her hips. "Let's leave that until the inspector checks things out tomorrow. We should see what the insurance guy says and then let's rebuild. I'll leave the construction up to Jimmy. At least with the front door closed, we can heat the house and start to clean things up a bit."

"You think it's that simple? Insurance money falls from the sky and we rebuild? We shouldn't be in this situation to begin with. What were you thinking lighting the wood stove? Now you've set the house on fire, and almost burned out our home. We'll probably never get things fixed. We'll probably never be able to open now."

"Oh, come on Jack! I lit the wood stove because it was a cold night. I didn't set the house on fire. It was a simple accident. It just happened."

"Sure, whatever you say. The way I see it, while I'm down in Boston working, you do something foolish and now the house is ruined. After all my work getting it ready to open."

"All your work? You're never home!" Keira shouted. "Jimmy and his crew did all the work. I've been here through all of it. Letting the workmen in and out. Meeting with Jimmy. And don't forget, my inheritance bought the place."

"Oh! So, you're going to throw that in my face? That you paid for it? Like I don't have anything to do with it, anything to say about it?"

"It's a small piece of my mother. That's why it matters where the money came from. Don't you understand?"

"I thought it would be a good thing to buy the house. It would give you something to take your mind off your inability to have children. But that doesn't seem to matter, does it?"

They stood, facing each other, both with hands on hips, both realizing that maybe they had gone too far already.

Slowly, quietly, Keira took a deep breath and spoke. "Sometimes I just want to go back to Boston. I just want to give up and go home. But now, with the fire damage, I can't. We're in so far already with the money we've put into the house. Even with insurance, we're committed to this."

Jack softened a little. Palms up, he started over. "Okay. Let's not fight about it. Remember how it was when we started? We'd been dreaming of owning a bed and breakfast someday. We've had such nice getaways together, staying at places like this. We wanted to run one ourselves. Now we own this house and we can fix it back up with the insurance money. We'll survive this setback. And we'll be fine here. I already feel like we've become a part of the town. You've got your friends, Lana and Michelle. And I'm playing hockey every weekend with Jimmy and the boys."

Keira paced and started in again. "Oh, be serious Jack. You have no idea what it's like being here all week. You run off to Boston every week while I'm stuck here alone. Playing hockey on the weekend doesn't begin to make you a native. I don't know what to do about the house or with you. I'm torn. I want to make this all work for us. But maybe we should just give up, cut our losses, sell the place and move back to Boston."

Jack began to push back but thought better of it and stopped. He ran his hands over his hair and stared at the damage in front of the woodstove.

In the tense silence, Keira's phone rang, and Lana's name appeared. Keira shrugged and muttered, "Let me take this. Hello?"

"Hi, it's Lana. I wanted to let you know, I just got a call from Michelle at the hospital. Peter's had a heart attack."

"Oh my God!" Keira sat suddenly on the couch in the parlor, her hand to her mouth.

"What is it?" Jack asked, concerned.

Keira held her hand up, silencing him, focusing on the call with Lana. "How is he? Did he survive? Dear God!"

"Yes, he's okay. So far, at least. But he'll be there a few more days. I'm going to run down to Manchester later today and take some clothes and things for Michelle."

"Oh, God, I feel responsible. This is all because he tried to rescue Smoky from the house. Is there anything I can do?"

"Not right now. You've got your hands full with the house. I'll let you know how Michelle and Peter are doing and when they're coming home. But I wanted to tell you since you might be staying at their place while the Metcalfe House is being rebuilt."

"No, that's all right. I think we'll be able to stay here in our house. There's a lot of smoke and water damage, but our apartment is okay. I just wish I could do something for Peter. And Michelle."

"Say a prayer. I'll let them know how you're doing and that you're thinking of them."

After she hung up, Keira sat on the grimy, soot-covered sofa, drained by everything. By the terrifying night, watching the house burn and firefighters swarming around the snow-filled yard. By the disorientation she'd felt waking up in a strange room. By the damage to the house. And now by her fight with Jack. And here was this call, with the disturbing news about Peter. One thing after another. So much trouble, in such a short time. She looked up at Jack, needing his love, craving his arms around her.

"What is it?" he asked. "What's happened?"

"Peter had a heart attack in the hospital in Manchester. He pulled through, but he'll be there a few more days."

"Michelle is with him?"

"Yes, she called Lana, and Lana called me."

"God." Jack sat next to Keira and held her. She tucked into the comfort of his arm.

"Is there anything we can do for him? And for Michelle?"

"Lana said just pray. She'll let us know how he's doing."

"We have to do something for him. I feel responsible since our house fire is what put him in the hospital."

They sat a long time, snug against each other, thinking, not talking. It soothed them after their fight, but tension remained. Finally Jack said, "Let's get a quick lunch and then we can start cleaning. There's really nothing we can do for Peter. We'll just have to wait and see how he is in a few days."

They went to the kitchen and began assembling sandwiches. Smoky wound her way between their feet, rubbing against their ankles. Despite the pervasive smell of smoke, the soot and the ashes they could see in the parlor, it was a pleasant moment, reminiscent of the idyllic earlier days of their time together.

After lunch, Jack took a large black trash bag and together they began to fill it with ash and debris swept from the front hall and around the wood stove. They continued cleaning on the stairs. They were relieved to see that, behind the closed doors of the second-floor bedrooms, everything appeared to be fine. The second-floor hall was wet, the carpet and walls water-stained. Everything held the sour smell of smoke and burnt plaster. Otherwise, it didn't look like much work would be needed to repair the second floor.

The rug on the stairs to the third floor squished beneath their feet as they climbed. Carpet throughout the third floor was sopping and filthy.

One bedroom on the third floor was damp but otherwise untouched by the fire. The bedroom next to the chimney was worse. A scorched patch darkened most of one wall. A hole had burned through the middle of it, exposing the cracked and blackened bricks of the chimney. Masonry crumbled when Jack touched it. The wall was soaked, the aged plaster soft and spongy to the touch.

Jack shook his head. "Not much we can do here right now. We'll leave this floor as is for the State inspector to see. And we really can't do much clean up until it's been seen by the insurance company. We can do a little on the first two floors today. That's about it."

"Our apartment is still clean. And the kitchen looks okay to use. Tomorrow morning, I'll bake something for Lana and Michelle to thank them," said Keira.

"That would be a nice gesture," Jack said. "Now let's get to work downstairs."

CHAPTER

Twenty-Nine

Thursday night

Jimmy Sanborn's two kids were upstairs in their bedrooms finishing their homework. Jimmy leaned against the kitchen counter watching Lynn put the last of the dinner dishes in the dishwasher.

"I need to tell you about what happened this morning down at The Sunrise," he began.

Lynn turned to him, her arms crossed, her expression deadpan.

"Wilbur and I stopped in on the way back after checking the damage at the Metcalfe House. There was a big scene. Rodney was going on and on, the way he does, with all sorts of crazy ideas."

"What did he say?"

"He started by blaming the fire on anybody and everybody, claiming it was arson. Then he blamed me. He hadn't noticed that Wilbur and I had come in." Jimmy paused.

Lynn paused. "I know how Rodney is. What did he say about you?"

"He said I might have burned the place to get more work. Then he went on to suggest that I might be having an affair with Keira Sullivan. I'm not. You know that."

Jimmy watched Lynn, assessing her reaction. She relaxed and smiled, leaning toward her husband.

"Yes, I know. The rumor already got to me. That's just Rodney. I didn't believe it. You've never given me any reason not to trust you."

Jimmy heaved himself forward from the counter and took a step toward Lynn. She came to him, and they held each other.

"Thank you for telling me," Lynn added. "I would have worried more if you hadn't told me about Rodney."

"Thanks. I'll be spending a bit of time up at their house over the next few weeks. Maybe longer. They'll want me to contract with my people and do what we can to fix the damage."

"Do what you need to do. I understand."

"You know what I can't understand? Why people assume that if I have work to do up there and Jack's out of town, that I must be having an affair with Keira Sullivan. What kind of a soap opera do they think this is? We don't live in Peyton Place, for heaven's sake!"

"No, we don't." Lynn giggled, relieving the tension. "That's down in Gilmanton. We're not like that here in Bennett Falls."

CHAPTER

Thirty

Friday

After the Thursday thaw, the air turned crisp again Friday morning. Jack and Keira dressed quickly and took their coffee and tea to the front porch. They were prepared for the outdoors in fleece jackets over sweaters, and, aside from their drinks, it would appear they might have spent the night elsewhere and come back to the house at dawn. Even though the air was cold, the sun warmed the porch and heated the wall of the house.

"We should remember how nice this is," Jack said. "Once we get things back to normal, we should make this a regular morning ritual."

Keira basked in the sun. "Remember the first time we did this, back last fall, right after we bought the house?"

Jack nodded. "A lot of water under the bridge since then."

Keira laughed. "Water under the bridge. And a lot of water poured down the stairs from the third floor Wednesday night."

Jack didn't laugh.

A pickup truck turned in the driveway, circled, and stopped at the base of the front steps. Wilbur Jackson climbed out. "Morning," he said, deadpan, playing out the charade of their accommodations the night before. "I hope you two found a safe place to spend last night."

"We did," Jack said. "We're all rested and ready to take on today. We cleaned up some of the mess on the first two floors yesterday, but we left the third floor for the guy from the state to see."

"That's good. I got a call from him a few minutes ago. He should be along shortly."

"Would you like a cup of coffee?" Keira asked. "I made a big pot. You could join us here while we wait."

"Sure. I'd appreciate it. Cream, no sugar."

Keira headed to the kitchen. Wilbur pulled off his fleece-lined leather gloves and settled on one of the padded chairs on the wide porch. As Keira brought him his cup, Wilbur said, "When the inspector gets here, you can tell him you made coffee in the kitchen. Offer him a cup. He'll appreciate the offer, and he'll understand that you could use the kitchen this morning even if you can't be staying here yet. He'll likely turn down the cup. He tends to be all business when he comes out for an inspection."

Moments later, a red truck with New Hampshire Fire Marshall marked on the door slowed, then turned into the driveway.

"Let me do most of the talking," Wilbur said.

Two men got out of the truck. One, an older, white-haired man approached, trailed by a quiet, bearded younger man carrying a clipboard. The older man reached out to shake hands. "Morning, Wilbur. Good to see you." Turning to Jack, he asked, "And you are the homeowner?"

"Yes. I'm Jack Sullivan. I own the house."

Keira joined the group. "We both do. I'm Jack's wife, Keira."

"Bob Bouchard. From the state." He handed Jack a business card. "You're welcome to come with us while I check the house but stay back so you're safe. You never know what we'll come across."

"Would you like a cup of coffee?" Keira asked. "I went in this morning and made a pot."

Politely, Bouchard smiled at Keira. He reached up and touched his forehead, as though he were tipping a cap or saluting. "No, thank you, ma'am." Turning back to Wilbur and Jack, he said, "Let's take a look at the damage."

Wilbur asked, "Should we start inside? It looks like it might be a standard chimney fire."

"Lead the way."

Bouchard followed Wilbur into the house, trailed by Bouchard's assistant and Jack. They started at the woodstove. Bouchard knelt, opened the stove doors, and shone his flashlight inside. He checked the black metal fitting and the pipe that ran through the fireplace and into the chimney. He leaned behind the stove and peered up the chimney. After a minute, he sat back on the floor.

"It's wet," he said. "But that's from your firefighters, I expect. It looks like it was installed properly, and everything looks to be in order. According to my records, it passed inspection after installation."

He rolled to his hands and knees and, grunting, slowly stood. "Let's see where the chimney goes. Let's check upstairs inside first."

The group climbed the stairs to the second floor. Keira picked up Smoky, watched them go, and retreated to the kitchen.

On the second floor, they surveyed the wall of the guest room next to the chimney. Bouchard tapped on the wall and ran his hands carefully over the smooth wallpapered plaster. "This wall is damp, but it looks okay," he said. Then, turning to Jack, he added, "You'll need to watch for mold, but that's not my concern. This room looks okay."

They went to the third-floor, Wilbur leading. "Ah," Bouchard said as they entered the guest room. "Here we go."

He went to the scorched wall and poked at the hole in the plaster, prying it back. He took out a pocketknife and picked at the brittle masonry between the old bricks. He pulled back another piece of the old wall, plaster crumbling, and shone his flashlight inside the slim gap between the wall and the chimney. He snapped pictures with his phone then stepped back and asked Jack, "How old is this house?"

"I'm not sure. We bought it last summer and we've spent a few months fixing it up. I think the real estate papers said it was built sometime in the late nineteenth century. Maybe a bit earlier, mid-century?"

"So it's around one-hundred-fifty years old?"

"I expect so. At least."

"Yes. It's very well built. The wall is solid plaster over wood laths. The problem is the old chimney has masonry that's falling apart. When the chimney fire started, it came right through the chinks in the mortar and hit the laths and here we are."

"So what do we do? What does all this mean?" Jack asked, anxious that the man from the State would condemn the house.

"I'm going to have another look at the chimney from the outside. I need to figure out why the fire started. But you'll have to replace the entire chimney. The whole thing is probably no good now. It burned through here, but it could happen again anywhere the entire length of the chimney."

"How about the rest of the house?" Jack asked.

"I expect you'll want to rebuild the wall here. And it'll need to be replaced everywhere it abuts the chimney once you replace the chimney. That means on the other floors of the house, too. I also want to get into the attic to see if there was a problem there and look at the underside of the roof."

Wilbur interjected. "How does the house look structurally? Is it safe for Jack and his wife to stay here while the work is done?"

"Let me check the roof," Bouchard repeated. "It'll be a hassle," he added, turning to Jack. "Living here with the smell of smoke and workmen all over the place redoing the walls and building the new chimney. Otherwise, it looks safe from what I've seen so far."

Jack showed him the door to the steep stairway into the attic. They all went up, ducking beneath the low beams, swiping cobwebs. "Yup,"

Bouchard said. "It's the same here as downstairs. This wall will need work when the new chimney is built. The roof looks okay so far. Let's go outside and check the chimney. You taking notes on all this?" he asked his assistant.

The assistant nodded. Bouchard led the party downstairs and out to the driveway.

"Get the ladder," Bouchard instructed his assistant, "and set it up next to the chimney."

The young man took a long extension ladder off the top of the truck and, with Bouchard's help, began setting it up against the chimney. While he worked, a car turned into the driveway and parked behind the two trucks. A man got out and approached the group.

"Which one of you is Jack Sullivan?" the man asked.

"That's me."

"I'm the adjustor from your insurance company." He handed Jack a business card. "Your agent said if I came this morning, the local Fire Chief and the State Fire Marshall would be here."

"We've got the whole gang right here," Jack said, smiling. He made introductions.

"How does it look?" the adjustor asked, handing around more of his business cards.

"A little too soon to be sure," Bouchard answered. "I need to look at the roof and the chimney from up top before I give my report. The owner will need to do some work."

"All set," called his assistant. Bouchard climbed the ladder while his assistant stood on the snow steadying the base. Bouchard leaned over the top of the chimney and shone his light down the flue. He took several pictures on his phone inside the flue and more of the roof near the chimney.

When he came down, he showed Jack the pictures on his phone. "The roof is fine. Most of the snow has melted off the roof either from the heat of the fire or from the sun, but it looks good, new, fire-retardant shingles from the look of things. But there's your problem," he said, sliding to a new picture on his phone. "See all that ash right there down inside the chimney? That was a nest of some sort. Maybe a squirrel, maybe a bird. It doesn't matter what made the nest. Things like to build nests in old chimneys that aren't being used. Warm air seeps up the chimney in the winter and keeps the critters nice and warm. But when you light a fire, a spark comes up the chimney and bam. There you go. It looks like you had a bit of creosote build-up, too."

"The nest burned?" Jack asked.

"Yes. I doubt whatever built it stayed around for the fun. The nest is toast, but that got the whole chimney going and then it broke through that old masonry and set the wall on fire." Bouchard turned to Wilbur. "Your boys got here fast and did a good job stopping the fire so quickly. Another couple of minutes and the whole place could have been gone."

Wilbur smiled and nodded. "I'll tell my men."

"Thanks," Jack said, putting his hand on Wilbur's shoulder.

"So, we're done here," Bouchard said. "I'll take a couple of minutes in my truck to put my report together before I leave. I can email it to you, Mr. Sullivan, and to you, Wilbur, and to anyone else who wants a copy."

"I'll take a copy," the insurance adjustor said.

"So, I can stay here while I rebuild?" Jack asked.

"Sure," Bouchard said.

Jack turned to the insurance inspector. "How long will it take to get my money? I'd like to start on the repairs."

"I'll get the paperwork rolling first thing Monday morning when I get back to Boston. I'll take a look inside to see what furnishings need to be replaced, and I'll base my report off the State Fire Marshall's report. You'll have the settlement figure probably late Monday. You might get the money by the end of next week."

The assistant secured the ladder on top of the State truck. "You're a lucky man," Bouchard said to Jack. "You almost lost it all."

After Bouchard pulled out, Wilbur eased over to Jack. "You heard what the man from the State said. If you and Keira want to move back in now, you can since he's given his okay. I hope you two found a safe place to stay last night."

He clapped Jack on the shoulder, got in his truck and drove away.

Jack gave the insurance adjustor a tour of the inside, showing him the soaked carpets and stained furniture. Jack explained, "The house passed an inspection when we bought it last summer. And the woodstove passed when it was installed. I don't understand how this could have happened."

The adjustor nodded. "Everything can appear normal and pass inspection. But accidents happen all the time. Nobody's to blame. I do have one question. How about your mortgage? We'll need to work with your mortgage company on this."

"That's one area where we don't have a problem," Jack explained. "We inherited some money last year and bought the place outright."

"Ah, yes." The adjustor nodded. "I see that here in my notes. So you're all set."

After the insurance man left, Jack and Keira were alone in the remains of their house. They looked around at the debris, breathing the pervasive smell of smoke. Finally, Keira broke the silence. "That's the first step. We're on our way to recovery."

Jack shook his head but said nothing.

CHAPTER
Thirty-One
Friday afternoon

Keira baked scones while the men conducted the inspection. She made two batches: one with sliced almonds, golden raisins, and honey, the second with dried cranberries and crushed walnuts. When they cooled, she stacked a mix of the two recipes on three plates, covering two of the plates with plastic wrap. The covered plates would be thank-you gifts for Lana and Michelle. The third plate Keira planned to keep for Jack and herself.

Jack came in, sniffed, and went straight to the kitchen. "How did the inspection go?" Keira asked.

"It looks like everything's okay. The man from the state said we can move back in." Jack chuckled quickly. "And the insurance adjustor said we might get our money by the end of next week."

"That's a relief!"

Jack sniffed again. "What's cooking?" he asked with a grin.

"Scones. Some for us, and some for Lana and Michelle to thank them for looking out for me during the fire."

"That's nice. We can run out after lunch and drop them off at their houses. Do you think Peter will be home?"

"I don't know. But Lana said Michelle leaves the door unlocked. We can leave them on her kitchen table with a note if she's not home. She'll have to stop by to get clean clothes even if Peter's still in the hospital."

"Good idea."

After lunch, they drove down the hill and turned left on River Road before the covered bridge. They had never been to the Briggs Farm, of course, but Jack and Keira had seen the big red barn from across the river.

They drove along River Road, turned up a short hill, and crested a rise. Briggs Farm loomed ahead. Up close, the immense barn had peeling, weathered red paint. Next to the road, a small, barren farm stand stood, swamped with snow. The fields were a smooth white expanse glaring in the winter sun, the furrows buried. The white clapboard farmhouse had two stories with black shutters framing the windows. A railed porch with gingerbread trim ran across the front. The driveway was plowed down to mud. Warren's battered pickup with a rusted plow blade was parked next to the front steps.

Jack parked behind the truck and walked up the steps, followed by Keira with a covered plate of scones. As he reached to knock on the wooden storm door, Warren pushed it open, unsmiling. "I saw you turn in. What do you want?"

Keira, gracious and smiling, stepped forward past Jack. She held out the plate of scones. "I baked these for you and Lana to thank her for what she did to help me during the fire."

"I suppose I ought to invite you in," Warren mumbled. He held the storm door back, pushed the front door open, and led the way to the living room.

"Have a seat," he said as he took the plate from Keira. He settled in a wooden rocker, setting the scones on a round side-table next to his chair.

Keira explained, "Lana saved me two nights ago. She got me away from our house after the fire. She put me to bed in Michelle and Peter's house and stayed with me 'til morning. I don't know how I would have gotten through that awful night without her."

Warren nodded. "That's Lana. She's a good woman. She told me what she did for you."

"Where is she today?" Keira asked.

Warren said nothing, staring at the scones beneath the plastic wrap.

Jack finally spoke. "You're a lucky man to be married to her."

Warren pulled back the plastic from the scones, took one, and sampled a small bite. "And you're a lucky man to be married to a woman who can cook like this," he said, waving the scone.

"I am." Jack nodded.

"So, where is Lana?" Keira repeated.

"Manchester. She picked up some clothes and things for Michelle and went down to meet her at the hospital. Michelle's still there with Peter."

"How's he doing?" Jack asked.

"He had a heart attack. How do you think he's doing?" Warren's voice held a touch of anger. He looked at Jack the way he would if he was explaining something simple to a child, hands out, palms up, his face implacable.

Neither Jack nor Keira replied. They looked uneasily around the austere living room. Some people might have called the furniture antiques. Others might have referred to them simply as old. To Warren, it was home.

Warren continued, "I guess it's no secret around town that I've been against your opening a bed and breakfast. Now look what all has happened. You two come to town and start fixing up the old Metcalfe Place. People are all up in arms. The town's divided over it. And when it burns, there's even more controversy, more anger and shouting going on. And one of our people is nearly killed? You two have really made a mess of our town, haven't you?"

"All we want is to open a bed and breakfast," Jack fired back. "There's nothing wrong with that!" He stood, preparing to leave.

Keira was on the edge of tears. "Why do you hate us?" she asked.

Distressed by Keira's statement, Warren flushed suddenly and shifted on his chair. Then he looked down and took another bite of his scone. Finally, he put the scone on the table, scattering crumbs, and looked up at them while he chewed. Eating bought him time to prepare what he should say. It also mellowed him.

Jack paused, then sat back down.

Warren swallowed and began, giving a dismissive wave of his hand, as if sweeping away an annoying insect. "I don't hate you. I might not care for what you're trying to do, that's all. But I don't hate you, or anybody for that matter. I'm not against everything that changes here in town. I went to school in the old school building, the place where they have all the town offices now, on the Common. I graduated from there two years after my good friend Andrew Holmes. Our lives have taken very different paths, but he's always been my best friend. He went off to college at Dartmouth after high school. Later, when he graduated from college, he took a job at the bank here in town and joined the National Guard to dodge the draft. His son Matthew went to Dartmouth, too."

Warren nibbled another small bite and looked at the braid rug in front of him as he talked.

"I didn't go to college when I got out of high school. I got drafted, and I left my parents to run the farm here on the river without my help. It was the first time I'd ever really been away from Bennett Falls. They took me through Boston and New York City and Texas, and I ended up in Vietnam for a year. Didn't see much good while I was away. The farther I got from home, the worse things were. Noisy and crowded and dirty. Dangerous, too. Not just in Vietnam, but in New York and Texas. I'm not a big fan of the rest of the world. I couldn't wait to come home and settle down, here in Bennett Falls."

Warren paused again, staring out the window at the bright sun reflecting off the snow. He shook his head and shuffled his feet on the braid rug, remembering the days after he returned to Bennett Falls from the fighting, recalling the relief he felt coming home to the clean air, the predictability, the safety and orderliness of his hometown.

"When I got home, the town was already starting to change. Some punk kids had lit the covered bridge on fire and burned it down. The town replaced it with a concrete and steel thing that was perfectly fine, I suppose. But it wasn't right, not at all like our old bridge. I led a push in town to make it back into a covered bridge, and thank the lord the town did. Andrew worked at the bank and he helped me, and people listened to me back then and followed me. They saw me as a patriot because I'd been in the army. Not all Vietnam vets in other places were treated well, but my town respected what I'd done. They rallied behind me. What you see out there now looks just like the original bridge, but the concrete bridge is right there under all that wood. So, it's still indestructible underneath, but it looks the way it should. Right away, people in town took it the wrong way. They built parking lots on either side of the river for the tourists. They printed up t-shirts and made souvenirs showing the bridge. Everyone was looking for a way to get rich off it. It took about a year for our town to be overrun with people coming to New Hampshire for vacation."

Jack and Keira sat quietly, entranced, listening to Warren's story.

"Then the same sort of thing happened to the old mill. The Metcalfe family saw their business going overseas during the seventies. They finally laid off all the mill workers and closed the place around 1980, I think. A lot of people lost their jobs. The place sat empty for years. Then some developer from somewhere away from here, probably from down your way in Boston, bought the big old building for a song and turned it out the way you see it now with all the little shops and the fancy restaurant and the expensive condos upstairs. I suppose that's all good in a way. It drove out the rats and brought in some tax revenue. But it changed everything again. It brought in rich folks from Boston and everywhere, people who don't appreciate what we had here in Bennett Falls. More of our little town's character was lost.

"In the midst of it all, my parents both passed away. I was fine running the farm without them for a while. Lana worked with me, and we kept it all going, selling our produce at a couple of nearby farmers' markets and the local stores and at the farm stand out front. Debbie bought her fair share of what we grew and served it up over at The Sunrise. She says she likes to serve locally grown food. But it got to be too much. The big supermarket past the new high school doesn't buy their produce from people like me. I can't compete. So, I'm out of business. I'm too old to farm now anyway. But it's still hard to watch my family farm go out of business. My family has farmed on this land for centuries."

Warren shifted in his seat and continued. "Now you two come to town with your bed and breakfast fantasy. Fixing up the old house is a good thing. Just like rebuilding the covered bridge and doing over the mill. But Bennett Falls doesn't need a bed and breakfast. You're just the latest thing to come along."

Warren took a moment and looked at Keira.

"You asked why I hate you? I don't hate either of you. This isn't personal. You're welcome to move to Bennett Falls. I'm just not a big fan of everything that's happened here in recent years. I remember what the town was like when I was a boy. It's almost all gone now. Things here certainly haven't gotten any better over the past few years."

Warren sat back in his rail-back rocking chair and took another bite of the scone.

"Now, this is very good!" he added, holding up the remnants.

Keira smiled. "I'm glad you enjoyed it."

"Is this the sort of thing you'll be serving if you ever open the bed and breakfast?"

"I hope so. I've been researching all sorts of recipes for breakfast."

"Do you have children?" Warren asked, changing his tack, hoping to soften his message with the couple. "They would enjoy a breakfast like this."

"No," Jack said. Keira hung her head.

Warren noticed Keira's reaction. "Oh, I'm sorry," he said. "What was I thinking?"

Jack reached across and took Keira's hand. "When we were first married, we were focused on our careers. A baby wouldn't have fit with our plans. Then a few years ago, we decided to try. It didn't work out for us. But we've talked it over. We're perfectly fine without kids."

Keira still said nothing, staring hard, straight ahead at emptiness. How could she talk about the pain, the loss, the emptiness, and the lack of fulfillment with this brusque old man? He had just opened up so much with them, but this was not a conversation she wanted to start.

Warren nodded. "Careers are important too, I suppose. And I expect you think kids would be in the way if you were running a bed and breakfast."

Hoping to establish a bond, Jack asked, "How about you, Warren? Do you have children?"

Warren brightened, sitting forward in his rocker. "Yes, Lana and I have a daughter, Susan. She's married and living down in Manchester. We have a grandchild, a boy named Jonah. My daughter is about your age."

"Maybe she can come back and take over the farm?" Jack asked.

"Nah, she doesn't want to be a farmer." He gave a wave of his hand, pushing the idea away. "Like everything else, she's gone. Kids don't want to stay in a place like Bennett Falls. They all go off and make their living elsewhere. Nobody wants to be a farmer these days."

Eager to change the subject, Keira said, "Back to my scones. Save some of those for Lana to thank her for saving me the other night with the fire. And what about Michelle? Do you know when she and Peter are coming home?"

Warren was also happy to move the conversation along. "I don't know. Lana says he's doing well, recovering nicely. She says it wasn't a serious heart attack, as though that sort of thing isn't serious. But you know how these things go. They'll keep him in the hospital in Manchester another day or so to watch him."

Keira nodded. "I have a plate of scones in the car for her and Peter, too. Should I drop them off at their house?"

"You can leave them with me. I promise not to eat them. Lana will be home in an hour or so, and I expect she'll be running back down there tomorrow morning. I'll see that she takes them to Michelle and Peter when she goes back."

"Thanks. Let me get them for you."

Jack and Keira went to their car. Warren followed them outside and waited on the porch. Keira wrote a short note, thanking Michelle. She tucked it inside the plastic wrap and took the plate back to Warren. He took the plate, nodded to Keira, and waved to Jack in the car. Slowly, he turned and went inside, pulling the storm door closed behind him.

Jack and Keira drove back to their house, mulling their conversation with Warren.

Keira brightened and said, "I guess we understand Warren better now. I can see why he's the way he is. He's not such a bad guy."

Jack shook his head. "I still think he's a son of a bitch. He had no reason to treat us the way he did at the town meeting. I don't like him one bit."

"Oh, Jack. Let it go. You heard what he said about things. He's okay."

At their house, they started cleaning again, working on the slight damage to the second floor. Finally they went to the third floor. Looking into the guest room where the fire had broken through from the chimney, Jack shook his head and closed the door. "Let's leave this for the professionals to handle when we get the settlement from the insurance company."

They spent the rest of the day working quietly, shadowed by Smoky.

Keira was preparing what she liked to call "special eggs" for breakfast: diced ham, mushrooms, onions, and cheddar cheese in an omelet with hash brown potatoes on the side. She knew Jack loved this meal. He came from their apartment, walked through the kitchen with only a brief glance at Keira at the stove, passed through the dining room and stood in the parlor looking at the orderly mess left from their clean-up after the fire. He ran his hands through his hair and surveyed the damage. He started toward the stairs, paused, then turned and came back to the kitchen.

"We need to talk."

Keira poured his coffee and took it to him as he sat at the kitchen table. "Okay," she said warily, standing with her hands on her hips. "What's on your mind?"

"A lot. I got so caught up in everything with the fire, I haven't had a chance to tell you my news. Last week, my boss told me they like the way things have gone with me working part-time. Our clients like me and the guy who was supposed to replace me isn't working out. They want me to stay on, working Tuesday through Thursday. Just three days a week. So, I'm thinking we could make a go of that. I'd leave early Tuesday mornings and be back for a late dinner on Thursdays."

Jack stopped and looked at Keira, waiting for her to respond. He suspected she wouldn't be pleased with his announcement.

She stood for a moment, one hand on her hip, looking at him. Then she turned back to the stove to tend to the eggs.

"If you take the offer," she said with her back still to Jack. "It would be back to the same routine we've lived with since September."

"Yes. I'd be down there only two nights a week, probably staying with my parents. I'd be here most of the time. Would you be okay with that?"

Keira turned off the stove and began dishing the omelets onto two plates. She handed Jack his plate and sat across from him, not eating. "I don't know. It's been difficult these past few months. You're always in Boston so you don't know how hard it is for me being alone here all week. I miss Boston. I feel like I'm caught half in Boston and half here, stuck in limbo somewhere between belonging in one town or the other. There are things in Boston I haven't found here. And I'm alone all the time, letting all the carpenters and workmen in, and trying to take care of everything. I was looking forward to having you home for a change. I need you to help out here."

"We both have lots of friends in Boston. And we've both got friends here, now too. You have Michelle and Lana. I have Jimmy and Peter and all the hockey guys. I can't say Warren's a friend, but after yesterday at least we know where he's coming from. This is a friendly town."

"So why don't you stay?"

"I was undecided about what to do when my boss first proposed it. But the fire changed everything. If I continue working down in Boston, particularly since our opening will be delayed a few months, maybe more, this gives us a financial cushion, some income to get us through this time. We can't be sure the bed and breakfast will be a success anyway, and now we'll be opening later than we planned. We need my income. And health insurance too. My boss says we can stay on their insurance."

Keira picked at her eggs. "We can't give up on this house. We put all our money into buying it. We're stuck here. And you're right. We'll need your income for a while. But this is our new home. Do you think you'll ever move here permanently?"

"I expect so. Probably. We've both talked about opening a bed and breakfast for so long, and now that we're finally on the edge of making that dream come true, we have a setback. That's all it is, just a setback. What if I go down to Boston Monday morning and tell my boss I'll take a year contract for my part-time Tuesday through Thursday job starting the following week? I'll keep our health insurance coverage too. Then, after the house is fixed up and open for business, we can make a more long-term decision."

"I'll need you here when we open. Running it will be a two-person job."

"But we'll need my income too, to tide us over."

Keira sighed. "I really wanted you here with me. I need your help. But after the fire, this is our reality. I guess we have no choice."

"Maybe this is the way it's supposed to be. Can it be a coincidence that the day before the fire, my boss in Boston makes me this offer? It will help us survive this catastrophe. Besides, we have a few friends here in town. But we may never fit in as locals. You probably have to be born here to be considered a local."

Keira smiled and picked up Smoky. "That means Smoky's our only local resident. She was born in Warren's barn."

"Maybe. It might go back further than just one generation." Jack reached over and scratched Smoky's head. "It may go back many generations. But I expect Smoky's family has been living in Warren's barn for generations. So you're probably right."

Smoky jumped off Jack's lap and strolled out of the room without looking back.

CHAPTER
Thirty-Three
Late Winter

Jack was up and out the door before sunrise on Monday. Keira got out of bed and watched from the living room window as his taillights turned out of the driveway, down the hill, on his way to Boston. She was irritable, alone again, and not sure where to start in the house. She leaned her forehead against the icy glass, noting the gritty soot on the windowsill.

We were so close, Keira thought. Jack was at the end of his contract with his old company. The house was finished. I was done with my old job, and I had everything ready for guests here. Now there'll be weeks, maybe months to rebuild because of the fire. How long will it take to build a new chimney? Will the insurance money cover everything? We'll need new furniture. There's nothing I can do until Jack and I get the figure from the insurance agent and talk to Jimmy. And now Jack is gone anyway. Again. It's up to me to make this right.

After a moment, she sighed and straightened. I should have talked more with Jack about all this. But he's gone. Time to move on. There's no time for feeling sorry for myself. It's time to do something. But what?

She scuffed into the kitchen in her slippers and robe and started water for her tea. When it boiled, she made a mug, added honey, and sat at the kitchen table looking out the window at the trampled snow next to the porch. Small piles of ashes and other debris from the fire dotted the icy yard. She dragged one of the scones onto a plate and began to eat. Aside from the rush of warm air from a vent as the furnace kicked on, the house was silent. Smoky sniffed at the vent and settled on top of its warmth.

After a few moments soaking up the heat, Smoky prowled the floor beneath the table looking for crumbs. Keira got up and filled the bowl with cat food. Smoky ran to the bowl and began gobbling. Keira assessed her situation. I'm almost out of cat food. And low on human food too. I'll need to go shopping today.

Keira showered, dressed, and was preparing her shopping list when she heard tires crackle on the ice in front of the house. Jimmy's pickup circled in front of the house, skipping on the frozen ruts. He got out and started for the kitchen door, waving when he saw Keira through the window. She let him in.

"Good morning!" Jimmy's tone was bright. "Is Jack still around?"

"No. He left early for Boston. I thought he was almost done there, but he's got a contract for a year more. It's probably a good thing though. Since we can't open for a while, we'll need his income."

Jimmy paused, frowning. "Oh. That's good then? I expect you both were hoping he'd stay home once spring arrived. But you're right. That regular paycheck will be nice to have right now."

Keira started the coffee maker. "Yes, I guess so. Anyway, we are planning to fix the damage and open as soon as possible. Can you help?"

Jimmy unzipped his coat and sat at the kitchen table across from Keira. "Of course. I made a few calls over the weekend. I've got a bunch of people ready to go. And I'm assuming you want me plowing the drive for you? They're saying more snow is coming later this week. I didn't get a chance to talk about that with Jack, what with the fire and all."

"Yes, thanks for keeping us plowed out." Keira had talked with Jack about the need for plowing and Jimmy's offer, but they hadn't committed to it. Keira spoke for herself, not for both of them.

Jimmy asked, "Do you have a figure from the insurance company yet? I'm thinking about a budget to repair the damage. You'll need someone to handle the smoke and water damage at the least."

"Jack should hear about that early this week, maybe today."

"Whatever amount they offer, I can work within that budget to set things right. Let me know when Jack hears from them." Jimmy thought about the money being raised in the jar down at the Sunrise. It was a gracious gesture, but it wouldn't begin to cover the cost of the repairs.

Keira brought him a mug of coffee and sat across from him. She pushed the plate of scones closer. "Help yourself."

"Thanks. These look delicious."

"Could you start before we hear about how much we get from the insurance company?"

"Of course. If you'd like, I'll call the smoke and water damage people today and schedule them for tomorrow. I expect the settlement will more than cover that cost. And I know you're good for the money."

"We're going to need to replace some of the rugs and the furniture too. Everything on the third floor was ruined. I feel like we're right back at the beginning. But it's not as much fun doing it all again."

"You'll get through this. By the end of the week, I can probably give you a time estimate for how long it'll take to fix everything. And when Jack hears from the insurance people, you'll be on your way. It shouldn't take long. It took four months for the complete do-over last fall. This time, from what I hear from Wilbur, it's really just repairs. I'll need to redo a few interior walls, but the plumbing and wiring are still good, and the house is sound. The new chimney is the only big project, and I've got a masonry guy ready to go with that. I expect he'll have to tear down the old chimney before he can start building a new one. That's not something I do very often, so I don't know how long that might take."

Keira looked out at the glaring white that surrounded the house. In the morning sunshine, snow was already melting, dripping from the porch roof. Birds clustered and pecked at the sand in bare spots in the plowed driveway. The yard might still be littered with debris from the fire, but Jimmy's optimistic mood was contagious.

"You're so encouraging," she said. "I was really feeling down about things this morning."

Jimmy took a bite of the scone and smiled. "Don't be. You'll get through this. And if you serve things like this to your guests, the bed and breakfast will be a hit."

He stood, finishing the scone and taking a final sip of coffee. "I'll have my smoke and water damage people here tomorrow morning and have the chimney mason look at things as soon as you have a budget to work with."

Keira stood, relieved after their quick talk.

Jimmy touched her shoulder, a brief gesture of support from a friend. "Everything's going to be okay. You'll see."

He was out the kitchen door, across the porch, zipping his jacket as he jogged to his truck.

After returning from a quick run to the supermarket, Keira straightened the kitchen and set to work with Smoky tagging along. She rolled the oriental rugs in every room where the water had soaked them. She dragged them down the stairs and out to the porch, spreading them to dry across the railing. When she had cleared the rugs out of the guest rooms, Keira took a break from the heavy work and sat at her computer, searching for rug cleaning services. She found a carpet store in Concord, called them, and set a time for them to pick up the rugs later in the week.

Next, Keira took a plastic laundry basket and went through all the damaged rooms, gathering the small knickknacks from dresser tops and bedside tables. The furniture on the third floor was scorched. A dresser was charred next to the hole in the wall in the third-floor bedroom where the fire had broken through.

It was chilly. A slight breeze blew through the torn plaster and the scorched hole. She closed the door and set a rolled towel across the sill as she left, hoping to block the cold air from the rest of the house.

Again, she fretted. *I wish Jack would have stayed to help with all the* work here. But we need his income.

Keira brought the basket of decorations to the kitchen. It took the rest of the morning to clean everything, sponging off the porcelain, polishing the pewter and brass. Once finished, she took the shining decorations up to a second-floor guest room.

As she worked, she was interrupted by a call from Jack. He started right in without even a word of greeting. "I got a call from the insurance adjuster. They're giving us a pretty substantial amount to fix everything. I called Jimmy and told him how much we have to work with, and he's scheduling everything. I'm holding out a bit to buy replacement furniture."

"Yes," Keira said. "He—"

"Could you possibly start to clear the rooms?"

Keira sighed, frustrated, her forehead in her hand. "Jimmy stopped by this morning. He's going to get people here tomorrow to start work on cleaning the smoke and water damage."

"Oh, that's good. But why can't you straighten things a bit? It'll make it easier for his men to do their work."

"I've already taken care of a lot of it. The rugs are rolled up and the knickknacks are cleaned and set aside."

"Oh. Good. Jimmy said he's got a guy for the chimney work. He didn't give me a figure for how much that would cost or when he would start, but he said he'd work within our budget."

Keira sat, running a hand across her head, smoothing her hair. *Jack has no idea what's needed here. How do I let him know what we're up against?* "We'll also need some big repairs," Keira said. "Patching the hole in the wall, painting, and other cosmetic work. What else?"

Jack gave a terse laugh. "Nothing. It feels good to be rolling on fixing everything up. If we're lucky, in a few weeks, it'll be like nothing happened. Listen, I've got to go. I have a meeting. I'll call later in the week."

Jack was off the line before Keira said goodbye.

What's with him? He's clueless about what I'm up against. And he's hardly got time to talk with me. But, it feels good to be moving on things. Now, what should I tackle next?

Keira's phone rang again. It was Jimmy. "Good morning again," he began. "I talked to Jack and got your insurance settlement figure, and I can work within that budget. Could the chimney mason come tomorrow morning to start checking it out? The guys cleaning up the smoke and water damage should be there a little after eight tomorrow."

"Of course. The sooner the better. There's a bit of a draft where the hole is next to the chimney."

"I can close that over, at least a temporary patch while the chimney guy is doing his work. I expect we'll have to rebuild that whole wall."

"I'll be ready early tomorrow for everyone to be here again."

Keira had barely ended the call with Jimmy when the phone rang again. It was Lana. "Hi Keira, how are you this morning?"

"Good! I've started the clean-up, and Jimmy Sanborn's got his guys ready to start working again. I'm making progress."

"That's good. Listen, Michelle brought Peter home this morning. You might want to give her a call or stop by to see them at their house."

"That's great news. How is he?"

"He's alive and well. I saw him briefly, and he seemed subdued. This might have scared him a bit, but he's such a tough old bastard, it's hard to tell."

"Okay, I'll run by their house this afternoon. I haven't seen her yet to thank her for what she did last week."

"She understands. Oh, and I took her the scones you baked for her. Warren actually left two for me on the plate you brought us."

"Only two? There were ten on your plate."

"Um hum. I can't imagine what happened to the rest of them!"

"I'll make you more."

"Take your time. You've got a lot going on. Michelle would love to see you this afternoon. If you've got time, take a run over there."

"I'll head over right now."

CHAPTER

Thirty-Five

Winter's End

It took Keira a moment to remember which house was the Lacroix house. Frenchtown was a maze of narrow streets, laid out in a haphazard grid by the Metcalfe family to house their workers when the mill was new. Most of the houses looked identical: small, white clapboard saltboxes with black-shingled roofs and black doors and shutters. Keira finally picked the correct house because she recognized Peter's truck parked in the snow and mud driveway.

Keira parked on the street, walked to the door, and knocked. Michelle came out onto the granite doorstep, hugging her without a word. She kept her arm tight around Keira, pulled her into the house, and led her to the confined living room. Peter sat stiffly on a sofa, his feet set squarely on the floor in front of him. His face was lined and tired, but he smiled when he saw Keira. Keira reached down and took his hand.

"Thank you for helping save my house. And thank you for saving my kitten. How are you?"

Michelle released Keira and sat next to her husband, her hand on his knee. Keira sat in an armchair across from them.

Peter grinned. "My pleasure. Happy to be of service. I'm okay." He gave a short, sardonic laugh.

"I'm glad you're home."

"It's good to be home. I've just got to take it easy for a while. How's your house?"

"Not as bad as I thought. It can be fixed. Jimmy's already got people lined up, ready to start."

"You might need a new plumber. I won't be doing much of that work for a while."

"I think the plumbing's fine. It's just smoke damage, some small repairs and a new chimney."

"Ah. That's good. So it's a setback, but you'll still be opening for business in a while. How's Jack? He was just about done with his work down in Boston. Is he home now?"

"No, he's back in Boston. His company asked him to stay on part-time. I suppose that's a good thing because we might be unable to open for a few months."

"He needs to be here with you at the house."

"I agree. But we need his income right now."

Michelle spoke up. "I'll be opening the store in a couple of weeks. I'll put you to work there. That should help give you a small income. And if you'd like to help set up the inventory, let me know. I'll be in there a few days each week getting everything ready."

"You don't need to stay with Peter?"

Peter gave a dismissive wave of his hand. "Nah. I'm a big boy. I can take care of myself. No need for Michelle to be hanging around, treating me like an invalid."

Michelle nodded. "We'd just be in each other's way and drive each other nuts. I can walk home for lunch every day. It's only a two-minute walk."

"And I can walk to the store if I get lonely. The doctor says I need to stay active and exercise. Or I can walk down to the VFW."

Michelle turned to him and pointed. "You be careful with that. The doctor also said to watch your diet and cut back on the beer."

"My friends are at the VFW," he fussed. "Or down at The Sunrise. I know what I can't eat or drink, but I need to walk and I need to see my friends."

Michelle relented. "Okay. But be careful. I can't always be taking care of you."

Keira was relieved to see the brewing fight abate. "Okay, listen," Keira interrupted. "I have to go. I don't want to take all your time. I just wanted to thank you both for what you did for me that night. I'm so glad you're back, Peter. Take care of yourself. I'll stop by again with Jack when he's home on Friday. Michelle, I'll call. I'd love to work with you at the store any time you'll have me."

"I'll have you anytime you want to come by."

Keira stood and went to Peter, slumped on the sofa. Leaning down, she kissed him quickly on his whiskered cheek. "Take care of yourself," she repeated.

"I'm fine," he insisted. "You say Jack's home in a couple of days? Bring him by. I'd like to see him."

"I will," Keira said. Then she hugged Michelle and whispered, "I don't know how I would have gotten through that night if you hadn't been there with me."

"Would you have expected me to do anything else?"

Keira gave Michelle's hand a quick squeeze. Then she let herself out and drove back to the Metcalfe House, feeling unsettled after seeing Peter's gaunt face, but relieved that he was alive.

The four of them walked from the Lacroix house heading toward the Metcalfe Mill along the narrow streets of Frenchtown. Michelle and Keira followed Peter and Jack. Keira cradled Smoky tight to her jacket in her cupped hands. When they reached Main Street, the women crossed and went to the Craft shop. The men continued down the hill, heading for the VFW and lunch.

"Ever since the fire, little Smoky hates being left alone at our house," Keira explained as she followed Michelle through the door of the craft shop. "I keep a big cardboard box in the car and put her in it to bring her with me when I go out. She hates riding in the box too, but she enjoys being with me wherever I go."

"That's fine," Michelle said. "She can join us in the store while we get set for our opening day."

As soon as Michelle closed the door behind them, Keira put Smoky on the floor. The kitten scampered across the store and found her place on the wide windowsill overlooking the whitewater river. She turned around twice and lay down to nap in the sun.

Peter led Jack into the bar at the VFW. They took seats on stools, side by side. Jack took a stained paper menu from behind the sugar and condiments and looked it over.

The bartender, a heavy older man with wise eyes and a gray and black beard, approached and greeted Peter. "Welcome back, old friend. How're you feeling?"

"I'm fine. Nothing to worry about. Just a bit of heart trouble. It's good to be home."

The bartender turned to Jack. His words slightly accented, he said, "And you're Jacque Sullivan. The new fellow fixing up the old Metcalfe place. Welcome to the VFW. Haven't you been here a couple of times after the Sunday night hockey?"

"Yes. I'm Jack. It's good to meet you." Jack reached out to shake the bartender's hand. "And you are?"

The bartender shook and introduced himself. "Phillip Mandeville. I work here during the day. I have another business I do in the evening. Cleaning and maintenance jobs up at the mill, around town, here and there. I haven't been up to your place yet. I hear it's turning out nicely. Or it will be when you fix it up after your fire."

"I hope so. It'll take a while." Jack studied the menu. "I'll have a cheeseburger with fries. And what's on tap?"

"Bud. Bud Lite. Coors. Coors Lite. Labatts. There's a list of other beer by the bottle on the back of the menu."

Jack flipped the menu and reviewed it for a moment. "Sam Adams," he ordered.

"How about you?" Phillip turned to Peter. "The usual?"

"Nah. Not anymore. I'll have a tuna melt and an iced tea or something else to drink. The doctor says I have to watch my diet."

"Sure. I'll take care of you." Phillip made a note on a scrap of paper and walked to the kitchen.

"This is the worst part of the whole deal," Peter said quietly, leaning over to confide in Jack, their shoulders touching. "Not that Phillip says he'll 'take care of me.'" Peter made quote marks with his fingers as he said it. "I actually enjoy Michelle making a fuss over me. And it's not that I hurt for the first couple of days. It was a mild heart attack, the doctors say. What really cranks me up is that I have to give up so much that I love. The doctors gave me a stack of papers telling me how to live now. What I should eat. I threw it all in the trash. I know what they're telling me. No more cheeseburgers. No more beer. I usually get a cheeseburger and a beer. They know just how to cook it for me here at the VFW. I don't know if a tuna melt is good for me or not. Honestly, I don't even know if I'll like it. But I'll miss my cheeseburger. And no beer. Maybe in a few months I might have a beer again. I don't know."

"It's a small sacrifice to make to stay healthy. It's not like you have to give up everything."

Peter gave a short chuckle. "Ha! I can't play hockey anymore. I've played hockey my whole life. Ever since I was a kid. And my plumbing days are over. I know a guy a couple of towns away who can pick up my business if I need him. So my regular customers don't have to worry. Jimmy knows the guy too, so that's finished. No more plumbing. Probably no hunting next fall. It's like my whole life, everything I love, has been taken from me."

"But you're alive. Can you still go fishing?"

"Yes, I can still fish. It's not much of a life without cheeseburgers, beer, hockey, my job, and everything, but I am alive. Do you fish, Jack?"

"I never had much chance in Boston. I'm always working. And we don't have a boat."

"I've got a boat. I'll take you fishing. Sometime this summer we'll go fishing up on Clear Lake.

"That would be great. You're on."

"So at least I can fish. Everything else is gone." Peter traced his fingers on the bar, following the grain of the wood. "Here's what I think. We're all going to die someday. I believe someone once said, 'live every day as if it was your last. Because someday it will be.' It's what we do about things between our birth, when we start to live, and whenever we die that matters."

Phillip set two glasses on the bar in front of them, iced tea for Peter and a frosted glass for Jack's dark bottle of Sam Adams Winter Wheat.

Jack nodded, startled by the sudden philosophy coming from Peter the Plumber. "Words to live by." Jack lifted his beer to salute Peter.

"Jim Morrison put it well," Peter added, clicking his glass with Jack's. "'The future's uncertain but the end is always near.'"

Peter sipped his iced tea. "Let me tell you something, Jack. You're a few years younger than me, so you missed Vietnam. And Korea. I went in the army right after we pulled out of Vietnam. I was in for three years. I try not to think about that time. Even though I wasn't in combat, it was no good. I try not to worry about the wars we have now in the Middle East; Iran, Iraq, Afghanistan, Syria. If I let myself think about what's going on over there now, I'd be right back in Korea. My youngest child went in and served over in Iraq. He was always in a bit of trouble before he left for the service. Not like my two older kids. The older ones have always done fine. College. Good jobs. Families. But Larry, the youngest… he was in trouble before he enlisted, and he's a bigger mess now, after he came home. He's in Texas these days and it's no good."

Phillip brought two plates: the tuna melt for Peter, the cheeseburger for Jack. Both plates had pale French fries, a leaf of lettuce, a tomato slice, and a quartered pickle slice on the side.

Peter took a nibble of the tuna and dabbed mayonnaise from his lower lip. "It's not just war. There's always disease. My heart attack. Drugs. Crime. But here's the way I see things. As a whole, the world sucks, but here we are, living in this pretty little town. I'm more or less retired whether or not I want to be, but my social security and Michelle's shop keep us afloat. You're still working down in Boston, and you have the bed and breakfast waiting for you here. So, we both have decent incomes. Great opportunities lie ahead. Winter's over, and the weather's getting warmer.

We have our wives and our lives. What more could anyone want?"

Peter sipped his tea, shuddered quickly, and shook his head. "So I say, 'enjoy today because tomorrow we might die.' I think some French philosopher said that. Maybe Shakespeare or some guy in ancient Greece. It doesn't matter who said it, it's a good approach to life when we have so many terrible things going on all around us every day.

He picked up a limp French fry, dabbed it in ketchup, and popped it in his mouth.

"I just wish I could have a cheeseburger. Or a beer." He took a big bite of the tuna melt, tuna salad spilling from between the slices of toast onto his plate. He pinched the spilled salad between his thumb and fingers and stuffed it in his mouth.

"Life goes on," Jack said.

"It's a hell of a lot better than the alternative," Peter concluded.

CHAPTER

Thirty-Seven

Spring

Spring was nothing more than a rumor in New Hampshire. Winter refused to end. Every day was cold, damp, and gray. The weather warmed, but there were still weekly snow squalls, the sodden snow accumulating, sometimes almost a foot of it, deep enough to be a nuisance. This time of year, the snow always melted in a few days, leaving mud.

The chilled woods were filled with a frothy, pointillist haze of buds, pastel yellow, green, white, and pink nubs and flowers. The ground became soggy. Snowbanks next to plowed roads were granular and icy, dotted with the dirt of winter. Water trickled in gutters day and night. Potholes cratered the streets, giving Bennett Falls the look of a shelled town in the aftermath of a war. The highway department spent most days stuffing raw, cold asphalt into the holes.

The river running under the covered bridge thundered with snowmelt from the mountains. Standing on the porch of the Metcalfe House, Keira could hear the deep-throated, booming roar. People came and stood along the river edge to watch the awesome force of the pounding white water, spray flying, an endless, rushing torrent hammering the rocks that lined the bank, slamming the concrete foundation of the covered bridge.

Away from the river, the mood was more cheerful and placid. Bennett Falls' early spring rituals became the talk of The Sunrise every morning.

The men's hockey games continued for a few more weeks. Jack found his way to the rink every Sunday evening, though he still didn't know the names of a lot of the players. Peter came by, sitting in the stands with Michelle and Keira. Jimmy suspended play in late March, saying something about it being time for other games.

Cub Scouts took their handmade, wooden pinewood derby cars to the post office where the postmaster weighed them on the postage scale and handed each boy a signed certificate declaring the weight of his little car. The postmaster knew the rules, and if a car was over the weight limit, he denied the boy his certificate and sent him home with a stern look and a warning to shave a half an ounce off, come back and re-weigh the car before the derby. The derby was scheduled for a Friday night in early April in the cafetorium. Families and friends filled the bleachers to cheer.

The cafetorium was also used for Little League tryouts on a Saturday morning in mid-March. The ball fields were still covered with a shallow bed of snow, but the players needed to be ready, and hockey season was finished. Six evenly balanced teams of boys were drafted by the coaches at a tense Monday evening session at the VFW that lasted late into the night. Practices started on muddy fields in early April. The games, held twice a week, would begin the first week of May and play until the town championship in June.

Wagers were settled at the VFW. The first bet was for the last ice fishing shack standing on Clear Lake. Peter Lacroix won, since he was unable to get up to the lake and drag his house off the ice as he usually did, toting it home on his pickup truck, leaving it standing in his back yard, ready for the next year. At first, Peter complained profanely about losing the shack, about how he'd polluted the lake, and how he now faced the hassle of building a new shack for the next winter.

"My so-called friends, the bastards! They left the house out in the middle of the lake! They knew I couldn't get it after my heart attack, but they said it was the only way to settle the betting fair and square. They said it wasn't worth anything anyway. Now I'll have to go buy another one of those big blue tarps and beg Jimmy for scraps from the Metcalfe House work. I have to build a whole new shack."

The second bet, for the day the ice vanished from Clear Lake, was settled a week after Peter's shack fell in. Both bets were celebrated with beer at the VFW and discussed over coffee at The Sunrise. Peter skipped the beer but joined the camaraderie at both locations.

Keira and Jack returned to their autumn routine. Jack left every Tuesday at dawn, driving two hours to Boston. He stayed with his parents in Quincy on Tuesday and Wednesday nights and returned to Bennett Falls Thursday evening for a late dinner with Keira. Keira let workmen come and go at the house all week. She revised and updated the Metcalfe House website, taking new photographs of the restored guest rooms as soon as they were finished. She hesitated to list an opening date or begin taking reservations, uncertain when the house would be ready for guests.

She went to The New Hampshire Crafts store several days each week, leaving home with Smoky mid-morning, once the workmen were settled in, returning late each afternoon. She and Michelle puttered around the store, stocking shelves with pottery and laying out quilts. Sometimes Lana joined them.

Keira was reluctant to leave the kitten in the Metcalfe House with the workmen coming and going all day. Smoky commandeered the wide windowsill in the back of the store above the roaring river, sleeping in the sun. She had a dish for food and a litter box hidden in an office of the store. Technically, the store was open for business, but no customers had arrived for the summer season yet.

One morning, as Keira sat alone on the Metcalfe House porch with her tea, enjoying the unusual new warmth of the spring sun, Jimmy came by.

He climbed the steps to the porch and asked, "May I join you?"

"Of course. Can I fix you a cup of coffee?"

"No, thanks. I just left The Sunrise." He sat in the padded wicker chair next to Keira. "I've had my fill of coffee for the morning. Have you checked upstairs to see how things are coming along?"

"Yes. It looks like we're getting close. What do you think?"

"I think so. We're just about there. We have some work to do in the room where the fire broke through. I had to rebuild that entire wall, and I need to paint the new trim, the baseboard, and that chair rail. It looks like the mason is making good progress with the new chimney."

From around the corner, they could hear the clink and the scraping of the mason laying bricks, spreading mortar, working now on a scaffold halfway up the second floor of the house.

"When do you expect we'll be done?"

"Two to four weeks. There are a few small details to take care of. The wallpaper, for one. The original wallpaper for both of the third-floor bedrooms isn't available anymore. People paint walls more than they use wallpaper these days."

"What can we do?" Keira asked. "Just paint the walls? I'd hoped for something more."

Jimmy sat back and smiled. "I have an idea. What if I paint the new walls a neutral color, maybe light beige or a gray or a lilac color? I know a woman from Gilford a few miles north of here. She does stenciling. Michelle probably knows her too, because the woman's got some little painted things in Michelle's craft shop. I could have her come in and stencil a border along the wall, next to the ceiling in those rooms. It would give those rooms a nice colonial-era feel. I could keep her work within the budget too. What do you think? Should I contact her?"

"Yes. That's a great idea. Yes, let's do it."

One of the workmen came out the front door onto the porch. He walked over to where Jimmy sat with Keira, and stood, hands on his hips, spattered with white smudges of plaster. Averting his eyes from Jimmy, he looked out into the budding forest beyond the bright, wet, early spring lawn.

"I saw you drive up, Jimmy. I want to check with you. I'm just about finished with the sheetrock on the third floor. I think it looks pretty good. Do you want to take a look?"

"Sure, Rodney. Give me a minute to finish up with Mrs. Sullivan and I'll come right up."

"Okay, boss." Rodney turned away and hurried back in the front door. They listened to him clumping up the stairs.

"Rodney's a pain in the neck," Jimmy confided quietly to Keira. "But he's the best man in town when it comes to walls, plastering and such. I think you'll like his work."

"I'll go up this evening and see how it looks."

"Jack's home on Friday?"

"Yes. He's very good about getting home in time for dinner every Thursday night."

"Great. Could you two meet me at The Sunrise for breakfast Friday morning?"

"I expect so. That would be nice."

"Great! Breakfast is on me. We can talk about the last few things we need to do to so you can open. Nine o'clock?"

"We'll be there."

"Perfect. Now, let me go see about that sheetrock upstairs." Jimmy stood and went in the house.

Keira sat back, happy, enjoying the morning. Her tea was cooling, but the world seemed to be settling down after the hard times of the winter and the fire. *We're almost there. Knock on wood. No more catastrophes.*

She leaned toward the wooden coffee table and rapped it with her knuckles.

CHAPTER

Thirty-Eight

Jack and Keira entered The Sunrise, welcomed by the bell ringing above the door. They crossed the room through the crowd to Jimmy's table. Seeing them enter, Debbie quietly removed the fundraising jar and set it out of sight beneath the counter. She would choose the best moment to share it with Jack and Keira, her new but infrequent guests.

"Good morning!" Jimmy stood and shook both of their hands. "How are you, Jack? I spoke with Keira yesterday about our progress on the house. Have you been able to look things over?"

"Yes, I checked things out this morning before we came down here. It looks like we're almost done."

Jimmy nodded. "I believe so."

Debbie came to their table, bringing two mugs and a steel teapot on a tray: coffee for Jack, tea for Keira, the string from a tea bag hanging from the teapot. "What can I get you two?"

They ordered bagels.

Jimmy continued, "I think we can finish inside the house by the end of next week. The mason says he can also be done with the chimney probably next week, or early the following week. I'll have that inspected and we'll be done. Do you like the way it's turning out?"

Jack answered, "Yes, it all looks good. Keira and I will still need to replace a few pieces of furniture and a couple of rugs, but we can afford that, given the insurance."

"What furniture do you need?" Jimmy asked.

Across the room, Debbie eavesdropped.

Keira spoke up. "Beds for both of the third-floor bedrooms, and a side table and a dresser for the room where the fire broke through. A couple of more pieces got water damaged down near the woodstove. We'll find replacements, maybe this weekend. I wish we had an old photograph or something showing the house from when it was first built. We'd like to find one, frame it and display it downstairs, in the hall or the parlor."

"Once the mason is finished, I expect I'll be done with my part of the restoration," Jimmy said. "That woman I told you about will still need to do the stenciling for you, Keira, but if you get that furniture, by the end of next week you might be good to open the bed and breakfast."

Keira turned to Jack. "We're so close! Once again, we're so close! Even if we need a few more weeks to buy the new furniture, we might be able to open before Memorial Day."

Debbie returned with bagels on two small plates and a white porcelain dish filled with cream cheese. As she served them, she said, "Those last few items you said you'd need for the house? The town would like to help."

She returned to the counter, retrieved the jar, and came back. "People have been contributing, chipping in to support your rebuilding. There's not a lot here, but we'd all like to help out."

Silence descended throughout The Sunrise. People watched Debbie and listened to the conversation at Jimmy's table.

Jack and Keira looked at the jar, stunned, reading the label: "Metcalfe House Fund" with the old, fuzzy photograph of their home Billy had found on the internet. The jar was almost full of rolled, folded, and crumpled bills. Change slid around the bottom.

"We're fine," Jack said. "We don't need the town's charity."

"This isn't charity," Debbie said. "This is the town coming together to lend a hand."

Jack shook his head and started to speak again, but Keira stopped him, her hand on his arm, leaning toward Debbie and speaking before Jack could. "That's a lovely gesture. Thank you. And thank you all," she added, speaking louder for everyone in the café to hear.

Debbie, speaking for all her customers, replied, "You're welcome. We're happy to help. I'll total up all the money and write you a check. Is that okay?"

"Yes. That's wonderful!" Keira smiled, thrilled with what the town had done for her and Jack.

Jack quietly added, "Yes. Thank you."

Debbie took the jar and returned to the kitchen.

Andrew stood from his seat across the table from Warren, weaved through the tables to Jimmy's spot, and greeted Jack and Keira. "Good morning. I don't know if you remember me, but I'm Andrew Holmes. I live right down the hill from you, across from the covered bridge."

"Of course we remember you," Keira said. "We've met a few times around town."

Jack, half-standing, reached to shake Andrew's hand. "I recall you speaking on our behalf at the town meeting. And I think I remember you telling a funny story one other time here at the Sunrise."

Andrew smiled. "I heard you asking about old pictures of the Metcalfe House, and I might be able to help. I'm the president of the Bennett Falls Historical Society. I'm about the only active member of the society, so that makes me the president. Anyhow, we have a small space on the third floor of the old school, the town office building. It's a sort of an archive of the town's history. We don't officially open until the first of May, and then we're open only on Tuesday and Saturday afternoons by appointment. But I'm the president, so I can open any time. I know we have a few old pictures of the Metcalfe House in our files, photographs and such. I could contribute one of those to the house if you'd like. You'd have to see about getting it framed, but I'd be happy to have you take a look through the files and pick out a good picture."

Keira was excited, her eyes glowing, beaming at Andrew. "Really? That would be fantastic!"

Beside her, Jack sat stone-faced, staring at the remains of his bagel.

Andrew ignored Jack and continued talking with Keira. "Could I meet you next Tuesday afternoon? How about right after lunch? Meet me here at The Sunrise and we'll walk over. Maybe one o'clock?"

"That would be perfect."

Debbie called from behind the counter. "Maybe you could use the money from the jar to pay for framing the picture."

Andrew had more to say. "I understand you've become acquainted with my old friend, Warren Briggs. He mentioned that you stopped by his house a few weeks ago with some pastries."

Warren, hearing his name, swiveled on his chair to watch Andrew.

"Yes," Keira said. "We wanted to thank Lana for what she did for me the night of the fire, so we took some scones to Warren and Lana's house."

Andrew nodded. "Were you aware that Warren's widely known to be one of the best farmers in the state of New Hampshire?"

"Really?" Keira laughed, sensing Andrew leading into one of his famous stories.

Warren leaned over his table, his forehead in his hands. "Here we go. God, Andrew. Don't say it."

Andrew turned from his friend and went on, addressing Jack and Keira. "Why, yes. It's easy to see. It's no secret. He's one of the very best farmers in the state."

Warren shook his head, still hiding his face in his hands. "Here it comes," he said.

"Why, yes," Andrew said. "People drive by Briggs Farm, and they see him there, out in the middle of his field, and they say, 'There's Warren

Briggs. He's outstanding in his field.'"

Jack and Keira and the crowd in The Sunrise laughed and cheered. Andrew basked.

Warren looked up and growled, "You know what they say, Keira? Every village has an idiot? Andrew is ours."

Andrew stood up straight and beamed. "Yes, I am," he replied proudly, patting his chest. "I'm the village idiot. But you know what else they say, Keira?"

"What? What else do they say?" she asked, enjoying how she had become engaged in the town's banter.

"It takes a village to raise an idiot. And everybody here has raised me. Blame them, not me."

"Bah!" said Warren. He pushed back from the table, stood, and walked to the door. "I'm done. I'm out." As he banged through the door, he called back over his shoulder, "Welcome to Bennett Falls, Mr. and Mrs. Sullivan. You've become official citizens when Andrew Holmes shares one of his jokes with you."

Debbie came over. "He left without paying his check," she said to Andrew.

"Again?" Andrew said. "I'll take it. Again."

"You shouldn't have to cover for him, Andrew," Debbie stated.

"Oh, I don't mind. He'll buy me breakfast someday. He'll find some way to pay me back. There's always payback."

On a breezy Monday morning, Keira sat in the sunshine at the back window of the New Hampshire Artisan Crafts store with Michelle and Lana. Smoky lay curled on the warm sill next to Keira, sleeping.

"What do you still need to do to get the house ready for guests?" Lana asked.

"Not much. Jack's up there with the workmen this morning. They're putting on the finishing touches. We found some new furniture this weekend and everything should be in place by the end of April. The mason will have the chimney finished, and I'll get it inspected by next week."

Michelle clapped quickly, a small celebration. "So, you're all set? Finally settled here in New Hampshire?"

"Maybe. I don't know. I'm meeting with Andrew Holmes tomorrow afternoon. He says they might have an old photograph of our house in the Historical Society, and he's going to help me pick one. I'll have it framed. But that's about all I'll need."

Michelle looked around, surveying her shop. "We have a few old pictures here in old frames. Antiques maybe. Or junk. They're inexpensive. When Andrew and you pick out a picture, let's see if one of the old frames here might work."

Keira nodded. "That would be perfect. An old frame would suit the old picture nicely once I pick one out. And they set up a collection down at The Sunrise to help us. I could use that money to pay you for the frame."

"Nonsense! That won't be necessary. You work here. Pick a good frame and it's yours. What else do you need?"

"Not much." Keira thought for a moment. "I do have a few questions. Things you might be able to help me with. Not to do with the house; more about general life in New Hampshire."

Michelle and Lana waited. At last, Keira opened up. "I've found my way around Bennett Falls. And I know how to drive from here to Boston. But I just can't find some things I need. People tell me everything must be here, but I just don't know where to start looking. I've been so busy with the house, I don't really know where to start."

"What do you need?" Lana asked. "The old saying is that if we haven't got it here, you don't need it, but I expect we are lacking a few things."

"Go ahead and ask us anything," Michelle added. "Give us a shot. Let's see if we can help."

"How about a hairdresser? I don't see any place here in Bennett Falls. And Chinese food. Where do I find a good Chinese restaurant? I've checked the internet, of course. But I don't see much here in Bennett Falls and I don't know where else to look."

Michelle laughed. "About the hair. I only get mine trimmed a couple of times a year." She fluffed her long, white waves. "When I do, I go to Lana's hairdresser over near Concord."

Lana added. "Yes, there is my hairdresser. If you turn left out your driveway and follow Concord Road maybe six or seven miles, you come to a little strip mall at a crossroads. It's maybe a ten-minute drive. Have you been up that way, going to Concord?"

"No. I didn't really see a need to go to Concord. I've been down to Manchester a couple of times, but really, I've spent most of my time right here or in Boston. I need to get out more and explore." As she talked, Keira recognized her insecurity, her need always to know where she was, where she was going, and what to expect. The uncertainty of exploring, particularly without Jack beside her, had frightened her into minimal exploration of the roads near her house.

"Maybe we can go with you sometime," Michelle suggested, seeing Keira's anxiety.

"Road trip!" Lana shouted. "Later this week maybe. We'll show you the way. While Jack's in Boston, the three of us could find a bit of trouble together!"

Laughing, Michelle added, "You know what? I think there's a Chinese place in that same shopping center. I don't usually go for Chinese food, but maybe we could try it for lunch."

"Sure," Keira said. "If you show me how to get there, I'll buy lunch for all of us."

"I think there's an Italian restaurant there too," Lana said. "Not just pizza, but lasagna and that spaghetti with a meatball. A full menu of Italian. You might like that, too."

"I'm meeting Andrew Holmes tomorrow. Maybe we could go on Wednesday?"

"Perfect!" Michelle cheered. "We'll meet here in the morning and run over there for lunch."

"Road trip!" Lana repeated.

Keira accompanied Andrew on the short walk from The Sunrise to the town offices. The early spring sunshine and the budding trees filled her with optimism. Birds sang. A small group of children played on the grass between the walkways on the town common while their mothers sat on a bench. It's almost too perfect, Keira thought. Like a postcard of the ideal small town in New England.

Andrew held the heavy door to the town office building and ushered her inside to the echoing, wood-floored hallway. Diffused sunlight reflected white off the varnished floorboards. What had once been classrooms were now offices, open doors facing each other down a long corridor. Nameplates reached into the hallway above the doorways, announcing the offices inside. Taxation. Planning Board. School Department. Public Works. This is where Jack came to get our business license for the B&B nearly two months ago, Keira thought.

Andrew escorted Keira up a wide stairway to the second floor, where there were more open doors for the less commonly sought-after town offices. They circled around a second-floor landing and ascended a narrower staircase to the shadowy third floor. All the doors on the third floor were locked, blank darkness behind their frosted glass panels. Andrew went to one with gilt letters on the glass: "Bennett Falls Historical Society." He took a long, old-fashioned key on a ring from his pocket and unlocked the door.

Keira followed him into a cluttered room. File cabinets and bookcases lined the walls on both sides. A wide conference table, set with eight ancient, leather-upholstered chairs, dominated the middle of the cramped room. A single dormer window gave Keira a tree-top view of the town common. The statue of the soldier was straight ahead. The flag flapped off to Keira's right in the middle of the lawns. The room smelled musty; dry air filled with old dust.

Andrew left the door open and turned on the lights. "Have a seat. Let me see what we can find on the old Metcalfe House."

Keira sat, pleased by Andrew's courtesy and touched by his offer to give her an old photograph of her house.

He stood before a dark wooden file cabinet, tracing down the tiny, hand-lettered notes tucked in steel slots on the front of the drawers. "Let's see now. Metcalfe. Metcalfe. Metcalfe Mills—that might have something." He pulled out a drawer. "Ah! Here it is. The Metcalfe House."

Andrew took out three thick, dark green cardboard hanging file folders, their edges bent and worn. He brought them to the table and sat next to Keira.

"Here we go," he said, thumbing through pages of old newspaper clippings and other papers in the top folder. "This folder has the history of the house. Here's a copy of the original deed to the property. It seems that it was first built on the site where you live in 1842, but it burned down in '46. Possibly a kitchen fire? That wasn't uncommon back then. The family rebuilt immediately and the house, as you know it, was finished in 1847."

He turned over a thin paper, yellow and creased. "It looks like they added the big front porch in1878. The little back area that I hear you've refurbished and turned into your apartment? That was the original kitchen on the new 1847 house."

"Jimmy Sanborn tore that off and built a bigger addition on the back for us," Keira said.

Andrew shook his head for a moment. "It always disturbs me when something old and original is taken down to put up something new. But I understand. You and your husband need an adequate place to live."

Andrew continued, turning through the contents of the folder. He stopped and lifted out a sheet of paper. "Ah. Here's a bit of history for you. Hiram Metcalfe, the first owner of the house, and his wife, raised his six children there. Hiram became wealthy with the mill, turning out fine textiles before the Civil War. Gingham. Wool and cotton. He made cloth for uniforms during the war, possibly supplying both sides, though that might have been frowned upon."

He handed the paper and the rest of the folder to Keira. She became engrossed in the papers, turning through them while Andrew watched. "This is fascinating! It's wonderful!" she said. "Jack and I are living there now, but it's so interesting to learn who lived in the house before us and see a little of what their lives were like."

Andrew pointed to another folder. "This one has more information about the Metcalfe family." He traced his finger down a list of names and dates, following the family history. "It would seem that Hiram's second oldest son, William, took over the management of the mill when his father became too old to continue. I don't know what happened with Hiram's oldest son, Joshua, why he didn't run the mill. We know he fought in the Civil War, and we know he survived and came home. That's about all we have on him. But William ran the mill a long time, until after the turn of the century. He raised his family in your house, and his son, William Junior, took over the business when his father stepped down. Junior never married and had no children, but he lived with his sister Sarah and her family at Metcalfe House for decades. Sarah's son, James, took over the running of the mill when William Junior retired. James seems to have lived elsewhere. Sarah lived in the Metcalfe House with the rest of the family until her death in the 1960s. Many of her children moved away, but a couple of the children continued living there until nearly 2000, long after the mill had closed. I remember them, though they all went to private schools, so I didn't really know any of them. Phillips Exeter Academy, I believe. Then, an old family from New York rented it from the Metcalfe children and used it as a vacation home for a year or two, but the place sat empty for years. It's very good that you've been able to restore it."

Keira smiled as she poured through the papers. "This is wonderful. May I borrow these folders? I'd like to make a short summary document tracing the history of the house to show our guests."

"Of course. Take care of them and bring them back when you've made copies of what you need. I like spreading this information around. People tend to lose track of their history if we don't pay attention. That's why we have the files here. Once every year or so we get an inquiry, a grad student writing a thesis on New Hampshire history or someone studying the industrial revolution and the New England mill towns. They come in and go through things and then they leave. I like to think I'm helping preserve the story of our town."

Keira laughed. "From what I hear, you're quite the town storyteller!"

Andrew gave a dismissive wave of his hand. "I tell a few stories but they're not necessarily about Bennett Falls. They're just old New England stories. They're traditional. Some people say they got started over in Maine, maybe at a famous little dive, Moody's Diner, a bit north of Boothbay Harbor on Route One. I had an uncle who lived over that way, my dad's brother. I learned the stories from my uncle and my dad when I was a boy. Folks seem to like it when I tell those stories down at The Sunrise. Everyone except my good friend Warren. But part of the fun is hearing him complain whenever I go off on one of my tales." Andrew smiled.

"But you seem to have a good sense of the history of Bennett Falls too," she said.

Andrew nodded. He straightened in his chair, clasping his hands on the old folder in front of him. "That I do. Maybe I'm a modern-day storyteller for Bennett Falls, keeping an oral history alive. I like to think that every little town has its own collection of stories, history, and traditions. There's enough drama in a typical small town to provide plots for a dozen classic Greek tragedies. Or comedies, for that matter."

He paused, assessing Keira's attentiveness to what he had to say. She nodded, her chin on her knuckles. "Go on," she said.

"I know all about Bennett Falls. I know how we got to be the way we are. I know how we came to be so in love with ice hockey and all the things that have gone on up at Clear Lake over the years. Did you know that back in the old days, for most of the nineteenth century, we had a thriving ice business up there, harvesting ice from the lake all winter, packing it in straw, and taking it to Boston and Worcester and even as far away as Springfield? Modern refrigeration put an end to that business, of course. But it's good to know the stories. You and your husband are adding to that story now by restoring the old Metcalfe House. Everyone here has a part in the story. Your good friend Michelle and her husband Peter trace back to the French-Canadian mill workers. They're part of that tradition."

Keira sat silently. "I'm pleased to become a part of the town's history, if that's what we're doing by opening the B&B in the Metcalfe House."

"And I'm pleased you're doing it as well." Andrew shifted their attention to the third folder. "Here we go. Here are a whole lot of old photographs of the house."

Together they turned through old black-and-white photographs. Most were exterior views of the house from the front. Some showed the house from other angles. A few displayed the Victorian furnishings of the original interior.

"This is incredible," Keira said. "To see the way the house was when the Metcalfe family lived there. May I take one or two of these old pictures?"

"Please do. Pick out any you like. If there are two or more of the same picture, you can keep one. Make additional copies for yourself of any single photos. Get a photographer to make good, crisp, quality copies of them for you to frame and hang in the house along with the history of the house. When you're done, return any you don't need to me."

Keira selected two. One was an exterior view, showing the front porch, with leafy maple trees on either side of the house. The other picture showed the original parlor, with heavy floor-length drapes at the windows tied back by thick braided cords. Rolled-arm sofas and side tables covered with lace doilies and whale-oil lamps filled the room. She tucked the old photographs in the folder with the history of the house.

Andrew stood and returned the two remaining folders to the drawer in the wooden file cabinet. "Is there anything else I can help you with, my dear?"

"No. You've been very helpful, very kind. I really appreciate you taking the time to show me all this."

"Not at all. Let me know when you're ready to bring the folder and the photographs back. You know where to find me."

Keira stood and followed Andrew out into the hall. She waited while he turned off the lights and locked the door. Then she followed him down the stairs, along the dark hall between the offices, and out into the bright springtime sunshine on the common.

"Can I give you a lift back to your house?" she asked. "I'm parked across the street, by the common."

"I appreciate the offer. But no. I believe I'll walk up to the VFW and see who's about and hear what's going on. Then I'll walk home. I like the exercise."

Andrew gave a smile and a little wave. Then he turned away, walking quickly up Main Street.

CHAPTER

Forty-One

Michelle drove, with Lana riding shotgun. Keira sat in the back seat, watching the road ahead between the two women, trying to memorize the route. They went from the Crafts shop, through the covered bridge, up the hill past the Metcalfe House, passed the turn for Clear Lake, and continued through budding forests, over low hills. Nearing the outskirts of Concord, Michelle slowed, signaled, and turned into a long strip mall of low storefronts. A tall sign at the entrance announced: Granite State Shopping Plaza.

Michelle parked across from Curls and Clips, and they went inside. In the back of the salon, a row of chairs in front of mirrors lined the shop. Customers sat in every chair, with young women tending to their hair. Next to the door was a high counter with a computer and a cash register. A young woman, her hair teased and dyed white, wearing excessive eye makeup and crimson lipstick, sat on a high stool behind the counter. Edgy rock music played. The store held the aroma of perfume and bleach.

"May I help you?" the girl asked.

"I'd like to make an appointment to get my hair trimmed," Keira said.

"You can do that online, if you'd like," the girl said. She made no attempt to make the appointment for her customer.

"Of course. But I'm new to New Hampshire. I thought maybe you could set my first appointment for me."

The girl sighed and tapped her keyboard. "When do you want to come in?"

"How about next week? Maybe on Tuesday?"

The girl stared at the computer screen, moving the mouse. "Here we are," she finally said. "Next week. We open at ten. Tammy has an opening Tuesday morning at ten. Would you like her to take care of you? Tammy works with a lot of our older customers."

Keira suppressed a smile.

Lana laughed. "Tammy does my hair."

Michelle nodded. "Me too."

"That's fine," Keira said. "Next Tuesday at ten with Tammy."

"I'll need your name," the girl said.

"Of course. It's Keira Sullivan."

"Could you spell that?"

"K. E. I. R. A."

"And the last name again?"

"Sullivan."

The girl stood staring at Keira, waiting. Keira didn't have to ask; she understood that she needed to spell out her last name as well.

"S. U. L. L. I. V. A. N."

The girl pecked at the keyboard. "Keira Sullivan at ten next Tuesday with Tammy. And I'll need a phone number to reach you, Mrs. Sullivan."

Keira gave her the number.

"Area code 617? That's Boston, right? You're coming all the way up from Boston for a haircut?"

"No, I used to live in Boston. That's still my cell number, but I'm in Bennett Falls now."

"Oh."

"Could I have a card with my appointment on it?"

"Sure." The girl wrote on a Clips and Curls business card with a purple gel pen and handed it to Keira. "We can get the rest of your information when you come in next week. Your home address and email address and so on. You do have email, right?"

"Yes, I do." Keira smiled, taking the card. "Thank you very much."

"Not a problem," said the girl, sitting back on her tall stool, staring beyond Keira at nothing.

Keira, Michelle, and Lana made it to the sidewalk outside the salon and lost it, breaking into laughter.

"God!" Keira shouted. "I hope they do a better job on my hair than the girl did making my appointment."

"Shh," Lana cautioned. "She might hear us."

"Not a chance," Michelle said. "She barely heard us when we were right in front of her. But don't worry, Keira. Tammy does good work. She'll take care of you, just like she does with all us old ladies."

"Welcome to the old lady club," Lana added.

They walked past storefronts: a pharmacy, a bookstore, a store selling discount toys, and came to the Lotus Garden Chinese Restaurant. Across the parking lot, they saw another business with a green and red sign, Venice Café.

"Is that the Italian restaurant you mentioned?" Keira asked. "Would you two prefer Italian for lunch instead of Chinese?"

"That would be nice," Michelle said.

Lana agreed. "I don't know much about Chinese food. Let's go to Venice."

They cut across the parking lot and went in the restaurant, settling into a booth beneath a wide mural of Venetian canals, gondolas, archways, and a piazza. Contrary to the northern Italian décor, the menu was limited to southern Italian, traditional red sauce meals. When they finished lunch, Keira was happy to admit that it was good; not at the level of the restaurants in the North End in Boston, but still very good.

They were back in Bennett Falls late that afternoon.

CHAPTER

Forty-Two

Late April

Friday morning, so Jack was home. He sat with Keira on the porch, Jack with his coffee, Keira her tea, watching the birds chase each other through the trees. It was still cool. Fog melted into mist as the sun tried to burn through the overcast. It hinted at a warm day ahead.

Jack turned to Keira. "Have you done something with your hair?" he asked.

"I got it trimmed earlier this week."

"Where? You didn't go back to Boston."

"No, I found a place over near Concord. Michelle and Lana showed me the way. I just took a bit off the ends. I hadn't had anything done to it since before Christmas. Do you like it?"

It was a tricky question. Jack gave a long, assessing look. "Do you?"

"Yes."

"Me, too."

"I wanted to look nice when we open for business. I think we might be ready."

"Let's go take a look at things." Jack stood, setting his empty cup on the coffee table. Keira joined him, leaving her half-full cup on the table. They went down the steps from the porch and began evaluating the look of their home from the driveway.

The daffodils had been a surprise, emerging throughout the wet yard, pushing from the mud and melting snow earlier in the spring. Having first seen the house in summer and closed on it in early September, Jack and Keira knew about the gardens that edged the lawn and driveway, but they had no idea that the perimeter of the house was lined with daffodils. Now a thick riot of yellow flowers surrounded the porch and filled the gardens along both sides of the house. Volunteer daffodils dotted the lawn.

As they walked on the damp grass surveying their house, Keira stopped, squatted to get a low-angle perspective and took a photo with her phone, the yellow blossoms filling the foreground, leaving the house and the porch in the background, set against a pale blue sky. "I'll add that picture to the gallery of house photos on the website," she explained.

They walked back to the house and checked the crisp lines of the new chimney. The mason had taken down his scaffold and ladders two days earlier and departed. The new chimney was almost too clean, too straight, in contrast with the antique Victorian look of the rest of the house. The ivy that grew on the weathered bricks of the old chimney was gone. But it was safe. The woodstove had been reconnected to the fireplace in the parlor. It had passed inspection. Ivy could grow back, climbing the chimney.

Jack ran his hand along the smooth masonry, noting the precise lines of mortar between the bricks. He smiled. Hidden among the daffodils, Keira saw small, ragged rocks, like pebbles from the moon, white mortar debris that had fallen into the garden. That's all right, she thought. As long as I won't have another chimney fire. She reached down, picked up one of the white pebbles and put it in her pocket.

Keira said, "The woman doing the stenciling will be done today, or no later than tomorrow. Once she's finished, there's nothing left to do."

"We're ready again!" Jack said. "When can we start having guests?"

Keira took a moment, calculating what she needed to do, drawing on her marketing experience. "I'll open the website today and start promoting the house. We can start having guests maybe by early May, certainly no later than Memorial Day. We still need to buy a few final pieces of furniture."

Jack hugged her. "We should have that open house for the town. Jimmy mentioned an open house at the town meeting, and he asked me again if we planned to do it when I spoke with him last week. We could invite all the guys who worked on the house. Maybe let people know down at The Sunrise. What do you think?"

Before Keira could answer, they were interrupted by two pickup trucks turning into the driveway. Michelle, Lana, and Peter were in the first one. Debbie, Billy, and another man, a regular from The Sunrise, rode in the second one.

"We can make an informal announcement about the open house right now," Keira said. "It looks like we have some of the people we'd want to invite right here."

Debbie led the way as they got out of the two trucks. "You remember that jar we set up down at The Sunrise? Collecting donations to help you get back on your feet?"

"Yes," Keira said.

Jack stood quietly, uncomfortable with what he still believed to be needless charity from strangers.

"Here's what we've done with that money," Debbie continued. "We were going to use it to help you find and frame a photograph of the house. But we know that Andrew helped you find a couple of pictures at the Historical Society. And, of course, we know that Michelle gave you two old frames from her shop. So, you're all set with that."

Keira nodded. "Yes, the photographs are already hanging in the parlor."

"But Michelle mentioned that you had a small sideboard in the parlor that got ruined by the water during the fire. We found it out at the landfill where you'd taken it. It wasn't that badly damaged. Water stains and the veneer had pulled away from the body."

"That's right," Jack said. "It was wrecked by the firefighters' water and the fire. I took it and a few of the other ruined things up to the landfill."

Debbie ignored Jack's comment, speaking directly to Keira. "This is Hugh," she said, indicating the man they hadn't met. "He worked a little on your house, restoring some of the finish work, the molding, the baseboards, and the stair banister. He has a side business doing furniture restoration. We rescued the sideboard from the landfill and used the money raised at The Sunrise to buy new veneer and finish and anything he needed to fix up the old sideboard you thought was ruined."

Billy and the other man pulled back a tarp in the back of Debbie's truck and lifted a small, shiny sideboard off the tailgate. They carried it over to Keira and Jack, setting it on the gravel driveway.

Keira ran her hands over the smooth finish, appreciating the sensation of the Victorian lines, the curved, carved wood. She pulled the new, gleaming brass handles to open the doors on the front and checked inside. It looked better than when they had bought it at an antique store in the Berkshires months ago.

"It's beautiful. Thank you. You've all been so good to us."

Hugh smiled and nodded, his quiet way of acknowledging their thanks.

Jack smiled and tried to show his appreciation, though he still felt frustrated by the unnecessary grace the town was giving him. "We'd like to thank the town for everything," he said. "We were just talking about hosting an open house here to show off how the place has turned out. Maybe a Saturday in early May? This weekend is Easter, so probably too much going on for a social event."

"Great idea!" Michelle said. "Take the first Saturday in May. Schedule it for four o'clock, though. There are Little League games at one."

"We still have a few dollars left from the fund," Debbie said. "Let me cater the open house. I'll put together some snacks and things to serve."

"I'll buy wine," Keira said.

"And beer," Peter interjected. "Not that I'll be having any. But a lot of the boys who worked on your house are more beer drinkers than wine people."

"The guys from the hockey rink?" Jack asked.

"That's them. I'll just have a Diet Coke. Or iced tea. I've found that I like tea." Peter shook his head. Michelle put her arm around him.

"The first Saturday in May." Michelle confirmed the date. "And the first Sunday in May is when I traditionally hold an opening event at my store. So that would be the next day. Back-to-back open houses for the start of business here at the Metcalfe House and for the start of the season at the Craft shop. Keira, you and Jack will come to my opening too?"

"Of course we will," Keira answered, speaking for Jack as well as herself. "I'm an employee of the shop. I'll handle all the customers."

CHAPTER

Forty-Three

May

The day of the first open house had arrived. Debbie set out an array of small sandwiches, pastries, and cookies on the Metcalfe House's long dining room table. Wine bottles were lined along the refinished sideboard with stacks of clear plastic cups nearby. A large cooler with bottles of beer and red plastic cups waited for guests on the front porch. A smaller cooler with soft drinks for the children sat next to the beer. The small cooler also had several bottles of iced tea for Peter.

The guests started to arrive before four o'clock, the official starting time for the open house. Some of the children, both boys and girls, were sweaty and dirty, still in Little League baseball uniforms. Men led their families in the front door, greeted Keira and Jack and began showing their wives and children the work they had done, leading them through the house and up the stairs.

Keira recognized all the men and knew many of them by name. Jack saw some of his hockey buddies but knew far fewer of the men than Keira. He pulled Keira aside and whispered, "You seem to know all the men by name. How is that? What's been going on while I've been off working in Boston?"

"Jack!" Keira slapped him on his shoulder, only half in jest. "How can you say that? I've been here all the time while they've been working on our house. That's how I know them. Besides, you've been playing hockey with most of them. Having a beer with them after the hockey down at the VFW. You know them as well as I do."

"I don't know their names like you do. Out of the rink, out of their pads and helmets, I don't know them at all."

Keira shrugged and turned away.

After their quick tours of the upstairs rooms and the open areas of the downstairs, jovial crowds gathered in the dining room, sampling the familiar food from The Sunrise. The living room and the parlor were packed. By 4:30, the house was noisy and jammed. The adults clustered, talking about their contributions to the refurbishment of the Metcalfe House, admiring the results of their work.

Children huddled in smaller circles outside, done with the grownup celebration, eager to go home. Small children played on the end of the porch. Younger adolescents gathered on the lawn in two groups: boys talking about baseball and girls talking about the boys. A crowd of older adolescents congealed across the grass near the trees, boys and girls together.

Michelle with a clear cup of rosé and Peter with his new addiction, the bottled iced tea, spent the afternoon beside Jack and Keira in the parlor. Lana came in briefly to chat with Keira and Jack, but mostly she stayed on the front porch, sitting in a rocker next to Warren, watching all the children. Warren never went inside.

Andrew Holmes strolled in, coming to Jack and shaking his hand. "Well done, neighbor! The place looks beautiful. And you'll be taking guests soon?"

Jack beamed. "Yes, we have our first bookings for next weekend. Finally! Our investment will start paying off."

Keira added, "It's been a long journey and a lot of hard work. But we're ready to go at last."

"This is all very exciting," Andrew replied. "I see you got the pictures from the Historical Society framed. I'm glad I was able to help. It's an exciting time here on the quiet side of the bridge, our quiet corner of the village."

Jimmy Sanborn joined the group, his arm around his wife's shoulders. "This is my wife, Lynn. Thanks for holding the open house so I'm able to show her how everything turned out."

Lynn, a gracious, dark-blonde, pretty woman, shook Jack's hand and gave a cursory hug to Keira. "All I've heard about for months is how your house is coming along. Every night at dinner, Jimmy goes on about it. It's turned out beautifully."

Keira laughed. "It's all we've talked about at dinner here, too, whenever Jack's home. I've seen you at the hockey games. It's wonderful to finally meet you. Jimmy did some amazing work."

Jimmy smiled and held up his hands. "Oh, it wasn't me. All I did was oversee the project. It was all the guys I hired who did the work. I think all of them are here today except the woman who stenciled the walls upstairs. But she's not local. She's from Gilford."

All the guests, except Debbie and Billy, had left the house by six o'clock. Debbie and Billy packed some of the leftover food and took the few bottles of wine with them. "I'll take this up to Michelle's store for her open house," Debbie explained. "I'll see you both there tomorrow afternoon."

"Thank you for your help," Keira said, shaking Debbie's hand.

"Not at all. I'm glad to be able to contribute," Debbie replied. Billy just smiled and carried the bottles of wine to their truck.

Shortly after noon on Sunday, Debbie set the leftovers, fresh sandwiches, and wine on a table at the back of the New Hampshire Artisan Crafts store. Michelle and Peter waited near the door for their guests to arrive for the second of the back-to-back open houses. Jack and Keira with Lana and Warren stood near the rear of the store. Warren was quiet, giving space to Jack and Keira, but supporting his wife, his arm around her shoulder. Smoky, content to be out of the box Keira used to transport her in, slept in her accustomed spot in the sun on the back windowsill above the river. Beneath her, the river roared, white water crashing over the rocks, late season snowmelt rushing toward the covered bridge.

The first guest arrived, a woman not from Bennett Falls. "I'm so glad you're open," the stranger said, clutching her handbag. "I come up to New Hampshire on the weekend several times a year, and I just love your store. I didn't know when you'd open for the summer season."

"Today's the day," Michelle replied. "Welcome back! We're holding an open house to celebrate. Can I help you find something?"

The woman looked around the store, assessing, with a finger on her chin. "I don't know. I'd like to find something different, a bit unique or unusual."

Lana laughed, walked to the front of the store, and interjected, "You can have Warren. He's different, unique, and unusual." She pointed to her husband, standing slump-shouldered beside a table of pottery. "How much will you give me for him?" Lana asked. "I can help you get him out to your car if you'd like."

"Ah, Lana. Will you never stop?" Warren shook his head in apparent disgust, ambling toward the front of the store. "You're no better than Andrew, always making me the butt of your jokes." He turned to the woman from out of town. "I'm not for sale." He paused, and continued straight-faced, raising a finger to emphasize his point. "Unless.... How much are you willing to pay? Lana could use the money."

Andrew came into the store in time to hear the exchange. "Let me suggest," he explained to the woman. "You could do better than Warren. He's damaged goods, as we all know. Take a look around. You're bound to find something better."

The woman, unsure if she or Warren was the butt of everyone's jokes, looked quickly around the store, picked out woven placemats, and hurried to the cash register without a word.

After the woman left, Bennett Falls people started to trickle in. It was less crowded than the Metcalfe House open house the day before. It was quieter too, with fewer children. Pleasant, cool sunshine flooded the store through the window in the back. Smoky woke up, stretched, turned around twice, and curled back asleep, oblivious to the happy people in the shop.

Late in the afternoon, with the visitors gone, Michelle cleaned up with help from Peter, Jack, Keira, and Lana. Of their non-working guests, only Andrew Holmes and Warren remained, companions as always.

Michelle locked the door as they left. "I've got a box with leftover sandwiches," she said to Keira. "They're yours since Debbie prepared them for your open house. I'll carry them to your car. You've got your hands full with Smoky."

The seven of them walked to the parking lot on the riverbank below the old mill building: Lana and Warren, hand-in-hand, Andrew following, walking alone, Jack with Keira carrying the kitten, and Peter with Michelle and her box of leftovers. Keira unlocked her car and prepared to put Smoky into her box on the back seat.

While they were putting the sandwiches on the back seat, Smoky squirmed out of the box and, happy to be free, jumped out of the car onto the paved parking lot. She gave a brief, taunting look at Keira, hopped over the curb, and ran under a gray, steel guardrail onto the sloping granite slabs that lined the riverbank.

Keira started after the cat.

"Damn cat," Jack muttered, pulling Keira back and chasing. "I'll get her."

Churning water hammered the granite only feet away from Smoky. The kitten froze and looked at the white water, her ears back. Jack climbed over the guardrail, cursing again. The game was on. Smoky edged her way along the wet granite, steering clear of the rushing water. Jack pursued, cautious on the wet slabs, slipping to his hands and knees once on a thin coating of slick algae. He stood, but fell again, scraping his palms on the stone.

"Do you need help?" Andrew called. Spryly, he hopped over the guardrail and onto the granite-lined riverbank, trapping the kitten between himself and Jack. Smoky froze. She saw no place to run. Below her, the white water roared. In front of her was Andrew. Behind her was Jack.

Andrew inched closer and reached for Smoky, stretching. He took one more step, crab-like on the slick granite, slipped and slid, bumping from one rock to another, into the rushing river. Jack lunged for him and missed, sliding on the algae-polished stones. In an instant, both Andrew and Jack were in the icy water, clinging to the edges of the granite slabs. The pounding river pulled at the two men.

In the parking lot, Keira screamed. "Oh God, Jack! Andrew! We've got to save them!"

"I'll get them," Peter shouted. He straddled the guardrail and started for the two men in the water.

"No!" Michelle screamed, pulling him back. "Your heart! Stay here."

Keira leaped over the guardrail, followed more slowly by Warren.

"Get your husband," Warren shouted. "I've got Andrew."

Keira reached Jack just as he dragged himself out of the water onto the granite riverbank. They hugged for a moment and turned to see how Warren was faring with Andrew.

Warren, on his hands and arthritic knees, leaned down across the granite, close to Andrew, stretching his arm to him. Andrew held onto the rock with one hand and grabbed for Warren with the other. Their fingertips touched. Then they clasped hands. Warren reached with his other hand, getting a solid grip on Andrew's arm, trying to pull his best friend to safety. But when Andrew released his grip on the rim of a granite slab, stretching for Warren, the force of the river pulled him away, dragging Warren with him into the water. Together the two old men were swept away, holding hands as they tumbled downstream toward the covered bridge. The river roared.

Keira and Jack watched in horror as the two men rolled past them, out of reach in the pounding river. A surge of bitter black water swelled over them, pulling them deep, out of sight. They broke through the surface ten feet past Jack and Keira, both gasping for air, clinging to each other, looking wide-eyed back at the bank. Again, dark water slammed the men under as it swept them downstream. They roared over a short waterfall, crashing over rocks, and bobbed up again as the icy river carried them along.

It took a moment for Michelle, Peter, and Lana to react, stunned by the calamity in front of them. Peter started after Andrew and Warren, running to the downstream end of the parking lot. He stopped at the edge, looking over a ledge at the two men. As they surged away, Peter spun and raced from the parking lot, jogging as fast as he could toward the covered bridge.

"I'll catch them at the bridge," he called back as he ran.

Lana and Michelle caught and passed him on the street, Michelle on her phone calling 911 as she ran, explaining the situation to the operator.

Keira scooped up a contrite Smoky and, with Jack soaked and shivering beside her, they climbed to the parking lot and chased after their friends.

They found Warren and Andrew sprawled on the rocks behind the Congregational Church, washed up on the gravel at the base of the covered bridge. Shallow water pooled at their feet, flowing slowly through the bridge. Warren cradled Andrew's limp body in his arms and moaned, his shoulders shaking. He looked at Andrew's frozen face and pushed wet, white hair back from Andrew's staring eyes. Softly, he touched a bleeding wound on Andrew's forehead. He hugged his old friend and keened, "Why? I tried. I did everything I could. Why did this happen to you?"

Peter and Jack slid down the grassy bank and sat beside Warren, offering comfort, but bringing no solace. Lana followed, joined by Keira and Michelle.

On the street above them, Jimmy Sanborn's truck skidded to s stop. Red lights flashed in the grill. Jimmy dashed down the bank to the two old men. He squatted beside them and tried to take Andrew from Warren's grasp, hoping to start CPR.

"No! No!" Warren pleaded. "He's my friend. I need him."

Jimmy rested his hand on Warren's shoulder. "I know. We all need him. Let me try to save him."

Warren let go. Jimmy dragged Andrew like a disjointed doll up the bank to the church lawn and started pumping his chest, trying to jump-start his heart. He blew breaths into his mouth. More trucks appeared above them behind the church. Volunteer firefighters took over from Jimmy, working on Andrew.

Lana helped Warren stand, leading him soaked, shaking and crying back up the riverbank. They sat. Warren caved in, his head on Lana's chest, his whole body shaking.

Michelle and Peter stayed below, next to the frothing river, next to Jack and Keira, giving Lana and Warren their space. Smoky nestled in Keira's hands, trembling.

"Damn cat!" Jack said. "First the house fire and now this."

CHAPTER
Forty-Five
Spring

Keira sat sandwiched between Lana and Michelle several rows from the front in the packed Congregational Church. Peter sat on the other side of Michelle. Warren sagged next to the aisle, holding Lana's hand. The hush of whispered conversations betrayed the solemnity of the moment. The omnipresent backdrop rumble from the rushing river behind the church reminded everyone that Andrew Holmes had died just four days earlier within feet of where the town now sat.

Through tall, paned windows, a swatch of the river was visible, sparkling in bright sunlight. Birds flew through the branches of the maple trees lining the bank. The cheery vision of an early summer day in New Hampshire was an incongruous, hard contrast to the mood inside the church.

Keira looked around and realized she recognized most of the people who crowded the church. She knew many by name. She noticed the back of a man she didn't know sitting in the front pew. He seemed familiar to her, and Keira tried to place him, noting his thinning, sandy hair, wide shoulders, and a blue, pin-striped suit jacket. After a moment she gave up and realized she had never met him. Next to him were four young men she remembered from the Sunday night hockey games.

"Where's Jack?" Peter asked.

"At work in Boston." She wished Jack could have been with her, but it being Thursday, he couldn't get back to Bennett Falls. Peter shook his head and turned away.

"Who is that in the front pew?" Keira whispered to Michelle.

"Matthew Holmes, Andrew's son. I'm glad to see he was able to be here. He got married and moved south for his job. I think he lives in North Carolina now. I don't see his wife with him, but she probably had to stay down there to take care of their kids and probably couldn't get time off from her job. He must have had to come alone. I'm glad he could be here on such short notice."

"I expect any business would allow someone time off for a funeral," Keira said. Again she thought of Jack, still working in Boston.

Reverend Thompson started the service with a short prayer. Then, in the echoing church, he climbed the stairs to the pulpit. For a moment he surveyed the jammed pews, his face lined, his eyes weary. He took a deep breath and began, speaking slowly, his deep voice booming in the cavernous sanctuary. "How can it be that God could take such a fine man as Andrew Holmes, having him pass from us so suddenly? Yes, Andrew had lived a long life. Still, I doubt that he, or any of us, was ready for this sad ending."

Reverend Thompson went on for several minutes, ending with words of assurance about salvation and eternal life. He concluded by asking, "If anyone would like to say a few words about the life of Andrew Holmes, you may come forward."

Amos Sanborn stood and walked quietly to the pulpit. "Andrew Holmes was the soul of our little town," he stated. "It wasn't just his stories. And I expect we've all heard some of his storytelling down at The Sunrise."

Muffled chuckles followed. Amos waited for the church to become quiet again. "What really mattered was how he cared for this town. For all our residents. We saw that in how he ran things at the bank when he worked. Even after he retired, we saw his love for Bennett Falls in so many ways. In his managing the Historical Society, and his involvement in many other endeavors. There is a massive hole left by his passing. I know I will miss him as a friend. We all will miss his stories and the way he cared for Bennett Falls."

Others spoke, all reflecting on Andrew Holmes' humanity, love for the town, and attention to anyone in Bennett Falls who needed any assistance.

The last to speak was Debbie Forbes. "It's been a hard week down at The Sunrise. Every morning for years, just after eight, like clockwork, Andrew would come in. He was like a ray of sunshine to start each day, even when it was cold and dark outside. Most of you have been there and seen how he was each morning. These past few mornings it's been so quiet in there. All the regulars are still there. But without Andrew… We shut down The Sunrise this morning to come to the service. We never close, except on Sundays, and Christmas Day and New Year's Day. But for Andrew, we're closed. I miss him."

Sniffling, Debbie walked back to her seat.

After Reverend Thompson waited a moment in the silent church, he stood and said, "Is there anyone else who would like to speak?"

Warren rose from his seat on the aisle, pushing up against the pew in front of him. Slowly, he walked to the front of the church and climbed the stairs to the pulpit. He turned and faced the town, his face a tragic mask. For several moments he said nothing, swallowing, his mouth moving but making no sound. He looked at the ceiling. He looked at his feet.

"Andrew has always been my best friend."

He paused, his jaw clenched, fighting for control. He looked at the vaulted ceiling again, took a deep breath and blew out slowly. Sweat broke on his forehead and his upper lip. His shoulders shook. Still he couldn't speak. Finally, he turned and stepped down from the pulpit, assisted by Reverend Thompson. Lana met Warren in the aisle and helped him back to his seat.

After the funeral, with the sunshine filtering through the new leaves, Keira stood outside in front of the church with her four close friends. Peter and Michelle held hands. Lana held Warren, standing behind him, wrapping both her arms around him. Keira was alone.

"Where's Jack?" Peter asked again. "He should have been here."

Keira looked at the long grass on the lawn. "Boston," she explained again, exasperated. "He couldn't get off work."

Warren shook his head and said nothing.

Peter nodded. "Sure. Work. It's good at least you were able to be here."

"Of course I came," Keira said. A trace of defiant anger laced her voice. "Andrew had become a good friend and neighbor."

Warren took a deep breath and blew out, his lips pursed, his breath almost whistling. "I wish you could have known him the way I did. There was so much I had to say today, so much I wanted to, but I just couldn't. God! I feel like half my soul is gone with him. He was a real pain in the neck sometimes, but I loved him like my brother."

They watched as Matthew walked by with his friends on his way to the cemetery a block away. "Poor Matthew," Michelle said. "Living so far away. I know he and Andrew spoke often, at least once a week. But how long has it been since he was able to come home to Bennett Falls and see his father? Maybe the last time was when his mom passed away and that had to be ten years ago."

"I wonder what will become of the house," Lana asked.

Warren began to revert to his usual self. "Ah…. Amos Sanborn will probably take charge and sell the place to another out-of-towner." Embarrassed, he caught himself and reached across touching Keira's hand. "No offense intended," he apologized.

"None taken." She squeezed his hand and smiled.

CHAPTER
Forty-Six
Spring

The day of the funeral, Jack got home in time for a late dinner. Tired from the long drive, he crashed on the sofa in the parlor. "Boy, I hate the traffic out of Boston! Rush hour. It's good to be home."

Keira's response was terse. "Dinner is ready. It's just the two of us."

Jack sat at the small table in their apartment behind the house. Keira began to serve chili from a crock pot. Smoky napped nearby, watching them through half-opened eyes.

"What's been going on while I've been away?" Jack asked.

Keira turned to him. "Andrew's funeral. Don't you remember? That was this morning."

"Oh, yes. Did you go?"

"Of course!" Keira gave a frustrated sigh, looking Jack in the eyes. "The whole town was there. The church was packed. They left the doors open so people who couldn't get in could hear the service while they stood outside."

"Oh. Well, what with my work and all. Anything else going on here?"

"We're booked with guests all the way into the fall. Almost full every day for weeks. That's something to talk about. But Andrew's funeral is front and center here in Bennett Falls."

"Back in Boston, nobody even knows about Bennett Falls or what's happening here. There's always so much happening there. I'm always busy. Down in Boston, aside from my job, it's all about the Red Sox. They're winning this year! One of my clients has season tickets, and he took me to the game on Tuesday night. We were right on the first base line a few rows back of the dugout. It was a great game."

Keira felt like screaming, but she held herself under control. She sat with her chili across from Jack. She took a deep breath and blew out. When she spoke, her voice was tense, straining. "Andrew Holmes died. You were there when it happened. That doesn't mean anything to you?"

"Of course it does. But it's not like we really knew each other. I care about him. I care about anyone who passes away. But he was old. It's not unexpected."

"Oh, come on!" Now she yelled, standing from the table, her arms crossed. "Our neighbor died, suddenly, right there with us. He was trying to save our cat. You don't care? You should have come back for the funeral."

Jack laughed. "So, it's about the cat. Ha! I had work this morning. Remember, it's my income keeping us afloat while we try to make this bed and breakfast fantasy work."

"The bed and breakfast is doing fine. We're making money, but I need your help running things. I'm checking guests in, preparing breakfasts, cleaning rooms, doing sheets and towels. All with no help from you. And this morning, I made sure our guests knew we had a town-wide funeral, so they were all fed and checked out early. You could have made arrangements in Boston to get away for the day and come to the funeral."

"Well, no, I really couldn't. There's always a lot going on down there. Every day. It's bad enough that I'm not there on Mondays and Fridays."

Keira shook her head, sat again, but pushed her chili away and looked at Jack.

Jack reached across and took her hand. "Look, I know it's hard for you, running the place a couple of days a week without me. You should try to find someone local who can help out and pick up some of the slack. Listen, if you find someone who can work here part time, you could even come down to Boston with me once in a while. That customer who's got the Red Sox tickets said I can use them any time. Come to Boston and we'll go to a game."

"You've got to be kidding!" Keira stood, her dinner untouched. "I've had it! Even with help, I need to be here to run this place. And what would I do all day in Boston while you're at work? I gave up my job to move here. Sure, I'd love to go to a Sox game, but my life is here now. I can't get away just like that."

She dropped her bowl of chili clattering in the sink and went in the bedroom followed by Smoky. She slammed the door.

Jack continued eating, finished his chili, and put his bowl in the sink next to her full bowl. Then he went into the parlor and turned on the television. The Sox game was on.

CHAPTER
Forty-Seven
Memorial Day

Weeks passed with Jack in Boston and Keira managing the bed and breakfast. On the weekends he came home, Jack moved carefully around Keira, making sure not to bring up the funeral again. For him, it seemed their fight had been about his absence on the day of the funeral. He couldn't imagine that there was more involved.

After serving breakfast on Memorial Day and checking out their full house of departing guests, Jack and Keira hurried down the hill, through the bridge to the Town Common for the festivities. It was almost like a reenactment of Veteran's Day, but with warmer weather and additional events. There was a booth where kids could get their faces painted. A man sold balloons. A crowd cheered on the finishing runners in the twenty-fourth annual Bennett Falls Four Mile Classic road race. Sweat-soaked runners wandered on the Common lawn, wearing finisher medals on ribbons around their necks, sipping small bottles of juice. With the race over, everybody turned their attention to the traditional parade route, waiting for the bands.

Jack and Keira found Michelle and Peter, Lana and Warren near the bandstand. Peter confronted Jack. "How are you, my old friend? I haven't seen you for several weeks. You missed Andrew's funeral."

"I'm fine. I've been down in Boston except for the weekends. Work is going well."

"Of course it is. You should have been here for Andrew Holmes' funeral. Keira says the bed and breakfast is doing very well, too."

Lana interjected. "Yes, and Keira is taking me on to help out a bit at your house. I'll be doing some of the small tasks, cleaning up, taking care of the linens. She and I meet Michelle to walk every morning once Keira and I've got the house straightened and the first load of bed linens in the wash."

Michelle carried on. "Lana and I used to walk at nine so I could open my shop at ten. We've all adjusted. Now we walk with Keira at ten and I open at eleven. I never got customers that first hour anyway."

"Well, that's fine," Jack said. He smiled and hugged Keira. "I'm glad you're all helping Keira when I'm out of town. I know she needs that."

Peter pulled Jack away from their wives. "We talked a while back about going fishing. Are you still interested?"

"Sure. I don't have any fishing gear, but it sounds like fun."

Warren leaned in. "How are you going to go fishing without any gear? Have you ever been fishing before?"

"Of course. Once, back when I was a kid, I went fishing at summer camp. That was in Massachusetts of course, but fish are fish, right? I'll just need to borrow the gear."

"I'll set you up with everything," Peter said. "Let's wait a couple of weeks, though. Its catch and release season right now."

"Catch and release?" Jack was puzzled by another oddity of rural New Hampshire life. "What's that?"

"For four weeks in late May and early June, they allow us to go fishing, but if we catch anything, we have to take it off the hook and let it swim away," Peter said. "It's like practice for us fishermen. Maybe for the fish too, practicing how to get caught. I don't bother to fish during catch and release time. I like to catch them and bring them home for dinner."

Jack nodded. "Sure. If we catch enough, maybe Keira and I can join you and Michelle for a fish fry."

"Only if you catch something," Warren sneered.

"Oh, we will!" Peter assured Warren. "If we catch enough, we'll call and have you and Lana join us for dinner."

"Do I need a license?" Jack asked.

"Nah. I've got mine. Anyway, there's no warden to check on us at Clear Lake. Wait a couple of weeks and I'll pick you up at dawn."

They set a date and turned to watch for the parade.

CHAPTER

Forty-Eight

June

Early Saturday morning, Jack and Keira worked quietly in the kitchen, setting up breakfast. Jack put out fourteen fruit cups for their full house of guests. He started coffee percolating in the big coffee maker. Keira put three quiches in the oven to bake. Smoky prowled the kitchen, winding between their feet, watching for fallen scraps.

Through the open kitchen window, they heard the grind of tires on the gravel driveway. In the gray half-light of pre-dawn, Jack looked out and saw Peter's pickup circling in front of the house. Behind Peter's truck, a low trailer carried a flat boat painted drab, camouflage.

"Peter's here," Jack said. "Gotta run."

"He's gone again," Keira mumbled. Her face passive, she watched him go and set back to work without a word, assembling baskets with breads and pastries.

The dawn was damp. A silvery haze hung in the air, barely lit by the yellow glow of the coming sun. Jack got in the truck and reached over to shake Peter's hand. "This is great!" he said. "Thanks for rescuing me from kitchen duty. This is going to be a real adventure for me."

"Fishing always is," Peter said. He shook Jack's hand and handed him a paper cup. "I picked up coffees down at The Sunrise. Did you have breakfast?"

"A couple of bites of some of the pastries Keira makes for the guests. I don't usually eat much breakfast."

"That's good. We'll be on the water for a few hours. And it's good to see you wore shorts. You might get a little wet."

They drove up the hill to Clear Lake. Peter carefully backed down the boat ramp. With the trailer wheels in the water, he turned off the truck and set the brake. "Get out," he ordered as he stepped down from the truck. Jack did as he was told.

Peter waded alongside the trailer and unhooked the boat. "Grab your side and help me float the boat off the trailer."

Again, Jack did as he was told and waded in. They lifted the boat clear of the trailer, assisted by the soft lapping of the lake.

"Now hold on to the boat while I take care of the truck."

Peter pulled the truck and trailer up the ramp and backed in, parking next to two other trucks and trailers. He locked the truck, lifted his equipment from the back, and rejoined Jack. He set a large, red plastic cooler in the boat, and dropped in two fishing rods and a foot-long gray tackle box. Finally, he held the boat and gave Jack more directions. "Climb in and sit in the middle."

Jack hoisted himself into the boat and sat in the center of the middle seat, holding onto each side to steady himself. Peter pushed the boat free of the concrete ramp and slid in, pulling himself over the square bow. Then, hunched, he worked his way past Jack and sat in the stern. He dropped the propeller of a small motor into the water and pulled the cord. The motor puttered to life. Slowly, Peter turned the drifting boat toward the center of the lake. Dawn broke through the overcast, but traces of fog, glowing bronze in the low sunlight, still laced the surface of the lake. Somewhere across the water, they heard a hooting, warbling sound.

"What was that?" Jack asked.

"A loon."

"That's some kind of a big bird?"

Peter nodded. "Yup. There's at least two here on the lake, maybe more."

Opening the tackle box as he motored along, Peter took out a spray bottle and tossed it to Jack. "Spray this on your arms and legs and rub it onto your face and neck. It's for the black flies. They're a bitch this time of year. And out here on the lake at sunrise… they'll eat you alive."

They crossed the open width of the lake and moved quietly, slowly into a cove. Water lilies covered much of the surface, their thick leaves floating, sliding against the steel hull, rubbery stalks rising from the water. Through the clear water, deep beneath the boat, Jack saw pond weed growing on the bottom, waving slowly with the current. Peter cut the motor, letting the boat drift to a stop among the lilies.

Surrounded by the quiet of the lake, Peter opened the tackle box again, stowed the repellent, and sorted through a tray at the top of the box. He put aside rubber worms and other imitations of things fish might like to eat and pulled out two lures. They looked like tiny, sculptured impressions of small fish as they might be imagined by abstract artists, painted bright red, white, blue and black, with spots and stripes added along the bodies. Hanging on the lures were barbed hooks. The lures also featured shiny aluminum fins flapping loose from rings. Peter flipped one and said, "These things wiggle when the lure moves through the water. It makes them look like little swimming minnows. Big fish like that."

Deftly, Peter tied the lures on two lines and handed Jack one of the rods.

"Watch," he instructed. He held his rod back and flipped it forward, sending the line with the lure arcing across the lily pads, hissing as it ran off the reel. It dropped in an open space, clear of the lilies that filled the cove.

"Now you try," Peter said. "Make sure the reel is set to allow the line to run. Be careful. Cast it straight out so the hook doesn't snag us."

Jack tried to imitate the smooth, practiced move Peter had made, but the line looped out only a few feet from where they sat in the boat, plopping in the water and going slack.

"Not bad for a first try," Peter coached. "Reel it back in. Use the crank handle and rewind your line." Peter pointed to the reel on his rod.

Jack reeled the line in. When he was ready, he looked to Peter.

"Try it again. Use your wrist and shoot it a bit higher in the air."

This time the line sailed out and landed among the lilies farther from the boat.

"That's good. Now reel it back in slowly. Like this." Peter began retrieving his own line. Jack followed. "Easy. There's no rush. Remember, I said the lure is designed so it'll wiggle in the water like a little fish. Take your time. Fish will chase it."

Their lines came in with no fish. They peeled pond weed off the lines. "Now we cast them out again," Peter instructed.

They cast again and reeled in several more times. Still, they caught no fish.

A splash. A ring of ripples radiated through the water lilies across the cove, the pads rising and falling, the stems bobbing.

"What was that? A frog?" Jack asked.

"A fish."

Without another word, Peter started the small motor on the boat and putted to a different spot on the far side of the cove. "There are plenty of fish in this cove," he explained. "And this is the time of day when they're feeding. We just have to find them."

He cut the motor, leaving them drifting among the water lilies. They cast their lines and waited, gently reeling them back. Jack's line suddenly went taut, and the end of his rod dipped. Across the lilies they saw a fish thrashing, splashing on the surface, wrestling with Jack's lure.

"You've got one!" Peter whispered. "Give your rod a little jerk. Set the hook! When you feel tension, the fish pulling on the line, give a quick snap of your wrist to make sure the hook is in there. Then reel him in slowly. Let him think he's still in control. Reel a bit and relax. Reel a bit more. That's it. Easy, easy. He's coming. You've got him swimming right this way."

The fish drew closer to the boat, fighting, splashing, writhing with the hook. Jack wrestled to keep the fish coming.

The big fish paused. The line, still taut, set in the water ten feet from the boat. Beneath the dimple where the line met the water, through the reflections, they saw a light shadow moving toward them. Then it was on the surface again, thrashing, its mouth open wide, trying to get rid of the lure and the hook. Water swirled around the gaping hole that was the fish's mouth.

While Jack continued struggling with the big fish, Peter opened the cooler, took out two bottles, set them on the seat beside him, and left the lid open. He found a net beneath his seat and waited as Jack fought the fish closer. When the fish was next to the boat, Peter reached the net into the water and brought it up beneath the flapping fish, lifting it from the lake.

"That's a beauty, Jack! Now grab him. Watch out for the spines and be ready for him to be slippery. Keep him over the boat so you don't lose him and be careful when you take the lure out of his mouth. Don't catch yourself on the hook."

Jack beamed, thrilled by what he had done. He grasped the wriggling fish with one hand, hugging it against his shirt, and, after a clumsy first try, removed the hook with the other hand. "Amazing! I've never caught anything like this. What kind of fish is it?"

"It's a bass. Clear Lake is full of them. Toss it in the cooler and let's catch some more."

Jack pitched the fish into the cooler and watched it flopping on top of the ice and bottles.

Before Jack could cast again, Peter popped the top off one bottle and handed it over. "Your reward for the first catch of the day. I got you Sam

Summer Ale. It's what you drink, right?"

"Yes, but it's still pretty early in the morning, isn't it?" Jack checked his watch. "It's only ten past nine."

"So. It's getting hot. We need to stay hydrated. Time doesn't matter when you're on the water."

Peter snapped the top off his own bottle and took a quick drink. "Peach iced tea," he announced, displaying the bottle. "My new drink of choice. Michelle teases me about it. Says it's not manly enough of a drink for me. But I've found I like it."

They took another sip of their drinks, put them aside, and cast their lines again. Time passed. They caught more fish.

Later in the morning, Peter reeled in his line and said, "We've got six good sized bass. Looks like we'll have Lana and Warren joining us for dinner."

Jack checked his reel. "Warren can be a pain in the ass. Why do we have to invite him?"

"Lana and Michelle are best friends. And Lana's married to Warren. That's why. He's okay."

At first, Jack seemed to agree, nodding without a word. But then he shook his head.

Peter caught it and said, "You would know better about Warren if you had been at Andrew's funeral. Warren's just a regular guy."

"I wouldn't know."

"No, you wouldn't." Peter turned to Jack, pointing, his voice raised, sudden anger controlled. "You should have been at the funeral. Andrew was his best friend. But it's more than that. Being there on the riverbank, holding Andrew, watching him die, was, for Warren, like losing a piece of his soul. Like watching another part of Bennett Falls taken away. You would understand Warren better if you had been there."

"I had to work."

Peter put the lures in the tackle box and turned again to Jack. "You were there on the riverbank when he died. You could have been at the funeral if you really wanted to. You could have told your boss you had a funeral to go to. What's the story? Are you in or out with your move to Bennett Falls?"

"What's it to you? This is really none of your business."

Peter spoke with even more assertiveness, his voice steady and contained. "You know where you should be, what you should be doing. Keira's here running your business. Why aren't you with her?"

Jack looked away from Peter's directness, scanning the vista of the lake. "I don't know. I've got my job in Boston, my career. I manage a portfolio of high-rise buildings there. There's always a new challenge every day. A lot going on. I have a good team of guys working for me. I love my job. My family's there too. A lot of friends. We bought the house here, but I'm trying to make it work living here on the weekends and working there during the week."

Peter shook his head, exasperated. "Sheesh! Make up your mind. What about Keira?"

"What about her?"

"You love her?"

"Yes. Of course."

"Then you belong here. End of story."

"She could come to Boston with me every week. I've asked her. She refused."

"She's got the business to run. She has to stay here. You belong here with her. You need to figure this out."

"Lana's working at the B&B now. Keira could come to Boston and let Lana take care of things. We could live in Boston and let other people do the work of running the B&B."

"Make up your mind," Peter repeated. "Is Keira more important than your job? If she is, quit your job and stay here. If she's not… If your job is more important…" Peter stopped.

"We can do both if Keira would just join me in Boston."

"She shouldn't have to. She's got a life here. So do you."

Peter stowed his line and, without another word, started the motor and circled onto the open lake heading back to the boat ramp.

"No. My life is in Boston, not here," Jack mumbled, the words lost in the hum of the motor.

Jack watched Peter waiting for a response, unsure if he had heard. Peter shook his head and said nothing, looking straight ahead at the far shore, aiming for the ramp.

Keira searched for bass recipes on the internet. Satisfied with what she found, she took the fillets, freshly cleaned and deboned by Peter, and stored them in the refrigerator until the evening.

Michelle and Peter, Lana and Warren came to the Metcalfe House after five. Being a weekend, all seven guest rooms were booked, but the guests had all gone out for the evening.

Michelle greeted Keira with a conspiratorial smile. "The Old Mill is full tonight," she said. "They asked me to come into work, but I told them I had an engagement of my own. I expect a few of your guests are at dinner down there."

"Could be," Keira answered with a quick laugh. "I told all of them it was the best place to go for dinner. I called and made a reservation for one couple."

They gathered on the front porch on the padded wicker seats around the coffee table, sharing appetizers. The three women shared a bottle of Sauvignon Blanc. Warren and Jack drank Sam Adams, left over from the morning fishing trip. Peter had his peach iced tea. When the snacks were gone, Keira led Michelle and Lana to the kitchen to start frying the bass.

Jack asked Peter, "Is Clear Lake the best fishing spot in the state?"

"I like it. Nobody knows about it. All the tourists go over to Lake Winnipesaukee."

"The way it should be," Warren affirmed. "Keep the tourists over there."

As they spoke, a couple of the house guests parked and walked to the porch. "What's cooking?" the woman asked. "Smells like you're frying fish?"

"Bass," Jack bragged proudly. "Peter and I caught enough for all of us this morning up the hill at Clear Lake."

"Really!" the man said. "I was thinking of doing a little fishing while we're on vacation. Where is Clear Lake?"

Warren interrupted. "Nah. Don't bother with Clear Lake. It's just our little weed-filled local pond. If you want good fishing, head over to Lake Winnipesaukee or up north to Squam Lake. That's where the best fishing is."

"Ah. Thanks for the tip." The man and woman went in the house and up the stairs.

Peter chuckled quietly. "Still at it, scaring away the out-of-towners."

"It had to be said," Warren answered.

"Fine," Jack said. "But we're trying to run a business here. Don't scare away our customers."

"They can stay here while they visit. That much is okay. But they should go elsewhere to fish." Warren tipped back his bottle of beer, swallowed, and sat back, staring across the lawn.

"Dinner's ready!" Keira called. "Fried bass with a cornmeal crust. Wild rice and asparagus on the side."

The mood in the dining room was polite. Peter didn't bring up any of his talk with Jack on the lake. Neither did Jack. Warren remained cordial with both Jack and Keira. The evening passed civilly.

CHAPTER
Forty-Nine
July

Several weeks went by. When he returned home on the weekends, the mood between Jack and Keira was quiet but edgy. As he packed to go back to Boston, Jack suggested, "My boss is having a cookout for his management team next weekend at his house in Weston. Spouses are invited. Why don't you join me Friday night? Then we'd have the cookout Saturday, and you could stay the weekend. What do you say?"

"Oh, Jack. You know I can't. We're booked solid on the weekends. I need to be here."

They let the matter drop. Neither was willing to discuss their new tension. They both found tacit agreement not to discuss their growing rift.

After the next week, Jack skipped the cookout and came home Friday night. He said nothing about the missed event with his boss, but he was grumpy and fussy all weekend.

On Monday morning, hot sun burned through the dawn haze of humidity. The Metcalfe House vibrated with what had become a bustling morning routine. Keira cleaned up the dining room and kitchen after breakfast for the guests who had filled six of the seven rooms. In the midst of clearing the dishes, Keira signed out each set of guests. Lana stripped beds as soon as the guests left, bundling the linens to the oversized washer in Jack and Keira's apartment. Jack sat at the kitchen table and checked his emails from work in Boston. With the housework under control, Keira and Lana headed down the hill to the covered bridge to meet Michelle for their regular morning walk.

An hour later, Keira returned from the walk, flushed and sweat-soaked. She found Jack on the sofa with his laptop open on his knees. He ran his hands across the top of his head and said, "Things are happening with one of my clients in Boston. There's a problem."

"I've got to take a quick shower," Keira announced, heading for their apartment. "I'll be working a couple of hours down at the Craft Shop this afternoon. You'll be around if any of our guests arrive early for a check in?"

"I don't know. Probably, if I have to. Where else would I be? There's no place to go, nothing to do all day. But I may have to run down to Boston."

Keira stopped and turned to him, hands on her hips. "One of us has to be here, Jack. If you're planning to be out, I need to know."

"Fine. Go shower. Go to your other job. I'll be stuck here. I'll just let my business in Boston go to hell. Just like when I skipped the cookout with my boss on Saturday."

Keira mopped sweat from her forehead with the sleeve of her t-shirt and pushed a wet lock of hair from her face. "Stuck here? This is our house, our business. You need to pitch in and help."

"It's your business. You bought it with the money you inherited from your mother. I don't know why we ever decided to start this. It's not like we're making any money with this place."

"What? We talked about doing this for years. It was our dream. You didn't say no when we bought the place or when we were fixing it up. And yes, we're doing fine financially. We have at least three rooms booked every night from now till well into the fall. Weekends we're full. All my marketing experience has us on the tourists' radar. We're bringing in at least five thousand, sometimes close to ten thousand dollars a week. There are expenses, of course, but we have a steady income already, and we've only been open a couple of months. Our income more than covers our expenses."

"Sure, fine. And I have my work in Boston. My career. That's where I need to be."

"No!" Keira spoke with newfound assertiveness. Pent-up anger burned to the surface. "No! You're a part of our business and you need to start helping out."

"I can't."

"What's wrong with us, Jack? We seem to be heading in different directions. Don't you want to be a part of running our business?"

Jack leaned back on the sofa. "I don't know. Maybe not. Yes, we seem to be heading in different directions. Maybe we should just end it all."

"What? What are you saying? That I should walk away from the B&B now that it's open and making money?"

"Yes. Maybe that and more."

"More? What do you mean? That we should split up? Go our separate ways? Get divorced?"

"I don't know. Maybe yes. I'm needed in Boston. I've asked you to join me there, but you won't. That's your decision. This is on you, not me. This is no way for us to live."

"What's wrong with us? Except for when we lost the babies, we never fought about anything. We've always been able to move on. What's happened to us?"

"The babies might be a part of it. I thought maybe if you got involved in something like this house. If we moved from Boston, maybe it would give us a fresh start in a new place. It would give you something new to occupy your mind, and we'd leave all the old memories behind. The baby thing is still an issue. But there's so much more now."

"I love you, Jack. Do you still love me? Maybe we should find someone and get marriage counseling." Her voice was pleading, filled with fear.

Jack looked out the window. Birds hopped in the shade on the lawn. He said nothing, watching the birds. This problem, he realized, might never go away.

"Jack?" Keira queried, feeling the hopelessness implicit in his refusal to answer.

"I don't know. Yes, I love you. But this isn't what I thought we'd be doing when we got married. I thought by now, either we'd be living in a nice house somewhere in the suburbs or maybe in a townhouse right in the middle of downtown Boston. We could have sold our little starter house in Quincy and used your inheritance to buy a bigger house out farther from Boston. Instead, we bought this place. I thought we'd both have our careers. There'd be kids. Instead, you've decided to live here in this big old house in the middle of the woods. And you can't have a baby, so there's that. Nothing's the way it was supposed to be with you."

"I don't want to move back to Boston. There's nothing left for me there. I love this bed and breakfast business. Does this all come back to my not being able to have a baby?"

"That's a part of it. Maybe a big part. I don't want to live here in this dead little town. I want to be in Boston. And I do want children. And you can't do either of those things for me."

"Oh, come on. We talked about adoption, but you wouldn't do that. There's more to me than making a baby. Is my uterus the only part of me you love?"

"No, I love all of you, I guess. But this is turning out wrong. You've changed, Keira. You don't seem to want the same things we've always wanted."

"I haven't changed. A year ago, we both wanted to live here and do this. You're the one who's bailing and wants to give it all up and go back to Boston."

They were at an impasse. Keira, still damp from her walk, standing in the middle of the parlor, and late for work at the craft shop. Jack hunched on the sofa with his laptop, wishing he was at work in Boston. Both angry and frustrated.

Keira mumbled, "I've got to go get cleaned up for work."

Jack replied, "Fine. Whatever. Go. And there are things going on in Boston that need my attention. It can't wait till tomorrow. I'm going to head down so I can be there this afternoon."

When Keira was dressed after her shower, Jack was gone. She phoned Michelle to let her know she had to stay at the Metcalfe House for the day.

"Jack had to go to Boston. He's gone. I have to stay here at the house. I can't come to the store today."

"Is everything all right?"

"Yes, of course!" Keira infused her words with a false lack of concern. "I just have to stay here today. That's all."

⊰⊱

Jack called Wednesday evening. "How are things going in Bennett Falls?"

"Great!" Keira replied, her voice lilting, infused with false cheeriness, hoping Jack would catch her excitement. "Five rooms are booked tonight. And here we are mid-week, which is usually a slow day! We had four reservations, and then I got a call late this afternoon. A young couple hoping we had a room available."

"That's good."

"I'm working down at the Craft shop a few hours almost every afternoon. Lana's coming in to help a couple of hours in the morning and then one or the other of us, sometimes both of us, goes over to the shop. It depends on if we have new guests scheduled to arrive. One of us has to be here to greet the new people."

"That's good." Jack moved abruptly from Keira's talk of her life in Bennett Falls. "Listen. I've just about got things back under control down here. But my boss says he thinks he'll need me to go back to working five days a week again. We can't let issues like what just happened here come up again. So, I'm staying over again until Friday, just like last week. I'll be home Friday evening, not Thursday."

Keira sighed, her exhaled breath audible to Jack over the phone.

"Come on, Keira. I have to be here for work. One of us needs to provide a reliable, steady income. That has to be me. We depend on my job. We certainly can't count on your bed and breakfast."

"I need you here in New Hampshire."

Jack's tone shifted. He spoke with sudden, abrupt authority, his voice stern, his speech clipped. "I've been giving this a lot of thought over the past few weeks. I think we should sell the B and B. You should move back to Boston. You can find another job in Boston if you want to. Or just stay home while I'm at work. I don't care. But I'm done with the whole bed and breakfast idea."

"I can't give it all up now. It's doing well, and I love it."

"If you won't let it go and come back to Boston, then we're done. My work is in Boston. Hell, my life is in Boston. It always has been. Now you seem to want to live in New Hampshire. I'll see you Friday night. We'll talk it out then."

He hung up before Keira could answer. She sat on the sofa, stunned, stroking Smoky's head. "Son of a bitch! What am I going to do?" She stared out the window at the sunlit lawn, numb, angry, and confused. She suddenly found no beauty, no happiness in the gardens or the sunshine. The cat purred and snuggled, climbing to Keira's neck and nuzzling her.

CHAPTER

Fifty

July

When he returned to Bennett Falls on Friday, Jack brought a sheaf of legal papers from a divorce lawyer with him. That evening, with all the guests settled in their rooms, he and Keira sat at their kitchen table. Jack set the papers on the table, squaring them in front of Keira.

"This is it?" Keira asked as she thumbed through the pages. "No more discussion? No counseling? We just get divorced?"

"What's to discuss? You want to stay here. My life and my career are in Boston. You won't support my career, and I can't live like this. You like this little nowhere town. I like Boston. And you can't have a baby. There's no reason for us to stay together."

"We could adopt. We've talked about that. If this all comes down to having kids, we could always adopt."

"No. I want my own children. We've gone over this off and on for years. I don't want to raise someone else's baby. We're probably too old to adopt now anyway. And my life is in Boston, not here in Bennett Falls."

"I left everything to move here," Keira said. "My friends, my home, everything. I'm settled here with a new life. And now you bail on me?

And why bring up the baby issue again?"

Keira got up, left the papers on the kitchen table, and walked into their apartment trailed by Smoky. She turned and closed the door quietly behind her, never looking back at Jack.

Jack heard the lock click on the apartment door. Agitated, he picked up the papers, thumbed through them, and put them back in his briefcase. "She has to sign them," he grumbled softly to himself. "Why does she always make things so difficult?"

He sat alone and watched the Red Sox game on television. When all the guests had come in and returned to their rooms for the night, Jack kicked his shoes off and fell asleep on the living room sofa. He woke often during the night, cramped and sore.

At dawn, he was awakened by Keira, dressed and ready for her day, starting the coffee in the kitchen. Jack rolled off the sofa, wrinkled and fuzzy from the restless night.

"Good morning," he said glumly.

She turned away. "Get up and get dressed. Our guests will be coming downstairs soon. How did you sleep?" she asked.

"Badly. The sofa's not very comfortable and it's too short for my legs."

"Good," Keira replied. Then she eased up. "You can sleep in our bedroom tonight and tomorrow if you wish. But stay on your side of the bed."

"Thanks. You need to sign the papers before I go back Monday morning. I'm meeting with my lawyer again this coming week. I've got an extra copy so you can have your lawyer look at them, but I need to get them to my lawyer later this coming week. You can keep this big, old house you bought with the money you inherited from your mother. And I'll let you have a bit of money every month, something to live on. Otherwise, you'll be on your own."

Keira said nothing, working on breakfast, her back to Jack.

Jack waited a moment for her to respond. When it was clear she wouldn't, he went in their apartment for his shower.

When he came out, Keira had breakfast cooking. Lana was setting the tables in the dining room and on the porch for the guests from all seven rooms. The guests began straggling down the stairs before eight, looking for coffee and inquiring about breakfast.

On Saturday, Jack and Keira stayed out of each other's way. Keira was busy with the bed and breakfast. Jack was distracted and, finding nothing else to do, sat on the porch staring emptily across the lawn at the forest. This has to be the most boring place on earth, he mused.

Sunday morning, as he packed his bags for his upcoming week in Boston, Keira asked, "Where are the divorce papers?"

He took them from his briefcase and handed them to her.

"You want out. I want out. I just don't care anymore. Where do I sign?"

He showed her. Without reading them, she signed. She folded her copy and tucked it on a shelf in the kitchen. She handed the signed copy to Jack, and he put the papers back in his briefcase. "When you come home next weekend, I'll have all your stuff packed up. You can get out of here then."

Palms up, like he was stopping traffic, Jack pled his case. "Not so fast. What's the rush? I'll have to find a place to live down in Boston. That could take a while. I may need to keep coming back here on the weekends for a bit. I'm staying with my parents during the week. But I can't crash with them on the weekends too."

"Not my problem. You're the one in a big rush to get divorced. I signed the papers. You're not welcome in my apartment here. We're usually booked solid on the weekends, but if we have an open room upstairs, you can stay there. You know what I charge per night."

Jack shook his head, frustrated. He slept on the sofa again Sunday night and left for Boston before dawn on Monday.

CHAPTER

Fifty-One

July

The last of the weekend guests checked out early on Monday morning. Keira worked quietly, clearing dishes from the dining room table, loading them in the dishwasher.

Lana came into the kitchen, her arms bundling a load of linens for the washer. "Jack left early this morning? Doesn't he usually stay 'til Tuesday? When he has to go on Monday, he takes his time before he leaves."

"He left bright and early this morning." Keira's face was cold, unsmiling. A deep crease formed between her eyebrows.

Lana caught the look. She had sensed the tension in the house the past few weekends, noting the distance between Jack and Keira, how they never seemed to have anything to say to each other. "He's given up on the business?"

"Yes. And on me, too, it would seem. We're done."

Lana dropped the sheets, pulled Keira to her and held her. Keira broke down, silently crying, shaking, and clutching Lana. She had held it together, grim-faced, all weekend. Now the enormity of her situation crashed down on her.

After a moment Keira pushed back, breaking from Lana's arms. Keira's face was flushed, her cheeks wet. She wiped her nose on her palm, then pulled a paper towel off the roll. She mopped her face but said nothing.

Lana picked up the linens. "I'll get these in the wash. Then we'll find Michelle. No walking today. The three of us will sort this out together."

They met at the Crafts store. As soon as they were inside, Keira walked to the back and sat on the wide windowsill above the river, setting Smoky in her accustomed spot in the window beside her. The cat stretched in the sunshine, turned around twice, yawned, and settled into a nap.

By the door, Lana whispered quickly to Michelle, filling her in briefly on Keira's situation. Michelle locked the store's door and came to the back of the shop with Lana beside her. "What happened?" Michelle asked.

Keira looked up at her two friends. She gave a long exhalation of breath, easing her tension. "Jack and I've been struggling for a while, I guess. At first, we both wanted to run a bed and breakfast. Or so I thought. We'd talked about doing this for years. And, right after we bought it, it was so exciting, buying furniture for it, fixing it up. But then, after the fire…"

Keira's voice trailed off. She looked out the window at the surging white water, its tumult matching her turmoil. She turned back to her friends. "He loves his job in Boston. He loves Boston too. So do I, but this is home to me now. I love it here. I love running the B&B and I love working here at the Craft Shop and being with both of you. Jack never really got into life here. I guess it just got to be too much. We've fought off and on the last few weeks, whenever he was home, and now he's filed for divorce."

"Just like that?" Michelle was incredulous. "He wants a divorce because he doesn't want to run the bed and breakfast? Why not simply go on the way it's been, with him only being home on the weekends?"

"We talked about that. He's done with it all. With me too, I guess."

"Is there another woman back in Boston?" Michelle asked.

"No. I don't think so." Keira stopped, looking again at the rushing water behind her. "There's more to it."

Keira had rarely talked about the loss of the babies with anyone except Jack and her family. Now, they were all lost to her; her parents had both passed away and Jack was gone. The only people left who she could share this with were Sarah, Michelle, and Lana. And Sarah was still in Boston. Talking about it always left her feeling like weeping, drowning in the emptiness, but now, with Jack gone, she no longer even felt tears. There was regret, a deeper sense of loss, but a feeling of inevitability had settled over her. Again, she took a deep breath and dove in.

"A few years ago, we tried to have children," Keira confessed. "No luck. We had trouble getting pregnant, and the two times I did, I lost the babies. Jack helped me through the miscarriages. He seemed supportive and we kept trying, but the doctors finally told us it wasn't going to happen for us."

"Why didn't you adopt?" Lana asked.

"Jack wouldn't. He said he wanted to raise his own babies, not someone else's."

"That's not the way it is." Michelle seemed angry, pacing as she talked. "You two wanted a baby. There are babies out there who need a loving home. You could have adopted."

Her palms out, Keira tried to explain what she herself didn't understand. "That's what I thought, but Jack wouldn't have it." She slumped forward, looking between her feet at the old planks of the shop floor. "Anyway, it was years ago. I'd come to accept that this was just the way things were for us. We would be happy together, just without a child. Lately it's been coming up again and again. He's not okay with it. Maybe he never was."

Michelle stopped pacing. "And now he wants a divorce?"

Keira hung her head. "Yes." She hugged herself, arms crossed tight across her belly. She rocked. "I've lost two babies. And now it seems like I've lost Jack, too." Her eyes brimmed. "He wants to stay in Boston, with his job and his friends. He asked me to sell the house and join him. I can't do that. I gave it all up to come here. I've so little left there. No family. One good girlfriend. No job, no house. Just about everything I have now is here. And then he brought up the baby issue again. He went to a lawyer a few days ago and now he's brought me papers filing for divorce. I could fight him, but for what? He's hell-bent on doing this. I've got the bed and breakfast and a life here. I don't want him tearing away at it, and at me, at everything I have. I still love him, and he says he still loves me, but he certainly doesn't show it. Right now, he's tearing up everything that brings me joy. I don't need him in my life. I've got everything I need right here and if he won't be a part of that, so be it. So I signed the damn divorced papers. I'm done."

Keira finished her speech and sat back, leaning against the glass above the white water, sagging, drained. That's right, she thought. I've got everything I need. She looked at her two friends. They were a part of what she had, and she was grateful for them.

"You've got us," confirmed Michelle, as if she could read Keira's mind.

⟞⟝⟞⟝

Late the following day, Keira sat in the parlor, waiting for new guests scheduled to arrive that afternoon. A knocking sounded at the front of the house. She went to the front door, but the porch was empty. The knocking sounded again so she ventured out to the porch. The noise came from above her. Braving the early fall chill in just her sweater, she walked out on the lawn, turned, and surveyed her house. A shutter next to a window swung back and forth in the breeze.

What to do? Usually with a situation like this before the move to New Hampshire, she would have called Jack. She could call Jimmy now, but she steeled herself. It's my house. I'll deal with it.

She went inside, climbed to the second floor, and entered a guest room at the front of the house. She raised the window and climbed onto the porch roof. The shingles crunched beneath her sneakers. She sat on the roof and slid her way over to the loose shutter, praying she didn't fall. Wouldn't that be perfect, for my guests to find me sprawled on the front lawn with a broken arm. The loose shutter hung on hinges next to the window but should have been clipped solidly to the house. Two large hooks on the end of the shutter were meant to fasten onto the rings attached to the house. One of the hooks on the loose shutter had somehow broken free. The other hook's ring had pulled loose from the old clapboards. The hook swung uselessly on the back of the shutter The ring lay on the shingles beneath the loose shutter.

She stood on shaky legs and refastened the hook that still had a solid ring in the clapboards. Then she picked up the loose ring from the shingled roof and put it in her pocket. Finished, she climbed back through the window into the guest room. For the moment at least the shutter seemed to be firmly in place. It wouldn't last like that. The first stormy day it would pull loose again. The hook and ring would need to be replaced.

When she was safely back inside, she called Jimmy to ask him to replace the loose hook and ring. He agreed to come the following morning.

Through the window, she saw a car pull in and circle on the gravel in front of the house. Her guests were arriving. She had no time to do more or to think about what she had just done. She went downstairs and signed her new guests in. Later that night, alone, sipping a cup of tea by the woodstove, she reflected on the afternoon experience. I've always been afraid of heights. I've never done home repairs, always left that to a man. But there I was out on the porch roof, taking charge of the situation. I stayed away from the edge, but I did it. Yes, I'll need Jimmy for the repair, but I handled the immediate crisis. In that moment, she felt capable.

That evening after her dinner, with her guests checked in and up in their rooms, Keira settled on the sofa in the parlor, across from the cold woodstove. She dialed Sarah's number in Boston.

Sarah answered enthusiastically, "Keira! I was thinking about you today. I'm so glad you called. It's been too long. How are you doing?"

"I don't know. Not good. Jack and I are getting divorced." Keira couldn't think of anything to say, except to get to the point of her call. She slumped, her forehead in her hand. After emptying herself with Michelle and Lana, it was painful to go through it all again with Sarah, but it had to be done.

"Oh, Keira. I'm so sorry. What happened? What can I do?"

"I don't know. There's nothing you, or I, or anyone can do about it. Jack wants to live in Boston and here I am with my B&B in New Hampshire."

"You wouldn't sell it and come back?"

"That's what he told me I ought to do. But it's not easy to sell a big place like this, not after all the work we've put into it. Anyway, this is my life now. This is where I live, where I work. Aside from you, there's nothing left for me in Boston."

"Oh, Keira. I remember when you lost the babies. It feels like this is that time all over again, only worse."

"Yes, he brought that up too. I had come to accept that our life wouldn't include children. Maybe we both thought buying this big house and running a bed and breakfast would help me move past that time. Maybe it has for me. I thought he'd moved on too. But he brought it up again. He feels that if I can't have children and I won't come back to Boston, I'm not right for him anymore and we're done."

Sarah let out a sigh of exasperation. "I know you discussed adoption back then. And he said no. He can be so self-centered at times."

"I know. I'm angry. But I can't blame him. I've grown through everything these past few years with the loss of the babies and my mom's passing and our move. I guess he's still stuck in his life and job in Boston."

Sarah paused. "Keira, listen. I'd come up there tomorrow if I could. But with the girls on summer vacation, I just can't. But let's keep in touch. Let's make a point to touch base every day. Can I come up there in a few weeks? Once the girls go back to school, I'll make sure to be there as soon as I can this fall."

Keira nodded to herself in the quiet, empty downstairs of her big house. "I understand. I know you're busy with Tom and the girls. I'll let you go. I just needed to tell you what's going on."

"Call me again tomorrow. Okay? Be strong. We'll get through this."

Autumn blazed into the New Hampshire hills. Surreal gaudy reds, yellows, and oranges coated the forests. Glorious blue skies lit most days. When it rained, the bright foliage washed the countryside with a glow, a shining contrast to the dense, gray, rainy-day overcast.

Keira, Michelle, and Lana had settled into a daily routine. Jimmy Sanborn's daughter Christine worked part-time cleaning the guest rooms. Keira and Lana took care of managing the rest of the morning business at the Metcalfe House. Each day, when the last of the guests departed and the linens were in the washer, they would call Michelle at the craft shop. Alerted, Michelle walked to the covered bridge, meeting Keira and Lana as they came down the hill. Then, together, the three women walked the path along the river. With their walk finished, Michelle turned up Main Street to the Craft Shop. Keira passed through the covered bridge and returned to the bed and breakfast. Some days, Lana joined Keira at the bed and breakfast; others she followed Michelle to her store. Occasionally, Lana returned to her farm to look after Warren if he wasn't at The Sunrise.

When the last of her duties at the bed and breakfast were done, Keira left the Metcalfe House and drove to the Craft Shop. She worked there until she needed to return, getting home most afternoons by three to meet incoming house guests. The busy routine took her mind off the divorce.

Jack had not been back to New Hampshire in weeks. The divorce was moving along, mostly a legal proceeding punctuated with rare phone calls from Jack. Keira already received a small check from Jack on the first of each month. But, with the bed and breakfast doing well, she was not short of cash.

Keira missed Jack. She wondered how he was, but she had established herself in her new life. It still made her angry to think about what had become of their marriage, but she accepted the reality of her situation.

Just before the Columbus Day weekend, Keira left the Craft Shop in the afternoon, heading back to the Metcalfe House to be ready for her arriving guests. As she exited the covered bridge, starting up the Concord Road, she saw a car parked in the driveway of Andrew Holmes' empty house. A tall man stood next to the car, arms crossed, surveying the house.

Watching out for her neighbor's property, Keira turned in the driveway and parked behind the man's car. She got out and called to him. "Can I help you? I don't believe anyone is home right now."

The man turned. "No, I expect not. I'm Matthew Holmes. I was raised here. My father passed away a few months ago. I've inherited the house."

"Oh! Mr. Holmes. I apologize. I didn't recognize you. I'm Keira Sullivan. I live right up the hill at the Metcalfe House."

"Oh! Yes! I remember seeing you at my father's funeral. My dad and I spoke every week before he passed away and he told me a little about you. How nicely you'd fixed up the Metcalfe House. How he'd set you up with some old pictures of the place. My dad really liked you."

"How nice of you to say so, Mr. Holmes. Everyone in town loved your dad. I did too. He was a real gentleman, and he'd become a good friend. I was with him at the river when he passed away. I'm so sorry."

"That's fine. I'm doing okay. Thank you."

"So, what brings you home to Bennett Falls?"

"Exactly that. I'm thinking of coming home. It's been a hard couple of years for me."

"With your father's passing, I understand. My mom died recently too."

"Oh. I'm sorry."

They stood facing each other. The late afternoon sunlight shone through the turning maple leaves, surrounding them with a golden glow. Keira had always been at a loss in conversations with strangers. Now was no different.

"So, we've both lost our parents," Matthew finally said. "I guess that means we're both orphans."

Keira hung her head, her honey hair swinging to hide her face. "Yes, we share that."

"I expect so. And my wife became ill two years ago. She died, so I was alone in North Carolina. The bank where I worked was struggling. My job had become uncertain. I figured enough is enough. I resigned from the bank. I've got nothing there, and I've inherited this house here. So, I'm moving back to Bennett Falls."

"What about your children, Mr. Holmes? Aren't they in school?"

"No kids. We didn't have children. And please. Call me Matthew."

"Oh. Please call me Keira." Keira thought about how to respond to his statement about the lack of children. She couldn't think of a thing to say, considering her own childless life.

Matthew went on. "I've put my house on the market in Charlotte. Whatever I make when the house is sold will tide me over a year or two while I live here. It'll give me time to figure out what I want to do with the rest of my life, what sort of work I'd like to do. My dad's passing has left me thinking about what really matters in life. I know it's not banking. That's just something I fell into after college, following in my dad's footsteps."

"Any idea what you'd really like to do?"

Matthew smiled then laughed. "I have no idea. Maybe this is my mid-life crisis. But I'll figure it out. There's something out there for me."

Impulsively, assertively, Keira asked, "Do you have dinner plans,

Matthew? Would you like to join me for dinner tonight? Most nights I eat alone up the hill at the Metcalfe House, and I'd enjoy your company."

"I would love to. I was going to run down to the store and pick up some things to cook for dinner. They've kept the power running in the house these past few months, but I expect I'll be making do here, figuring out meals and such day-to-day. It would be very nice to have a meal I don't have to throw together. And your company would be nice, too."

"Good. Come on up to the Metcalfe House any time after six. I have three rooms booked, so I might be getting our guests checked in. Do you like Italian?"

"Sure. That sounds fine. I'll see you this evening."

Keira gave a quick wave, got in her car and turned up the hill to the Metcalfe House. *He seems nice,* she thought.

Matthew brought a Cabernet Franc with him. Keira prepared a shrimp recipe with cherry tomatoes and arugula in a cream sauce over linguine. The guests were all checked in. She and Matthew were alone in the big dining room.

Matthew poured the wine. Keira served salads, a basket of bread and brought out the shrimp and pasta.

"Tell me about North Carolina," Keira asked, as she served the salad from a big bowl into two smaller ones. "I've never been there."

"In some ways, it's a lot like here, only warmer. Charlotte was nice. It feels like Manchester maybe, only bigger and without the old mills. But it's not home. I missed Bennett Falls."

"I love Bennett Falls. After a little more than a year, it feels like home."

"You moved from Boston? I've been there, but I've never spent much time in Boston. People say it's a wonderful city. What's it like living there?"

The evening passed slowly, filled with the exploratory conversations of a new friendship. Late in the evening, with the dirty dishes in the kitchen and the wine finished, Matthew left.

Keira settled in with Smoky for the night. "I like him," she said to the cat. Smoky purred.

CHAPTER

Fifty-Three

Late October

Understanding Keira's need for support, Sarah came to visit over a long weekend late in October. Some of the leaves were down. The remainder glowed in the sunlight, but the trees were becoming bare, and the world of Bennett Falls was settling in for the winter. Nights were crisp, days were still brilliant, but there were hints of the gray weeks to come. Sarah found Keira in surprisingly good spirits, given the slow movement of the divorce.

The Metcalfe House was booked almost to capacity, even during the weekdays, filled with leaf peepers and retired couples enjoying the late-fall beauty of the White Mountains. Sarah's room on the third floor was the smallest guest room. Keira had reserved the larger, higher-priced rooms for the paying guests. Now, on the weekend, the house was packed.

Saturday morning, with the breakfast dishes cleared, Sarah sat with Keira on the porch sipping her second cup of coffee. Across from them, Smoky curled in a patch of sun, licking a paw and dragging it across her ears, then down her face. Her bath finished, Smoky shifted to center herself in the warmth of the sunlight, circled into a ball and fell asleep.

"It was a little over a year ago," Sarah said. "I sat right here with you and Jack. You had just bought the house and you were both so optimistic about fixing it up and opening the bed and breakfast."

Keira nodded and put down her teacup. She watched the deer that came every day to forage in the remains of the small, untended orchard on the far edge of the yard. "I remember," she said. "A lot has happened since then."

"You seem to be doing okay."

"I think so. I *am* okay." It was a declaration, delivered with a lift to Keira's voice. "Jack and I were together so long, but I feel like a burden has been removed with his leaving. He never really committed to the move, or to this house. Maybe not even to our marriage, as it turned out. At least the divorce will be final in a month or so. It's still hard at times, but I'm doing fine."

A pickup truck turned in the driveway, circled and parked at the end, next to the guests' cars. Michelle and Lana got out and approached the porch.

"Wonderful!" Keira exclaimed. "Here come my two Bennett Falls friends. I'm excited you'll be able to meet them."

"Is there still coffee?" Lana called as they climbed the steps.

"Yes. I thought you might be coming so I made plenty."

"Don't get up," Michelle said. "We'll help ourselves."

While the two women headed for the kitchen, Keira explained to Sarah. "They're my two best friends here in Bennett Falls. They've done so much to help me these last few months. Getting me out during the fire, being with me in the early days with the bed and breakfast. Seeing me through the divorce. Lana helps out here a few days a week. When my schedule here allows, I work up at Michelle's craft shop. We all walk together most mornings during the week."

Lana and Michelle heard the last statement as they returned to the porch. "No walking today," Michelle stated. "It's Saturday. Today is all play until I open the store. Then we work, right Keira? This time of year, there'll be lots of business."

"Yes, I'll come down for a few hours. Can Sarah join us?"

"Of course. Bring her, along with Smoky of course."

"Count me in too, then," Lana said.

They rearranged themselves in the chairs around the white wicker coffee table on the porch, Keira taking the seat closest to the front door and the stairs to the driveway so she would be available if any of her house guests still lingered.

"Let me make formal introductions," she said. "This is my old friend Sarah from Boston. And this is Lana. And Michelle."

"We're Keira's new old friends," Lana smiled. "We all seem to belong together."

"At first, we seemed to bond over how we cope with our husbands," Michelle said. "My husband Peter is a bother at times, but I love him."

"I've got Warren. So mine is a bother all the time," Lana laughed. "Lord, love him!"

"And mine is gone, which is a blessing," Keira added.

Sarah absorbed all the banter and joined in. "My husband is fine. My burden is my adolescent daughters. You remember them from when we visited at New Year's?" she said to Keira. "They're growing up. They still think their mother is clueless. But they've smoothed out a lot in the last few months. A lot less teenage drama and angst."

"Nothing stays the same," Keira said. "We all grow. We all change. And right now, we all find ourselves together here on the porch on this sunny morning. It's hard to complain."

Lana nodded. "It wouldn't do any good if we did."

"Life goes on," Michelle laughed. "Enjoy the day."

A car swung into the driveway, its tires crunching on the gravel, and parked next to Michelle's truck. Matthew climbed out and came to the porch, grinning. "Good morning, ladies."

Keira stopped him. "Matthew, I'd like to introduce my best friend from my Boston days. This is Sarah. She arrived last night. She'll be staying through the weekend. And Sarah, this is my friend and neighbor from down the hill, Matthew."

"Nice to meet you." Matthew leaned down and shook Sarah's hand. "Keira's told me about you. It's nice to put your face with your name."

"It's good to meet you as well," Sarah said, wanting to know more about this stranger and his relationship with Keira.

"Well, I'd best get started inside," Matthew said. "There's a lot to do to keep things tidy, even with all the guests staying over tonight. No new guests coming in, right?"

"That's right. We're booked with the same people all weekend."

"Good. I'll go take care of the dishes and check on the laundry. It's nice to see you, Michelle. Lana. And it's so nice to meet you, Sarah."

He leaned down and touched Keira briefly on the shoulder, not quite a caress, as he turned for the front door. Then he was gone, closing the door behind him.

Alone again on the porch, the four women sat in silence for a moment. Sarah opened the conversation again, her eyebrows arching. "Oh! My! Keira, you've got some explaining to do."

Michelle and Lana broke down, laughing.

"Stop it!" Keira said, her voice attempting to find a serious tone, hoping to stop the teasing. "He's just a good friend who stops by to help out, taking care of things for me here. That's all."

Michelle and Lana kept giggling like middle school students gossiping about boys.

Michelle stopped laughing long enough to say, "Does he do a good job taking care of things for you?"

Lana tried to appear serious, though she continued giggling. "I try to take care of things here, too. But, now that you've got Matthew? Maybe my helping out isn't the same?"

Sarah interrupted the hilarity, asking again, "Enough joking around. What have I missed, dear Keira? What can you tell me about this gentleman?"

"He's become a good friend. That's all I'll say." Keira sat back primly and smiled.

A warm breeze blew up again from the valley, the river and the lake, moving the yellow and crimson early autumn leaves on the trees. Above the tree tops, a chevron of geese honked past, seeking their traditional path south. Birds hopped on the lawn. Sparrows chased through the branches of a maple tree. High above it all, a hawk circled. Beyond the lawn, over the bright treetops they could see the narrow river valley, a white steeple and the rooftops of Bennett Falls a half mile away. Down the hill through the trees, they heard a church bell strike nine o'clock. Other than that, and the sounds of the birds and the breeze, it was silent.

CHAPTER
Fifty-Four
November – Saturday morning

Late autumn. Only the last remains of drab foliage showed on the trees. Frost glazed brittle leaves scattered on the ground. Most of the leaf peepers were gone, and tourism slowed in Bennett Falls.

With no tourists to manage, Michelle, Lana and Keira finished their morning walk at the covered bridge and cut across the Common for a stop at The Sunrise. Lana gave a quick wave to Warren as she came in but allowed him his space, alone at his table. Warren nodded to Lana and her two friends and turned back to his breakfast, cutting a piece of sausage and mopping it through the egg yolk.

The women came to enjoy the cheery mood of the regulars and share a cup, coffees for Michelle and Lana, tea for Keira. They shed their coats and scarves and sat at a table with a view through the window to the lawn of the Common across the street. Debbie brought their cups.

A black Mercedes pulled to the curb in front of The Sunrise. The Sunrise patrons turned to watch who came from the car and see what the stranger would do. "New York plates," Michelle noted. Throughout The Sunrise, people heard her and nodded.

Leaving the motor running, the driver climbed out and rushed through the door. He stopped, holding the door open, and looked around, distracted by the bell ringing over his head. Then he turned back to his business. Seeing Debbie standing by the counter, he called to her, "Do you sell *The New York Times* here? I need to keep up with the news."

"I've got copies of *The Manchester Union* and *The Boston Globe*," she replied. "One of each. People have been reading them while they have their breakfasts. They're mostly done with them, so the papers have been opened and read already, but I can take a moment and gather them together. They're yours at no cost."

"No. I want *The New York Times* and I can't get any WiFi out here. Where can I find a copy?"

"Head down the road about a mile," Debbie advised. "You'll come to a shopping plaza on your right. There's a CVS and a Cumberland Farms there. I don't know for sure, but one or the other of them might have The New York Times."

"Thanks." The man turned and hurried back out the door, letting it swing closed behind him.

"You're welcome," Debbie said to the closed door.

Someone laughed quietly. "New Yorkers," another Sunrise patron said. "Always in such a rush." More chuckles followed.

Slowly, Warren pushed back from his breakfast and stood. He dabbed at his mouth with his napkin and formally took a position beside his table. This was not a usual action from Warren. He took his breakfast seriously. Everyone turned to see what he was doing. Debbie paused at the counter, her arms folded. Billy leaned out of the kitchen door to listen.

Warren cleared his throat and began. "That New York fellow reminded me of a story my old friend Andrew used to tell. You all remember Andrew?"

Murmurs of assent followed from throughout The Sunrise. "God rest his soul," someone called out.

Warren shuffled his feet for a moment. He was always uncomfortable in the spotlight. "Well, I think it's time for me to share one of Andrew's stories. It seems that something similar to what we just witnessed here happened to Andrew's cousin who lived over on the coast of Maine a bit north of Portland."

"We all know where Portland is," someone shouted.

"Quiet!" cried another person. "Let Warren tell Andrew's story."

"Well, it seems that another New Yorker, just like our visitor, drives up to the general store over there down Maine. And when he stops in front of the store, he sees an old man sitting in a rocking chair on the front porch. Don't you know there's always an old man sitting on the front porch of a general store?"

The Sunrise patrons sat, rapt, attentive to their new storyteller.

"And the New York fellow calls to the old man, 'Do they sell *The New York Times* here?'"

"'Ayup,' says the old fellow on the porch."

"And so the New Yorker starts to get out of his car to go buy his New York Times. Just like the visitor we just had. But there was this big, ugly, vicious looking dog lying there sleeping on the porch right next to the old man in the rocker. That dog sprawled at the top of the stairs next to the door to the store."

"So the New York fellow is nervous about the dog, and he calls to the old man in the rocker, 'Does your dog bite?'"

"'Nope,' answers the old man."

"'Are you sure? This dog sure looks mean. You're sure your dog doesn't bite?'"

"'Yep, I'm sure my dog doesn't bite.'"

"So, the New Yorker feels better about things. He gets out of his car and climbs the stairs to go in the store and buy his *New York Times*. And don't you know, just as he reaches the top of the stairs, that dog wakes up, jumps, and bites him. And the New York fellow runs back and hops in his car."

"'I thought you said your dog doesn't bite,' he shouts to the old man on the porch rocker."

"'That I did,' answers the old man."

"'But the dog just bit me.'"

"'That he did.'"

"'But you said your dog doesn't bite.'"

"The old man in the rocker nods. 'My dog doesn't bite. But that's not my dog.'"

Warren stood alone beside his regular table, abashed, staring at the floor in front of him. Around him, The Sunrise patrons stood and clapped. Debbie walked over and gave him a quick hug and a kiss on the cheek. "Breakfast is on me this morning," she said. "Welcome home to Bennett Falls, Andrew!"

Warren smiled and eased back into his seat. Lana joined him, bringing her cup of coffee. Michelle and Keira followed with their cups and they all sat together.

"That was beautiful," Lana said, reaching to her husband and taking his hands.

"It had to be done," Warren answered. "Nothing lasts forever. Somebody's got to keep Andrew's stories alive. It might as well be me for a while."

EPILOGUE

Life rolled on in Bennett Falls.

As it had since time began, as it would forever, the river flowed through the town, defining it, pounding over the falls next to the mill, swirling in eddies as it passed under the covered bridge, pooling more gently in the wide shallows beyond the common, moving south to join the Merrimack, and so, down to the sea.

ACKNOWLEDGEMENTS

I wrote Bennett Falls in 2020 and 2021 during the Covid pandemic. I'm not sure how this time of unrest contributed to this story but it certainly changed the world. We saw massive rates of illness, hospitalizations and death throughout the world. National and global economies and world trade were impacted. In the United States, we were exposed to rampant racism, hate, and corruption. We lived through a divisive election and an attack on Congress. People lost their jobs and the ways we approach work may never be the same. I am confident the world and the United States will recover from these changes over time. Things will be different but life will go on.

I depend on my two Williamsburg writer critique groups for suggestions about my writing. For months, these groups met virtually. Their thoughts were shared with me, and mine with them from the isolation of my home office. This was a new and not optimal way for us to critique each others' work, but we made do. I finished the last few chapters of Bennett Falls with critiques and reviews resuming in person. I am indebted to my fellow writers for polishing my book, even if most of the work was done remotely.

I also wish to thank five beta readers: Anne Mercier, Ellen Smith, Jocelyn Callister, Mike St. Laurent, and Rick Bayko. Their suggestions on everything from literary style to the unique challenges of bed and breakfast ownership, and daily life in small town New Hampshire contributed to the clarity and authenticity of my story.

Narielle Living and her team of editors, proofreaders and graphic artists at Blue Fortune Publications have added the finishing touches to Bennett Falls. I continue to enjoy working with them.

Finally, Bennett Falls could be a love story; the tale of my love for small towns. I am grateful to the many friends I have in towns in New Hampshire, Rhode Island, and other parts of New England, in Virginia, South Dakota, and elsewhere. This story is set in New Hampshire and inspired by several towns I know and love there. It could be a reflection of life in many small towns.

ABOUT THE AUTHOR

Peter Stipe is the author of five books. His first book, *Finding Our Way*, a collection of short stories, was released in 2015. His second book and first novel, *The Art of Love*, was released in the summer of 2017. In 2019, *Remember Me*, Peter's third book was published. This book chronicles Peter's emotional search for the truth behind his family stories and includes an account of the lives of his great-grandparents in upstate New York and New Jersey during the late 1800s. His fourth book, *The Fairy Garden*, follows the growth of a young girl into adulthood, inspired by the fairies that live in her grandfather;'s garden in Williamsburg, VA. Bennett Falls is his fifth book.

Now retired, Peter has enjoyed a long career that has included time in education as well as work in Human Resource Development and Training for a variety of businesses. He has a Bachelors degree in History from Boston University and a Masters in Education from Tufts. In addition to his writing, Peter is an accomplished artist, working with photography and in watercolor. His photography is on display at On The Hill Gallery in Yorktown, Virginia.

A competitive long distance runner for many years, Peter has completed numerous marathons with six finishes in the top fifty places in the Boston Marathon and participation in the 1972 U.S. Olympic Trials. A New Englander for most of his life, Peter and his wife, Debra, now live in Williamsburg, Virginia, where he continues to write.

9 781948 979764